Al

First-time author Brianna McMahon met her Developmental Editor, Salima Ali Khan, on Reedsy to edit her book *Hidden Ancestry in the Middle East*. Together, they developed a methodical approach to address these critical human rights issues in the book. Brianna McMahon and Salima Ali Khan bonded over their shared experience with xenophobia and Islamophobia. They both emphasized the crucial need for positive voices of change within these marginalized communities, which became the backbone of curating the story. Brianna's goal is to resonate with the next generation and foster a sense of community, making the audience feel included and part of the journey.

Hidden Ancestry in the Middle East

Brianna McMahon

Hidden Ancestry in the Middle East

Vanguard Press

A CIP catalogue record for this title is available from the British Library.

ISBN 978-1-83794-344-9

The opinions expressed in this book are the author's own and do not reflect the
views of the publisher, author's employer, organisation, committee or other
group or individual.

Vanguard Press is an imprint of
Pegasus Elliot Mackenzie Publishers Ltd.
www.pegasuspublishers.com

First Published in 2025

Vanguard Press
Sheraton House Castle Park
Cambridge England

Printed & Bound in Great Britain

Dedication

I dedicate this book to my grandmother, Maunifa Ghadban. Her story is one of beauty and strength. Her roots began in the Kafala system in Lebanon. She unknowingly experienced discrimination in Lebanon for being a part of an ethnic group. Her resilience is admirable. When she perished, my world came to a standstill. It became my mission to vindicate her modern-day slavery through journeying through history and tracking past colonization and immigration. My movement became more impactful than expected. I got recognized by the head of Aboriginal Affairs in the Canadian government. Maunifa is a woman worthy of idolization.

Acknowledgments

After graduating from the University of Ontario Institute of Technology, Cultivating cultural research through first-hand sources has been both enlightening and transformative. I want to acknowledge the profound influence of two Peruvian nationalists, Thomas, an Incan, and Paulina, an individual with Spanish conquistador roots. Their exceptional insights, combined with my personal experiences, have been instrumental in my pursuit of rectifying the generational trauma caused by cruel colonization and the mistreatment continuum that persists today. Their presence, particularly their exceptional insights, has reshaped my perspectives on culture, colonization, and the marginalized First Nations community. The culmination of my research and personal experiences has permanently rearranged my understanding of mass immigration worldwide. I weaved my inspiration to write my fictional novel from the movie True Spirit, which chronicles Jessica Watson's solo sailing trip worldwide. The movie credits mention her dyslexia and how she overcame this barrier by writing two best-selling books. I resonated with her learning disability, as I, too, have a formal diagnosis of Nonverbal Learning Disability. Her persistence and success inspired me to embark on this writing journey. I met Thomas and Paulina. They both came from Peru. Thomas claimed to be indigenous. Paulina claimed her Spanish conquistador roots. The three of us began analyzing how we could rectify previous trauma caused by the cruel colonization and continuous mistreatment of the indigenous in the region. I researched indigeneity for a year. I began debunking the concept of race across the globe. One afternoon, I watched *True Spirit*. Here is a quick synopsis of the movie. Jessica Watson is an avid sailor with dyslexia. She felt determined to break a sailing record and prove she had capabilities despite her learning disability. Upon completing her world-sailing expedition, she published two books. I felt inspired by the movie. It planted the seed that I wanted to accomplish that goal too. It is the reason I decided to write this book I have been honored to be surrounded by influential people. They were the ones that pushed me to write this book. I want to thank them for their positive encouragement and reinforcement. It has enabled me to look beyond the surface of race. When I started, I was a neophyte in learning history. I quickly immersed myself in academic journals of ancient civilizations. I did extensive research in Lebanon. My findings were mind-boggling. I reconstructed history to find my ancestral lineage. I reclaimed this history for myself. It would not have been possible without my roommate. Paulina! Paulina is a mixed-raced individual from Peru. We both had a curiosity about Peruvian racial demographics. Paulina and I learned about the historical events that led these tribes to the Americas. Paulina had a particular interest in equality for Aymara and Incan tribes. Together, we watched *True Spirit*.

The movie resonated with me. Jessica Watson is an Australian celebrity.

She is a dyslexic woman who wrote two books. It resulted in me wanting to empower the disabled community. I took the initiative to curate a novel. My philanthropic endeavor has become more significant than I ever expected. It became a large-scale social rights movement. It changed the racial demographics of the world.

Most importantly, I would like to thank Salima Ali khan. She is an editor, an author, and a professor. Salima is a bi-racial Muslim-Indian woman. She was looking to mentor other Muslim women. We wrote this book to be about female Muslim empowerment. She challenged my ideologies, which helped the evolution of the book. Lastly, I want to dedicate my book to my deceased grandmother, Maunifa Ghadban. I felt inspired by her. She lived in Majdel Balhis, Beqaa Valley, Lebanon. She resided in the area where the Mamluk and Ottomans once were. Maunifa worked as a maid in the Kafala system. Our family perceived her as indigenous to the region.

This journey taught me that this was the furthest from the truth.

Preface

I am Yura Jignyasu. I am in high school. I am about to enter college. It is my ascension into womanhood. It is a transitional period. I am experiencing an identity crisis. It became imperative that I develop a fundamental understanding of who I am. From the outside looking in, I am an ordinary girl balancing a heavy school course load, family/friends, and navigating my love life. I have had to overcome harsh adversity. A rocky family dynamic with divorced parents and a twisted aunt. Did I mention I was born Muslim? I have a transgender sister. Our family gets ostracized in every community. I have faced various types of discrimination.

I need to focus on finding a suitable career after college. My academic journey has been tremendously thought-provoking. My educators challenged me immensely. It furthered my (Yura) education. My professor would rather fight for truth than the culture he grew accustomed to. Hanau and his brother, Pilip Bravebird, focus on empowering their community. He wants to foster young individuals to become educated. Hanau Bravebird does not care if his statements are controversial. He only cares about morality. He is a human rights activist.

Hanau and Pilip are actively mobilizing their students to speak truth to power. The brothers are fact-based learners. It is the Bravebird initiative. It is to teach young people to learn the truth rather than be misled by misinformation. They are slowly reshaping racial demographics throughout the world. The brothers speak of more than indigeneity in North America. Hanau Bravebird re-writes the history of the world. His pursuit is noble. He has been a positive influence in my (Yura) life. He has helped me become captivated by the subject. He was not alone. In grade 12, I was fortunate enough to meet an archeologist. Aliyah Smith spoke up for black human rights.

Coming from Saint Thomas, she knew her ancestors descended from African slavery. So many influential people have fought for justice and won. Hanau and Pilip believe in their students. He encouraged me (Yura) to research this. I was surprised that something as simple as looking into your heritage would not change the world's demographics. The Bravebird brothers' ability to critique themselves helps my (Yura's) personal growth. I have always felt enamored with those who have been game-changers. People need to become more inquisitive. That is the most effective way society will grow. That is how I plan to illuminate the world. My immediate family is full of trailblazers.

My family and I are concerned with the world's trajectory. We decided to become proactive. My family and I have a mantra. We want to be the change. Speaking for myself, I would love for women to become more empowered.

Foreword

I am honored to say I have formed a kinship with Brianna McMahon. She is a quirky and light-hearted woman. Her mother immigrated to Canada from Lebanon. When her mother was in her twenties, she met a European man. The two had one child together. At conception, he realized he felt unequipped to be a father. Brianna's parents parted ways. Brianna spent the duration of her life having an identity crisis. Brianna is bi-racial. She needed to find out where she fit in. Being Lebanese resulted in Brianna enduring incredibly harsh racism. Her race ostracized her. She experienced countless rough days. She continuously rose despite all the hardships she faced. I watched her pour her heart into this book. Brianna advocates for an increased awareness of scientific discoveries. She wants to spread this message to a larger audience. Brianna wants to be the voice for change.

In the second grade, she was diagnosed with nonverbal learning disability. She only learned to read in her early twenties. Brianna has defied the impossible. Her diagnosis allegedly ensured her fate. Chances were, she was going to spend her entire life struggling. In grade eight, she had difficulty reading children's stories to kindergarteners. Her mother believed in her capabilities regardless. Brianna learned about the human rights injustices occurring in history. Since then, she has been an outspoken advocate. She specializes in restorative justice for racialized groups. Brianna does so by speaking out against the trend of whitewashing history. Brianna spreads the truth about historical facts. She has revived a forgotten Asian history innovatively. She is on track to change the world. Engaging with her through her writing process has been delightful. It has been a long journey for her to be able to reveal her final project. It is a good read.

Introduction
Chapter 1: Grade 11 – The Struggle of Being an Astute Student

We had an assignment on leadership in business. The teacher assigned us to speak with confidence. The purpose was confidence-building. The topic was our heritage. When I got informed of the assignment, I took in what the teacher demanded from us. Growing up, I was under the impression that I was Lebanese. As I got older, I started to want to connect to my roots.

My mother, Nadia, informed me that we came from a tiny village called Majdel Balhis. I was curious why my family lived in the Beqaa Valley. I vaguely knew that it was the location where the Ottomans and the Mamluks once resided. I started to challenge everything about the world around me.

I learned about the inter-mixing that occurred around the world. Indigeneity was a loose theory that people fall back on. Our assignment required innovation. Students needed to stay engaged throughout the speech. The professor set the guidelines for the students. I felt overwhelmed. I had other projects in other classes. I needed to learn how to balance the workload effectively. The teaching methodology has changed since I was in elementary school. The government enacted a law that

17

limits the use of cue cards in the classroom. Over the years, the use of cue cards has become increasingly restrictive. The teacher stated that props were permitted; however, we could not use them verbatim. It would result in an automatic failure. Speaking in front of the class gave me anxiety. There are moments when I feel self-conscious.

I fret about the perceptions my classmates have of me. I get closed off when I receive enormous attention. It was something that I wanted to change. I took a public speaking course in the past. I made some progress. I need to continue making positive strides. Students must memorize their speech. My teacher handed out the rubric. As an astute student, I analyzed her criteria. It was a litmus test. My work needed to match the requirements. The grades are marked by our effective message conveyance. We needed to be well-versed. When prompted, we had to defend our stance. I jotted my process on a notepad.

I noted that my preparation entailed covering different perspectives. I knew that by doing so, I would strengthen my speech. It would become more dynamic. It would improve my grade. I felt nervous about my speech. Last night, I stayed up to complete my assignment. This morning, a wave of exhaustion hit me. I looked disheveled. I did not want my weariness to be on display. My teacher was an observant individual. He grades us on our professionalism. He was training us to be work-ready. I stood in my bedroom doorway. My nerves were visible. My mom, Nadia, called, "Yura, time for school."

"Okay, Mom, I will be down in a minute." I walked downstairs. I have dreaded this moment all week. I recognized it was a short-term angst I felt determined to overcome. While I walked down the stairs, I made a concerted effort to maintain my composure, my determination shining through. "Yura, you look presentable. I am proud of you, sweetheart. Summer vacation is only a week away. You need to pass today. I know you will." My mother's confidence in my abilities and reassurance helped calm my nerves, but I remained timid. I stared down at my manicured hands. "You tend to downplay your intelligence. I have watched you tirelessly work on your speech, and you are well rehearsed."

"Okay, Mom, I will be down in a minute." I walked downstairs.

"Yura, you look presentable. I am proud of you, sweetheart. Summer vacation is only a week away. You need to pass today. I know you will."

"Thanks, Mom." I felt appreciative of the reassuring words. It boosted my confidence. As I left the house, her words began to fade. I felt my anxiety resurface. I needed to overcome this.

I needed to conceal my internal battle. It felt like a difficult task.

I needed to be mentally strong. Giving in to my exhaustion will result in my failure. All my hard work would have gone unrecognized. I needed to reorganize myself and gain a new perspective. This assignment was worth only a tiny percentage. I could pass the course without passing this assignment. My doomsday rhetoric was loud in my mind. Failing the project would put me at a disadvantage. Thus, it increased my chance of flunking the course. I have worked tremendously hard to graduate from school since my formative years. Dropping out of school would leave me destitute for the rest of my life. I thought of the worst-case scenario.

I would need to re-enroll in the course. I could go to summer school. In grade nine, I went to summer school. Summer school taught me that I appreciate the two-month break. The last thing I wanted to experience was burnout. I needed to have positive thoughts. It would serve me no purpose to feel discouraged. It would likely increase the chances of my failure. The power of ideas is a mighty one. These thoughts might permit my worst fear to come to fruition. People need to be confident to pass. All of my hard work would have been for nothing. I needed to put myself on a pedestal. Only momentarily. I would utilize that esteem to deliver a strong performance. I hushed those voices.

I was aggrandizing my assignment. It was my last semester before summer vacation. This course was almost a thing of the past. The solution was to get a good grade today. My speech was well-written. It was an intriguing topic. I created a presentation to accompany my lesson. I experienced imposter syndrome. It occurred to me throughout the semester. Today, those feelings became exacerbated. My grades were at the top of the class. I felt inept and worried about my delivery. I needed reaffirmation that I would excel. My chances of being successful through my speech started to look more positive. I needed to get through this assignment. I reminded myself that the following week was summer vacation. It would be a mental break.

I required one desperately. I needed to push through today. I needed to put my best foot forward. On the bus ride, I watched a *TED Talk* about the power of positive thinking. I wanted to try it out. To boost my confidence, I spent the morning reiterating my self-affirmation. I noticed slight alterations in my confidence level. My confidence levels shifted throughout the morning. I knew that my parents depended on me. I also looked to make my familial line centuries prior proud. That meant I needed to rise to the occasion. I did not want to let everyone down. I had to be ready for the presentation. I was representing all the past events that led me here.

One minute, I felt capable, and the next, I reverted. Nevertheless, I noticed improvements. It was a productive activity. It did not soothe my upset stomach. My stomach felt queasy. Although the power of positivity boosted my confidence, it was not a cure. It did not resolve my predicament. My eyes felt fatigued. They burned. I needed to assess my needs. I need to be alert to deliver a good speech. It meant a change in my demeanor. Therefore, caffeine has become a necessity. I watched a documentary on the dangers of caffeine. It was insightful. I dismissed the entire purpose of its messaging. Caffeine was critical to my ability to function.

Humans have changed their lifestyles drastically since the Paleolithic era. I am okay with these changes. I find it disturbing that our bodies have yet to adapt throughout the centuries. On my way to school, I made a pit stop at a coffee shop. Steve's Cup was a small, family-owned business. The shop needed help to generate revenue. Customers gravitated toward chain restaurants. Corporate companies have more monetary resources. It was dirty money. Corrupt corporations have contributed to a toxic political atmosphere. I never thought that the competition was fair. Most customers are not concerned with the socio-political environment when they make a frivolous purchase at a convenience store.

The politics of business can both positively and negatively impact lives. I knew Steve. He was a family friend. My mother, Nadia, told me that you cast your vote with your money. I chose to support small businesses. It felt good. I ordered an extra-large latte. I suspected that I would return later in the day. I hoped that this would hold me over until my speech. Caffeine has served me well in the past. It will help me complete my assignment effectively. In middle school, I attempted to quit caffeine. The impacts were detrimental. I failed a class assignment. I was forced to redo the class assignment. The second time, I used caffeine as an aid. The second assignment went smoothly.

Steve McLeod could not afford to rent a building. Steve talked to his friend about cohabiting. McMahon agreed to the terms. They formed a business partnership. They were close friends. I thought it was business savvy. Fred McMahon wanted to expand his ventures. Steve McLeod did not share the same sentiments. Money was a corruptible entity. Fred had grandiose visions. He wanted to become a franchisee. Fred placed a bid to buy the coffee shop. It enraged Steve. He was a man of principle. He was by the book. He detested Fred. It was a callous act. He was going to refute this offer. The men were negotiating the terms. Fred offered a large lump sum for cash.

Steve folded. This amount was more than what he had generated at the store. Steve had to put his family first. He would face eviction in three months. I hoped Steve could continue renting his condo. He still needs to provide for himself and his family. I am worried about his financial security. Steve took all the appropriate business precautions. I wondered if he could land back on his feet. My loathing expressions became apparent. I was in a rush. I browsed the selection regardless. I purchased a handful of protein bars. All of the protein bars contained high concentrations of caffeine. I perused the ingredients printed on the back of the protein bars.

Chapter 2: Nefertiti Bust

They contained fifty-five milligrams. I searched for a higher quantum to no avail. I stuffed them in my purse and headed to school. Once I arrived, the campus bombarded me with light-emitting diode lights. The exuberant energy was infectious. I felt myself waking from my slumber. My classmates did not seem to have fatigue. The school had boisterous characters. I got energized. It helped calm my nerves. I needed to reduce my stress. I turned on my phone and searched through my playlist. Different playlists were required to suit my moods. Today, it is about female empowerment. I needed to remember my capabilities. I got pumped up.

I felt encapsulated by the lectures throughout the day. I love learning topics imperative to social rights. My main interest was the disenfranchisement within various ethnic groups. I find acquiring unfamiliar knowledge life-changing. My teacher was a profound individual. I get a lot of great takeaways from class. I have developed my listening habits since high school. I am a more attentive listener. I walked into history class. I waited five minutes for the lecture to begin. I took the time to check my social media feeds. I had three new notifications. It was nothing major. I received a like on one of my photos from my aunt. The desire for likes began to consume me.

"Hello, class. I am your new teacher, Pilip Bravebird. Christina R. Davis needed to take a maternal leave of absence. I want to introduce myself. A bit about me: my parents descended from the Algonquin/Ojibwe tribe. My brother teaches at the local college. My family is changing the misconceptions of indigeneity. I decided to change the teaching curriculum accordingly. I have made it my mission to change your perceptions about indigeneity. Please leave my class with solid takeaways. Our goal as academics is to remove colonization. Canada is a multicultural country. Canada is considered an inclusive region. In some parts of the world, it is illegal to practice culture.

"It was a generational misfortune that happened to the Hawaiians. It took a negative toll on the ethnic group. These laws infringed on the rights of Hawaiians for generations. Human rights activists have thus removed this barrier. Hawaiians are now able to practice their culture. Laws get enacted and get dismantled. Cultural disputes have also led to violence. Genocide has resulted from intransigence in culture. One tribal view can conflict with other cultures in the region. The unification among tribes is what the world ought to strive for. Have a great rest of your day." I walked out of class. I thought about Hawaiians I knew personally.

They never spoke about the cultural erasure they experienced as Europeans settled in the region. I wondered what impact this had on them psychologically. I want to make the world a better place. I thought about helping with their reconnection. I had started to anthropomorphize my teacher. I enjoyed listening to the lecture. I knew that this teacher was going to be an influential professional. I needed a positive male role model at the time. The teacher captured my attention. Something many men in my life have not been able to get. My stepfather was the other exception. I valued the teacher's opinions and what he thought.

I respected his endeavor to use his platform to influence the next generation. I found his desire to heal the indigenous communities to be philanthropic. I knew that I needed to deliver my speech in my next class. I felt prepared. I also felt nervous. I had a fifteen-minute break before my leadership class. I unzipped my backpack. I pulled out my lunchbox. I grabbed a Ziploc bag of cookies. I gobbled them down quickly. I rehearsed my speech. I visualized myself delivering the speech. I took a deep breath and made my way to class. My teacher broke down the class schedule. He would call on students to present. I fulfilled my role as an attentive listener. I found myself interested in the topics.

One girl named Dana got called to present. She talked about her uncle, Zaid, owning a Siberian tiger. Dana was from Saudi Arabia. "Hello, class. I am here to talk about how the culture of wealthy oligarchs in Saudi Arabia changed my family's connectivity to our heritage.

"The wealthy once had wild animals as pets back in my country. Seeing Saudi oligarchs have tigers influenced my uncle's decision to get one. In 2018, the government banned owning exotic animals. My uncle, Zaid, rejected this. My uncle, who came from money, decided to move to

Florida. He liked that America did not regulate the animals people were allowed to own. He bought a home. He had a gated area where the animal could roam. Zaid claimed to be an atheist. Ironically, he wears a kaffiyeh. My uncle kept the tiger in captivity. The Siberian tiger is considered endangered.

"My Uncle Zaid thinks captivity prevented extinction. He raised the cub and formed a strong bond. His culture influenced his entire life. It was not limited to his driving. My Uncle Zaid drove his car on two wheels. Florida road regulations prohibit this. He has had to pay multiple fines. His neighbors have called the police for minor offenses. My uncle is dark-skinned. He could pass as a black man. It is a hate crime. I feel nervous every day. I talked to him over the phone and sobbed about the situation. That could have killed him. Zaid viewed that as a homicide attempt. He promised to seek vengeance. Unbeknownst to his neighbor, Zaid trespassed on his property.

"He opened the backyard door. My Uncle Zaid released his tiger into their yard. He left. The next thing he heard was his neighbor's excruciating scream. My Uncle Zaid was on his front porch eating popcorn. He claimed he did not know how the tiger got there. The neighbor temporarily disappeared to call animal control. My Uncle Zaid retrieved his tiger. He never got charged for releasing the animal. One day, he forgot to feed the Siberian tiger. It changed the course of his wife's life forever. The tiger bit my aunt, Arwa. She felt the pain in her spinal cord. The tiger chewed off a piece of her back before releasing her.

My Aunt Arwa had a stint in the hospital. She made a full recovery.

"Her life will never be the same. My Aunt Arwa now requires a wheelchair. She does not blame the tiger. The couple pleaded with the courts to keep the tiger. The Florida justice system debated sentencing the tiger to death. My Uncle Zaid was terrified by the thought of a lethal injection. He knew the onus was on himself and not the tiger. He succumbed to his guilt. Ultimately, the judge decided that neglecting to feed the animal resulted in my aunt's new living situation. My uncle won. He still has the tiger. I have debated whether that was the right choice. Both parties remain content with the decision. It is a matter of free will.

"The government should have less control over people. People are intelligent enough to make their own decisions. The tiger is a beautiful animal. I am proud of my uncle for deciding to keep it. It was a horrific freak accident. We pray it never happens again." I noticed my classmate looking online to see price ranges on cubs. Dana looked at the blackboard before continuing with her presentation. "I have never gone to Florida and visited my Uncle Zaid. That is something I want to change. I want to meet the animal that put my aunt in a wheelchair. I need to forgive the tiger for this freak accident. I plan to move to America after I graduate. I respect my aunt and uncle. I am going to purchase a Malayan tiger after graduation. Living in Canada, the law has prohibited me from owning one. That is my speech. Thank you for listening." I put a considerable amount of thought into her speech.

I understand the government banned owning undomesticated animals. It was for their safety and the safety of others. I could picture a scenario where a wild animal escapes from its confines. Imagine a human getting caught in the crossfire. Canada has plenty of top predators that pose a threat to our survival. Generally, tigers thrive in warmer climates. The Siberian and Amur tigers live in Russia's harsh environments. They could easily get transported to Canada. I thought she was deranged. Tigers are undomesticated animals. They should not be pets. I cannot imagine owning a tiger. Dana went back to her seat. I nodded. Some of the students gave her congratulatory nods.

One gave her a pat on the back. Dana seemed to blush a little. I thought that was sweet. I wondered if she fully understood the assignment. I thought there was a chance she would flunk the class. Dana somehow managed to speak about her heritage. I hoped, for her sake, that it would enable her to pass the course. The teacher had a monotonous expression. I was unable to predict what he had written on his grading sheet. The teacher called on me to present. I felt crippled by my anxiety. I was paralyzed. I pulled myself up using my desk. I walked in front of the classroom. I stood in front of my classmates. I felt exposed—my confidence, which I had this morning, diminished.

I followed online advice. Avoid making eye contact. Try to imagine that there is no one in the audience.

Chapter 3: Terracotta Army

I went over my speech last night. I successfully delivered my message with confidence. I was worried that I would buckle under pressure. I stared at a mental health poster at the back of the wall. This irony did not get lost on me. I was experiencing a significant amount of distress. I should leave class and dial this number. It would have been unacceptable to my teacher. My teacher should not be touting mental health. The students gave me their full attention. A student would conclude their speech. The volume would increase. The teacher silenced the students to permit the new speaker to present. I appreciated the respect from my classmates. Standing in front of the class was humbling.

The room was silent. You could hear a pin drop. All eyes were on me. I was able to taste my leftover lasagna. I swallowed it immediately. I did not want to throw up in front of my classmates.

I folded both of my arms. I hugged myself. My eyes did a sweep of the room. I had broken my gaze from the wall. I was experiencing full-heart palpitations. My mind went blank. I froze up. I felt vulnerable. I rarely felt like this. I debated the severity. I may have been experiencing a panic attack. I did not know what was happening. Despite my mental state, I managed to compose myself. I soothed myself. I reminded myself that I was a professional. My teacher became impatient with me.

"Whenever you are ready." The teacher gave me a reassuring smile. It gave me a boost of confidence. I was grateful for that. I hoped my speech would live up to her expectations.

I nodded. "Hello, everyone. Today, I will talk about my genealogical history. Have you ever searched for ancestry? I can speak only for myself. In my formative years, my stepfather, Omar, told me we were Lebanese. I am sure it was the same way for my classmates. It is basic knowledge. The majority of the population knows their ethnicity. The rest considered their nationality to be their race. I began thinking about this. How much of the population's ancestral lineage is unknown?

"Some families need the luxury of tracing their ancestry past a century. That was the case with my family. I believe it is a hidden human rights violation. It is what I will discuss today. My ethnicity is a word-of-mouth concept. It goes unchallenged. This information was passed down to younger generations. How many classmates had to rely on verbal storytelling adaptations to their family history? Could you put your thumb up if you had that experience?" Four people put their thumbs up. "Thank you for your participation. The word-of-mouth concept needs to be more verifiable. I had to find a more academic source that would back their sentiments. It is what I sought out.

"Scientific journals were my best resource. It allowed me to become an educated woman. It is my goal to empower my classmates to do the same." I felt confident talking about this concept with the class. "I challenge my classmates to do the same. However, this remains controversial."

I paused for a moment. I felt on edge. In the next part of my speech, I stole the information from an online forum. I replaced the word Asian with Lebanese. I was scared.

Getting in trouble for plagiarism was no joke. I knew I needed to personalize the sentiments. The teacher needed to think these ideologies were coming from me. People need to be more comfortable with new concepts.

It challenges the ideologies they grew up with. The backlash insinuated that it would be a battle. Online Middle-Eastern critics claim that being from a subgroup was self-hatred. I thought their ideologies were tone-dead. In their minds, learning heritage equated to racism. One should seek knowledge. People should be obligated to speak the truth to power. Regardless, I pondered their criticism. Was I feeding into Lebanese self-hatred? Chances were they were ignorant people. The opinions of others could not hold too much clout. I needed to think about why I was doing this. I did this to retell the story of my forgotten heritage. I was empowering my ancestors. The criticism was meaningless. I am a Lebanese Muslim social activist. Having a Lebanese lineage means that I am a mixture of the world. I still remember the prehistoric migration patterns that make up Lebanon. Denying history does not change it. I experience national pride. In the upcoming portion of my speech, I switched back to using my own words. It was not always the case. I struggled astronomically in my younger years. Racism took my pride away. "Being Canadian, I occasionally chose my nationality over my heritage. It was a dilemma I faced daily. I do not want to get teary-eyed about this. What I am about to say contradicts this statement. Ethnic groups in Lebanon are the key to social rights within the region. People from these ethnic groups come from other countries. All of them call Lebanon home. Lebanon has accommodated some of these ethnic groups. In some aspects, Lebanon is racially inclusive. Lebanon has split between the Christian and Muslim communities.

"That makes Lebanon stand out from the Middle Eastern countries. I watched a documentary on Asian influence in ancient Middle Eastern civilization. It was life-changing. You are assigned a race at birth. If the individual gets misinformed, people tend to discount it. It means, a need for more education. I need everyone to overcome these barriers. You deserve to know your roots. Has anyone in this room taken an ancestral deoxyribonucleic acid test? Please raise your hand. I can discuss this after my speech." I did a sweep of the room. I noticed that many people were uncomfortable. Would my question encourage further inquiry into their genealogy?

Two people raised their hands. I only knew one of my classmates who raised their hands personally. Her name was Serena. I have known her since elementary school. The other was outside our program. Alice took this course as an elective. I found it odd how many people never inquired about their heritage. "Thank you." Serena smiled.

Her expression triggered a poignant memory of us collaborating on a history group project in grade five. It

33

was during this time that our friendship took root. We were placed in different classes the following year, a change that tested our bond. The memory stirred a mix of emotions, from nostalgia to regret. It made me realize the significant amount of time I had spent dwelling on the past, prompting me to refocus my thoughts on the present moment and the valuable lessons learned from the past. These lessons inspire hope for the future

"Serena and Alice have both taken the initiative to find roots. The question remains: How do we identify our ancestral lineage? It becomes more challenging when there are no records. Academic journals are excellent resources of information. It enabled me to become an advocate." I felt cathartic.

I stared at the rolled-up Persian carpet in the left-back corner of the room. I needed to de-center my thoughts. Had I stayed distracted, I would have spoiled my entire presentation. At random, I blurted out, "I have mathematical guesstimates of my heritage." I felt trapped between a rock and a hard place. I needed to continue. "My maternal line came from a village in Lebanon that spoke Turkish. The majority of the Lebanese population speaks Arabic. It is an indicator that I come from Altai. I am ethnically part Kazakhstani." I knew that certain villages in Lebanon spoke Turkish. My town spoke a dialect of Arabic.

I should not have told that class that tidbit of information. It needed to be more accurate. The statement, however, could be true. A more precise statement would be that my grandmother may be from Altai. It was an absolute word. I did not know what led me to make this misleading statement. I NEEDED TO SELL THE LIE. That meant doubling down on this inaccurate statement.

The guilt that I lied to my classmates ate me up inside. I was full of fear. What if someone in the class got word that I was lying about my heritage? I did not know what I got myself into. I did not know how to backtrack on this statement without looking demented. It came from a book I had read last night. I had copied verbatim what the author of *Islam and Altai* had written about her heritage. I was nervous that if the teacher found out, I would be deducted marks or fail the assignment. I knew it was my job to be persuasive and convince everyone in the room that this was my heritage.

The book has been a constructive tool in helping me navigate my heritage. I began understanding the racial demographics of the region. The Altai is far from Lebanon, yet it has made a significant dent in the country. It helped me begin figuring out where to start this research. My family is part of a disenfranchised ethnic group. We did not have access to any historical documents. I could only go by hearsay told to me by my family. My parents told me I was Lebanese.

"Our family lacked the economic standing to have rights such as properly recorded records. We do not have access to familial history that dates back a century ago. I felt enraged by this. It is a fundamental human right. All religions should have equal entitlement to this. The importance of it is monumental." I felt jarred by my lie. I knew I could not sit and stew about this. I needed to continue with my presentation.

"I have done extensive scientific research. This assignment has been life-changing. I perused the prehistoric era of Lebanon. I have a solid understanding of the topic. I seek to expand my repertoire. I assure you that I am qualified to attest to this." In actuality, I vaguely thought that my mind was teetering on insanity. I knew that I needed to expand my knowledge. I already had a solid understanding of who I was.

Chapter 4: Phaistos Disc

I needed to be more invested in this avenue of research. My limited amount of effort was disheartening. I took advantage of the assignment. I challenged myself half-heartedly. The assignment intended to help me gain an understanding of myself. I should have taken the time to do it properly. The only thing I cared about was getting a good grade. I got more focused on passing the course than reaping the benefits. Occasionally, I get nervous that this attitude will follow me into the workplace and hinder my success. I paused.

My thoughts became scattered with nervous apprehension. My mother emphasized that my ethnic lineage meant I was required to work harder than my counterparts. Discrimination in the workplace is an inevitable hardship that I must overcome. I saw my success in this course not just as a stepping stone, but as a crucial milestone in my journey to future job prospects.

One student muttered, "She caused the Islamic revolution. She is the biggest terrorist of them all."

I felt chastised and ostracized. I was part of a minor, marginalized ethnic group within the classroom. I noticed that my pulse began racing, and I started experiencing heart palpitations. The teacher noticed a shift in my demeanor.

The teacher piqued up. "Get out of my class. Go to the principal's office."

Joseph got up from his seat and marched out of the class. He seemed upset. I knew it was not my fault that Joseph got in trouble. I bet he thought he was clever. It was a shared sentiment among the indigenous population throughout the Middle East. I just thought he was an arrogant prick. History got written. I cannot undo it. Racism has the intention of hurting others. Make them feel inferior. It was beyond damaging. I am powerless. I am responsible for myself. I am not responsible for my ancestors in the 15th century. I stared at the individual blankly. I did not retaliate. I felt powerless. No one protected me. A hate crime had just occurred, but I was a professional.

I needed to continue my speech. "Most of us are on a quest for these a-a-answers." I felt veins on the back of my neck twitch. I had been toe-tapping. I was concerned with my state of mind. I decided to improvise. I rummaged through my bag and pulled out the book. I rented it from my local library last night. The library had the book *Islam and Altai* in stock. I skimmed the entire book last night. In a shaky voice, I said, "I perused the ancient civilizations of Lebanon. The Islamic Revolution originated in the Altai region. Mongolia and Kazakhstan reshaped the Middle East. I am of that lineage. When I realized that, I felt shocked.

"Far Eastern Asians were the first believers in Islam. They have spread this message across Asia. Colonization is controversial. Muslims respect the ancient Islamic Empire.

Those indigenous to the region or liberated Arabs loathe the Islamization. The critics say the beliefs are stuck in the 15th century. This empire was at the end of the First World War. It is a document in literature. The war occurred between Mehmet and Vlad. Some Ottomans were in cahoots with the Russians. They worked to dismantle the Russians. The Russians infiltrated Lebanon and Syria. The First World War affected Syria. It led to the collapse of the Ottoman Empire.

"The war resulted in the division of Syria into several zones of influence, with France and Britain taking control of different parts of the country. The war brought about significant changes in Syria's political landscape. The Arab Revolt against Ottoman rule played a role in shaping Syria's future. It paved the way for Arab nationalism and independence movements. The First World War had devastating impacts on Syria. Many people lost their lives or were displaced from their homes. Russia's military intervention secured Lebanon as its strategic interest. The Russian army provided ammunition and trained them to fight. Russia's involvement had negative consequences for Lebanon.

"The war caused significant damage to infrastructure, disrupted trade, and caused political instability and economic hardship. It led to widespread famine and disease outbreaks. The Russian soldiers suffered heavy casualties. The war exposed the weaknesses of the Russian government and military. The war began in 1914, and by 1917, the Russian army was suffering from severe defeats and shortages of supplies. The economy was struggling, with inflation skyrocketing, and food shortages. It led to widespread protests against the government. In February 1917, these protests culminated in the overthrow of Tsar Nicholas II. It paved the way for the Bolshevik Revolution in October 1917.

"It led to a transformation into a communist state under Soviet rule. A large subgroup in Lebanon is of Russian ancestry. The population comes from Altai. Kalmyk is Mongolian. This province complements Lebanese history. This province is a vulnerable, marginalized community. The Mongol invasion affected Russia as well. The largest subgroup in Russia is the Tatars. Tatars have ancestry from Altai. The Altai is an indigenous nature reserve. This nature reserve intersects China, Kazakhstan, Mongolia, and Russia." The first part of my speech came to a close. "Pilip Bravebird, I created a PowerPoint. I need access to the projector for the next part of my speech."

"Okay. I will assist you. Pull the projector screen down."

I turned around and pulled the lever down. I did a sweep of the classroom. I noticed that this action spiked intrigue in my classmates. I then started asking questions and encouraging participation, making my presentation more interactive. I believed this would improve my overall grade. It put my mind at ease temporarily.

"I need Internet access." He got up from his desk and allowed me to sit there. For a moment, the teacher and I switched roles. I took in the power dynamic. I felt a momentary air of confidence. I was a powerful woman. I enjoyed the feeling. I playfully looked down on my classmates. I pretended I was no longer in the hot seat but rather the grader. No one was aware of my thoughts. Had they heard, I would have risked ruining friendships. I am thankful for internalized dialogue. I logged into the email domain. I opened my PowerPoint and hit the start button. The first slide appeared. The slides contained both written text and imagery.

The images consist of ancient traditions. "I want to recognize a heroic figure. Bashir Khan. He rose to power in the 1700s. He was a Rotgut-Kalmyk prince. It means that he was the leader of the Oirat tribe. The majority of the Oirat tribe worked as farmers in northern Mongolia. The Kalmyk tribe has altered their nomadic lifestyles since then. In the 21st century, the government conducted a crackdown. The crackdown was effective. This lifestyle dwindled. The Kalmyk tribe once resided in Tuva, Oirat, and Xinjiang. Ubashi Khan made a decision that changed history. He chose to engage in bipartisanship. Ubashi refused assistance with Manchu. He did not want to harm anyone.

"His tribe was unwilling to join the army. The Oirat tribe became an enemy. It was not their intention. He made this decision based on Buddhist values. The Manchu Army disagreed with these decisions. The Manchu tribe decided to wipe out the Oirat tribe. It is known as the Dzungaria genocide. It is an Altai tragedy. The heart-breaking event occurred between 1755 and 1758. I want to take a moment to recognize who they were. The Dzungaria Khanate is Tibetan and Mongolian. They were the last powerful nomadic tribes in Asia. This genocide annexed 80% of the population. The cultural history got diminished. It is traumatic for those in the tribe.

"I feel humbled to be sharing this tragedy with you. The tribe now faces the threat of extinction. Historians claim that 500,000–800,000 people perished. These people were grandmothers, grandfathers, mothers, fathers, and children. Families got wiped off the face of the Earth. The memory of the Oirat tribe gets forgotten. Kalmykia honors their memory. I want everyone in the class to close their eyes. Think about if someone came to your house and killed everyone. How would you feel? That is the pain of those who experienced genocide. Their loved ones are left with an unhealed scar. It is identical. Another similar example is when your country goes to war.

"The result is the same. A high percentage of the population perishing is always a tragedy. It is easy to sympathize with the situation. Manchu men claimed Oirat women. The women were collateral damage, becoming sex trophies. The women divorced their Oirat husbands. They married the Manchu men. Ubashi devised a plan to preserve their race. He needed to consult the Dalai Lama. All his decisions had to align with Buddhism. I respect that he stuck to his moral compass even under dire circumstances. It demonstrates to me that he was a man of character. Ubashi Khan departed. Once he returned, he mobilized his clan to leave. The Oirat tribe became forced refugees.

"I know refugees. Their endurance is beyond respectable. These humans are heroes without capes. Refugees pushed the limits of what a human should ever get subjected to. In my opinion, the Oirat tribe consists of some of the most resilient people. The Manchu gave land to the other tribes. The demographics of Oirat province are telling. Very few Oirat tribes live there. It was a dark period in Mongolian history. Kalmykia is now a Russian territory. The Oirat community got disenfranchised by being far away from Mongolia. They feel disconnected from their traditional way of life. The two other territories are Tuva and Buryatia. They were both seized by Russia in the 1500s.

"The Russian-Asian community has a higher quantum of European blood. More so than other Asian demographics. The seizure of Far East Asia occurred because of Russia's desire to expand its influence in the Pacific region."

Chapter 5: Bronze Bells

"The expansionist policies of the Russian Empire led to its annexation of vast territories in Siberia, Manchuria, and Korea. It was a direct result of this territorial expansion. The influx of Russian settlers led to tensions with local populations, while the exploitation of natural resources disrupted traditional ways of life. I am going to state my opinion.

"I think the choice to expand into Far East Russia was wrong. It had some upsides. It created new jobs that helped strengthen the country's economy. The downsides outweighed the positives. That decision killed the majority of the population in the region. In the province of Yakutia, seventy percent of the people were slaughtered. Yakutia and Kalmykia shared the same horrific fate. Their pain is unrecognized. It gets minimized. Doing environmental damage and murdering the population is immeasurably catastrophic. No monetary currency is worth it.

"Mongolians and Kazakhstanis had Russian culture and language imposed on them. Russia wanted to solidify and consolidate the two ethnicities to become one nation. It was an initiative to promote power within the region. It led to a loss of cultural identity. It contributed to cultural homogenization and political unrest. The Oirat tribe's presence in Kalmykia dates back to the 1600s. It once belonged to Astrakhan. The Oirat people have a long and complex history, with the earliest records dating back to the 8th century. The Oirat tribe has been shaped by the rise and fall of the Mongol Empire, the Qing Dynasty's conquest of Mongolia, and the Soviet Union's influence on the region in the 20th century.

"One of the most distinctive features of Oirat culture is its language, which is a member of the Mongolic language family. The Oirat dialect came from Uyghur. Uyghurs are the Chinese Muslims. That indicates Kalmyk's influence on the ancient Islamic Empire. My initial assumption would be that they were of the Muslim faith. My assumption was wrong. The Oirat tribe believes in Buddhism. This ideology got embedded in the culture. In the medieval ages, the Oirat tribe left its mark on Lebanon. I have debated whether their presence in Lebanon occurred later on too. The Oirat tribe moved to Kalmykia in 1771. It happened simultaneously with the *Russo-Turk War*.

"Ubashi ordered 30,000 of his men to fight. In 1774, the fleet occupied Beirut. The fleet dropped its arsenal in Bourj Hammoud. The military marched into the Beqaa Valley. When I compiled this information, I realized there is a large ethnic group of Russians living in Lebanon. The Ottomans assisted them in dismantling the empire. The Lebanese Ottomans are from the Altai region. The Mongol Empire impacted the history of Europe, as it opened up long-distance trade routes and led to the spread of ideas, technology, and goods. Considering Mongolians pushed for Islam, one could dismiss their contributions to society. Far East Asian innovations have advanced the world.

"They have since the beginning of time. The Mongols helped spread new technologies to Europe. One innovation was gunpowder. It came back to haunt them when Europeans discovered America. The Europeans saw the ethnic group as a blight. The tribes were in the way of the Europeans' plan to advance infrastructure. If it were not for the Mongols introducing gunpowder, the genocide would not have occurred. The Mongols helped to re-establish the Silk Road, which linked Asia, the Middle East, and Europe. They facilitated the exchange of goods, ideas, and even diseases. The Mongol Empire also contributed to the formation of the modern nation-state system in Europe.

"It encouraged the rise of strong, centralized governments. The *Turko-Russian War of 1877–78* between the Ottoman Empire and the Russian government. They fought over territorial disputes in the Balkans. Russia declared war on the Ottomans. Several battles ensued. One included the Siege of Plevna, where Ottoman forces held off Russian attacks for months before surrendering. *The Turko-Russian War of 1700* lasted over two decades. Russia emerged victorious in the end, gaining control of several territories previously held by the Ottoman Empire. Russia emerged victorious. Russia gained control of several regions previously held by the Ottoman Empire.

"It was the first time the Middle East had not been ruled by a foreign Islamic empire. The impacts of the Islamic empires are evident. Removing the empire does not remove colonization." I plopped down onto the chair next to the microphone. I prepared myself for the next part of my speech. There was a time-lapse. My mind went blank for a moment. In a raspy voice, I said, "I will summarize this book." I held up *Islam and the Altai* in the air. I took a sip of my bottled water. I took a deep breath and exhaled. "Take the opportunity to understand your colonizers. I did. I understood what led Lebanon to adopt Islam. It invoked empathy. I developed more compassion for my country.

"I became an educated woman. I was no longer susceptible to misinformation. I have advice for my classmates. Fact-check your resources. Verify their validity. There are ways to improve your research techniques. There should be overlapping documents. Be sure to verify the information is correct. The Oirat tribe adapted and settled in Kalmykia. They did not expect further hardships. The tides shifted against the racial group. In the Second World War, Russia was villainous. The government appointed Joseph Stalin. Stalin allied with Hitler. Hitler wanted to eradicate the world of Jews. I do not know if anyone in the class is Jewish. Hitler was a homicidal maniac.

"Hitler was a deplorable human. He took the lives of millions. Stalin's decision to align with Hitler was callous. Russia got outcast by the Western world. Russia is the enemy. The Kalmyk tribe realized that Stalin had supported the Holocaust. They no longer supported his regime. The Kalmyk tribe became mobilized into action. Joseph Stalin went against Buddhist ideologies. Kalmykia has a provincial government. They decided to undercut Stalin. The province got caught conspiring against the government. The Kalmyk tribe became the enemy of the

Russian Republic. I find the decision to stand up for what is right noble. It takes courage for someone to go against the tide and fight for what they believe is right.

"The Kalmyk tribe sought sovereignty in Russia. It is not how you thank your savior. Stalin no longer approved of the Oirat tribe living in Kalmykia. He called for ethnic cleansing. The Oirat tribe needed to find a new place to live. Kalmykia would revert to those tribes indigenous to the region. The Oirat tribe experienced deportation and displacement. Stalin ordered cattle cars to Kalmykia. Russians felt appalled. The Russians must have felt the same way I have retelling the disturbing history. The Russians sided with Stalin. The Kalmyk tribe deserved a punishment. The Oirat tribe must have loyalty to the country above all. They were traitors.

"Stalin created deportation. It was race-based. Stalin sympathized with the white populace. He only wanted to get rid of the Far East Asians. Stalin proposed a marital act. He incentivized the white partner to divorce their spouse. He attempted to break up interracial couples. The white partner would not experience brutality. They could remain in Kalmykia. The Far East Asians did not have that privilege. Many white people broke up with their spouses. Some couples persisted and endured this hardship. They had set deportation dates. The Russian government transported the Oirat tribe to Siberia and Europe. The conditions were atrocious. There was a shortage of food. These conditions were almost inhabitable. It killed twenty-five percent of their population. They arrived at their destination. The indigenous despised having them there.

They received harsh brutality. They were gas-lighted. Their treatment was inhumane. Living in a foreign environment, they were outcasts.

"The Kalmyk tribe received malicious verbal jargon. The hurtful gossip took a toll on their self-worth. These were preposterous claims. They insisted that the Oirat tribe were cannibals. These tactics dehumanized them. These conjured-up ideologies led to violent acts. Violent confrontations were common. One hate crime involved throwing them in fires. Their bodies got eviscerated to ash. Many longed to return to Kalmykia. Under the new Russian leadership, they were able to return. A sub-sect declined this invitation. They did not view their violent treatment as acceptable. Those who declined settled themselves within the new region. They have now entered a Putin era. Putin is committing ethnic genocide. New generations are less interested in learning Oirat.

"Speaking different languages would make the entire country more innovative. The way to balance this is through racial tolerance. It needs to be embedded in our political system. It helps us strive for equality."

Chapter 6: Narmer Palette

"The Oirat tribe cares about preserving their heritage and is challenging these measures. Community members attend town halls where they preface the ethnocide they are experiencing. Western media does not cover Kalmykia. It is an unrecognized province within Russia. Putin and his cronies attract the Western world's attention. Political leadership is debatable in Kalmykia. I have subscribed to a list of Russian-digitized newspapers. I translate the articles from Russian to English. One of my neighbors is a lonely, widowed, eighty-years-old Russian woman. I keep up-to-date on Russian news to bond with her. I have formed a kinship with her. She enjoys talking to me about her country. The articles discuss Russian affairs. I perused *Putin versus Buddha*.

"A store owner took a stand against the war in Ukraine. He fled. Another individual held a high position in the monastery. He went against the war in Ukraine and got fired. Those in favor of the war lash out in a fit of rage. Russian news intends to brainwash the public. The government tailors newspapers to their political agendas. The government is unable to force ideology on constituents. Tell what is moral. That is up to the individual to define their character. Buddhism contradicts killing innocent Ukrainians. Some people in the Oirat tribe are more loyal to Russia than Buddha. One individual dismembered the bodies of Ukrainians. It caught the Ukrainian humanitarian social rights attention.

"To a Canadian, preserving Oirat is not the top priority. It is for me. It is a Mongolian human rights issue. Kalmykia receives little attention. I want to change that. These men were equal to Manchu strength-wise. They chose to adhere to peace and pay with their lives. I want to pay homage to the genocide. Society should learn about the Oirat culture, which includes their customized Mongolian attire. Every tribe had different traditional clothing. Language was the differentiating element. To ignore the language is to ignore the history. That concludes my speech." I got a round of applause. The teacher asked the students if they had follow-up questions.

I felt mentally prepared to give well-informed answers. I wanted to leave a positive last impression of myself. I needed to put my best foot forward. My job was to convince the class that I was well-versed in this topic. It would reflect my overall grade. Erica raised her hand. "Go ahead, Erica."

I looked at Erica compassionately, hoping to instill a short-term bond. Her body language reciprocated my professional intentions. Erica had exceptional social mannerisms. In a soft-spoken tone, she began formulating her well-thought-out commentary. Thank you, professor.

"Thank you. I thought your speech was exceptional. Did you learn anything else interesting about Russia?"

I nodded in recognition of her question, understanding the weight it carried. As I digested the information, I realized that this moment was not just a question-answer period, but a crucial part of my overall grade, accounting for ten percent. I quickly formulated a well-thought-out response, aware of its impact.

"Thank you for your question, Erica. I learned more about Circassia. Circassia was once an independent country. It is now part of North Caucasus, Russia. The Russian Empire aimed to eliminate the Circassian people, who were indigenous to the Caucasus region. The Circassia Genocide was a tragic event in the 19th century. It was a sectarian conflict. The Russians were Christians. The Circassians were Muslims. Circassia wanted to remain an independent nation. Circassia had a parliamentary system. The Russians were not interested in a democratic process. Russia decided Circassia would become a part of its empire. These civilians were subjected to brutal violence and forced displacement, resulting in thousands of deaths. The genocide began in 1864 when Russian forces invaded Circassia and terrorized the local population. Circassia had unequipped fighters.

"Circassia did not have the funding to fend them off. Russia had a weaponized arsenal. They fought for their sovereignty nonetheless. Russia engaged in war crimes. The Russians burned villages, destroyed crops, and killed anyone who resisted their rule. Circassians needed to flee into concealed areas. Families left en masse. They ran into the forest. The forest led to a river. The Russians caught on to their escape method. They mobilized their army to find them. Many Circassians fled. Their peregrinations resulted in them finding refuge in neighboring sovereign countries.

The descendants of those who survived this tragedy continue to honor their heritage and remember those who lost their lives.

"The culture gets revived through their language. The Circassian language has its own unique alphabet and grammar system. Circassians also have rich arts of music, dance, and storytelling. The Circassian people have managed to preserve their unique cultural identity. The estimate of Circassians living abroad is indeterminable. Many families did not keep track. They may have thought it would prevent their children from being exposed to racism. Being a foreigner may have proved too difficult. Many Circassians go unreported. It is the bloodiest genocide in Russian history. It is a forgotten history. Russia renamed the country Sochi. I hope that answers your question."

I sensed my response made Erica uneasy. Erica was half-Muslim. Circassia was a Muslim tragedy. Her ability to sympathize was no surprise to me. I share those same depressed feelings. It was worse than the region receiving no recognition. "Thank you. Anyone else."

As I swept the room, I couldn't help but notice the substantial change in energy. I longed to return to my desk, but the teacher's call for more participation in my speech compelled me to stay engaged.

Paulina raised her hand. "I am from Dagestan. Did you learn anything about my country?"

Her comment indicated her blatant disregard for the Republics of Russia. I wondered whether her comment would be well-received by other classmates from Russia.

My research revealed Russia's diverse and complex political divisions, which distinguish it from other countries. Russia's division into eighty-three federations, twenty-one republics, nine territories, forty-six regions, and one autonomous region is a testament to the country's rich and varied governance. This unique structure, along with four autonomous districts and two subordinate cities, Moscow and St. Petersburg, is a fascinating aspect of Russia's political landscape that I felt compelled to share with Paulina and our classmates

"Thank you for your question. Dagestan is a republic known for its diverse ethnic and linguistic groups, including Avars, Dargins, Kumyks, and Lezgins. Dagestan got infiltrated by an aberration of ethnic tribes in the region. It has faced invasions from neighboring regions and conflicts between ethnic groups.

"Dagestan has managed to preserve its unique cultural heritage. It is known for its stunning mountain ranges, lakes, and forests. *The Dagestan-Russia War* was a conflict in the Republic of Dagestan in 1999. The war began when Chechen militants crossed the border into Dagestan. It launched an attack on Russian forces. The Russian military responded by launching a counter-offensive attack and eventually defeating the militants. The conflict was significant because it marked the Second Chechen War. It lasted until 2009. Many people had to flee their homes. The alternative was to become caught up in the fighting. It also resulted in significant casualties for both sides."

I paused for a moment. "War is a taboo subject. Both parties tend to know people caught up in the conflict. It takes lives and separates humans from their humanity. The weapon manufacturers do profit from this. There are monetary gains in inciting wars. Therefore, people have decided that diplomacy is not profitable. War is the way to go."

Matthew raised his hand. "Yes, Matthew."

"You did a fantastic job on your presentation. It was well structured. I found you tied in the topics nicely. I found myself enamored with this topic. I learned a lot from you today. My question is, what influence do you think Putin has in Russia?"

"Thank you for your question. Putin has immense power. He displays megalomania. Putin uses his military Intel to spy on the public. He does not tolerate those who challenge his ideology. Those who take a stand tend to receive some form of punishment. There have been cases of doctors getting thrown out of windows. It resulted from the failure to follow political protocol. Putin uses the media to propagate the public. Every Russian president has reshaped the country. The president determines the trajectory. Ethnic groups oppose a threat to their political agendas. Ethnic groups go against this ideology. The government dismantles them. It happened to Circassia and Kalmykia.

"Circassia got annihilated for their beliefs in Islam. The Altai region was the first place on Earth to adopt Islam. Tying the North Caucasus together. The Western World often neglects this part of the world. People tend to ignore the socio-politics of the provinces. Russia is a federal entity. Putin and wealthy oligarchs control the narrative. It is not an equal platform to voice different ethnic views. It is a suppressive regime.

"Russians experience victimization to an extent. Their human rights get minimized. Russia is the largest country on the planet. The Western world tends to view every province the same. People equate Circassia and Kalmykia. I am going to ask a question. What is the first associate you make when you hear the word Russia?"

Matthew responded, "Moscow."

Anticipating the comment, my serious countenance changed, and a half-hearted smile appeared. It aligned with my concocted response. I had prepared my response to this question well in advance. My anxiety had plateaued, and I hoped I would not fumble this. I quickly reverberated my rehearsed response.

"I agree with you, Matthew. I would go even further. The first thing I would associate with Russia is St. Basil's Cathedral. Circassia is Muslim, and Kalmykia is Buddhist. That is a poor representation. It does a disservice to their struggles.

"I refer to these ethnic groups as the 'invisible people.' It is a human rights violation. The Russian Caucasus is near the Middle East. It is a tragedy that their history is untold.

"I felt honored to be sharing this history. Russia has many hidden, untold stories. The entire conquest of Russia was full of bloodshed. Cultural erasure was a common practice. It is not only Russia. It is the expansion of a region. It is a tragedy."

The teacher selected another student, Parker. "How did you prepare for your speech?" Parker and I had a unique relationship. We went on a date. It did not go well. We shared a kiss. He ghosted me. I felt immensely awkward talking to him in front of the class. I took a sip from my water bottle before answering his question.

While taking a sip, I observed that the water had a zesty lemon flavor. The flavor piqued my interest, but I refrained from commenting out of respect for Parker's preferences. I chose to provide a compassionate response, considering the situation and the feelings of others.

"Good question, Parker. I rehearsed. I was well-versed in this topic before my speech. I went through my main talking points this morning. I tried to elicit emotions throughout my presentation. It would enhance my emotional connection to the class. On my cue cards, I wrote passages to regurgitate. I emphasized the Oirat tribe. The Oirat tribe was in the Mongol Empire alongside the Jalairs in the 1500s. I had compiled research on Ubashi. The Altai, the ancient perpetrators of colonization in the Middle East, got victimized in the 1700s.

"Lebanon will never revert to the Syriac era. The population is now ethnically diverse. Colonization is demoralizing. Lebanon needs social empowerment. One way the Middle East can accomplish that would be to claim ethnic groups. It is a way for the Arabic population to gain more empowerment substantially. I hope my presentation has taught you something.

"I hope that I answered your question."

[As I turned to the teacher, I could see the contentment in her eyes. The relief of having satisfied both the teacher and the student with my reply was palpable. After my response, I found myself yearning to be an active listener once more, back at my desk, feeling a sense of connection with the learning process.

Parker nodded. He appeared to be slightly flustered.

Chapter 7: Tutankhamun's Mask

As far as I am concerned, Parker had his chance with me. He blew it. I could care less about his childish antics. I was over it. I was here as a professional woman. All I cared about was receiving a passing grade. The teacher informed me that I could take one more question. I chose Adonis. He was a shy person. I am surprised that he raised his hand. I rarely heard him speak throughout the course. I pondered the reason that he spoke up. My best theory was that the students in class get graded for participation. He was most likely nervous that he would not pass.

I felt touched that he chose my assignment to raise his voice. I understand how difficult that must have been for him. I gave him a sweet smile to encourage him. He asked his question. "Did this research help you gain a further sense of self?"

The assignment had stirred an identity crisis within me. I had assumed that my classmates would resonate with me, but the irony of the question was not lost on me. Nevertheless, I endeavored to craft a response that would offer valuable insights to the young learners in the room.

"Great question. Yes. I have an understanding of heritage. I understand how I became a Muslim. When I was in my formative years, I celebrated Eid. The majority of Kindergarten classmates celebrated Christmas. It isolated me. I was unsure why I was different. My classmates noticed that I was not the same. I was six years old when I experienced my first racial attack. I ran to my mom, Nadia. I asked her why a forty-year-old man wanted to hurt me.

"I have knowledge that will permit me to educate others. I want to be a voice for change. Thank you for your question, Adonis." I went back to my desk. I had completed my last class assignment. After class, I thought about how my speech went. I found Joseph's callous remarks disturbing. He made a racist comment, and I felt it had hindered my speech. I would like to know if I would get penalized for that. I felt concerned that it would reflect on my grade. That was one area I needed to remedy. My self-worth had diminished. I felt isolated during the occurrence. I needed to soothe myself. The majority of my speech was fact-based knowledge. Parts of my remarks were fictitious. I needed to connect my story to Altai.

My grandma displayed Asian facial characteristics. I was in desperation for a subgroup to claim. I had been touting my genealogical research. In my speech, I stated that my grandma was from Kazakhstan. This fib deviated from my character. It was an erratic decision. I blame sleep deprivation for my abnormal behavior. It was the only way I could talk about Ubashi Khan. Being from Lebanon, I felt disenfranchised. All the information came from my book. The teacher would have prohibited me from blathering about Mongolia. I needed to deceive my class. I did not expect the callous comment. That was a racist attack on Kazakhstan. It was the principle of the matter.

Ottomans are people. Being attacked for being a Lebanese Muslim is identical. It is out of a person's control. I sympathized with myself. It was easy to judge myself for lunacy. My family never referred to themselves as Ottomans. It was plausible that my family was once Ottomans. I wanted to investigate. I felt shaken by the attack. I went to the bathroom and cried. Women heard but chose to ignore the sobs. I calmed down. I was not going to let a racist take away my joy. I reassured myself I had a good speech. I am stronger than the racist. The dubiety that I failed remained. I was worried about that. I knew I could not let that consume me. It would ruin my vacation.

I would not let that happen. The next day, I woke up and signed onto my computer. The teacher had tallied up our final mark for the course. I passed. Five more days of school until summer vacation. I eagerly anticipated its arrival. My patience wore thin. The week flew by. I had a jammed-packed summer vacation planned. I thought about how different my summer vacation would be from last year's holiday. Luckily, change is inevitable. This time last year, my life was in freefall. My life had a snowball effect of catastrophic events. The revolving door of disastrous events was too much for me to handle. I remember this time last year vividly. I was on the precipice of graduating from high school. My life had unraveled. My grandmother, Maya, had passed away. Her death occurred a month ago. Time heals all wounds. Time moves forward. I stay stagnant. Maya was my favorite person. I tried to reason with myself. I grappled with myself. I needed to put some semblance of normalcy back into my life.

I turned around, and a month had gone by. My room was in a state of disorganization. I needed to do something constructive. I had not gone to the gym in a while. My mother, Nadia, bought me a gym pass. It had barely been used. Strength was never my strong suit. Being in excruciating pain was not enjoyable. I knew when the starvation kicked in. I would get up. I wondered if the pain would ever diminish.

She lived to ninety-one years of age. Her quality of life was poor. Maya had dementia and physical conditions. Maya lived with chronic pain. She was no longer in pain. In her 90s, she became dependent on her daughters. They orchestrated a rotation schedule. The daughters struggled with the duties. The tasks took a toll on their mental health. It led to plenty of animosities. The sisters bickered. The passive aggression led to a fight. Their good intentions took an unexpected turn. One that my family would never bounce back from. As her dementia worsened, they hired a support worker. The personal support worker could not tolerate her.

Maya's aggressive demeanor proved to be too much. There was a revolving door of support workers. On one fateful day, she was rushed to the hospital. This time, it was terminal. The family decided to pull the plug. At the time of her death, the family mourned together. It was a brief moment of tranquility. I stood there in shock as she took her last dying breaths. Her family gathered around her bed in the living room. Her face appeared almost unrecognizable. A spacious room was jam-packed with people. People were left standing in the hallway. Some gathered in the kitchen. The family decided to hire a nurse. He specialized in palliative care. He monitored her pain levels.

The nurse made a journal of her progression. Maya had a fighting spirit. She was off all medications for three days. On the third day, my grandmother passed away. She journeyed into the unknown. She left her family behind. Our family was in distress. Tears fled everyone's eyes. Losing my grandma brought out my vulnerable side. I hope that people can see your personality in me.

I aspire to overcome a tremendous amount of adversity and come out victorious. The backbone of our family is resilient women. I hope my name will be as respectable as my grandmother's one day. She was the most influential person I have ever met. I hope that our paths cross again someday. My mom, Nadia, told me it would be lethargic to express my emotions. She suggested putting my feelings into a letter. I sat down on my bed. I retrieved my notepad and pen from the floor. I placed the notebook on a table near my bedside. I started organizing my thoughts in a way that would do her justice.

Most people have experienced the pain of losing their grandmothers. It does not make it any easier.

The pain was beyond words. My grandmother was my anchor, my haven. Her calming presence was my refuge. The thought of her not being there was overwhelming. Amidst this emotional storm, I found a way to express my feelings- in a letter she would never read.

Dear Maya Jignyasu,

Grandma, you raised me. You influenced my ascension into womanhood. I had a strong female presence in my life. I was at a loss for words. Death is final. My world crumbled. I connect to you through my memories. I can recall so many.

I watched you frequently marvel at birds. Their freedom was enticing. I wanted you to experience that freedom. I saw you struggle with illiteracy. I attempted to teach you how to read. You were able to memorize words. You showed more interest in the Arabic language. I know you learned how to read during your Quran studies.

While our views on religiosity may differ, I wholeheartedly acknowledge the significant role it plays in your life. Your devotion to a deity has not only become the backbone of your identity but has also fostered your personal growth, validating the person you've become. The joy you find in your religious practices is a testament to this growth and has strengthened our bond.

You kept pushing yourself to try new things. We were inseparable. My mom, Nadia, always wanted to go to Walt Disney. It was her childhood dream. I was hesitant. I gave my mom, Nadia, an ultimatum. You had to come. My mom caved. I wanted you to be with me through all of my milestones. You attended my grade six graduation.

We cooked Lebanese fusion-style dishes. You taught me to steal grape leaves from grapevines. Your desire to cook blinded you to commit illegal activities. You got caught trespassing. You got off with a warning. On one eventful day, we were picking grape leaves. A white lady noticed foreigners.

She stood a foot away from us, shouting racial slurs. My mom, Nadia, felt upset.

She was not going to let the racists win. It did not deter us from practicing our culture. We even had shawarma nights. The two of us talked about the female Arab takeover. You believed I could do anything. You gave me self-confidence. You boasted about my successes. When you did, I beamed with pride. I know your mother died during your formative years.

It left our family with questions. We wanted to piece the family together. This forgotten lineage intrigued me. You were only able to recollect your upbringing. I wish I could have pried out more of you.

Love, Yura

P.S. I attached a photo of us.

Chapter 8: Mask of Agamemnon

Her funeral did her a disservice. It happened during Covid-19. It limited the attendees she got. The mosque had a restrictive building capacity. The Imam locked the mosque doors. The prayer service took place outside the mosque. I let out an excruciating sob during the service. No hardship could equate to losing your grandma. My mother, Nadia, allowed me to grieve. She felt scared of my academic standing. It was now September. I had missed the first two weeks of school.

I got homeschooled during this time. It became clear that I may not graduate. My mom, Nadia, told me that I was to re-attend classes tomorrow. That night, I anticipated my reintegration. My anxiety prohibited any shut-eye. In the morning, I needed to get ready for school. I laid on my back and put a pillow over my face. I let out a gigantic scream. Why was she making me do this?

I did not want to go back. I hated everyone at that school. I got up and made a U-turn for my closet. I plucked out a raggedy beige coat and a pair of jeans. I put on meditative music to calm my nerves. It was time to go to class. I left my house and trekked to school. It was a fifteen-minute walk.

I entered the school and made my way to the office. I informed the staff that I had returned. The administrator welcomed me back. She told me to sign my name in the attendance book. I obliged. I went to my locker and grabbed my textbooks. The students operated at a fast pace. Everything seemed surreal. My movements did not match my peers. I moved in slow motion. My world had to come to a halt. I did my best not to let my outer expressions show. I was dying inside. I followed people making their way to science class. The teacher recognized my resurfacing. He appeared surprised. I resented my mom for this. He re-welcomed me back to class.

I wished that I could have gone unnoticed. My attempt to go under the radar failed. I barely engaged with anyone the entire day. The school finished. I survived. Days like this were sure to follow. By the end of the week, I saw slight improvements. I reverted to isolation during the weekend. On Monday, I heard we had a school speaker. All grades were to take part. Grade 12 got slotted for the fourth period. The classes lagged. I limited my social engagements. It differs from my usual behavior. I was extroverted. My teachers described me as a well-mannered, friendly girl.. I feared that once I got out of this funk, I would no longer have any of my friends. I needed to think of my life post-grief.

In the thick of healing, I forgot to treat people properly. I got into a tiff with my friend, Mia. She, fortunately, understood that my sarcasm got misconstrued. She understood I was not myself and let it slide. It reminded me that I could not blame my poor behavior on grief. I knew that even though I was healing, I would need to follow social protocol. I struggled with everything. An archaeologist stood center stage in our school auditorium. She appeared to be ambiguous. She went by the name Aliyah Smith. She was a well-organized individual. She had replica skulls placed on a table. Aliyah had a projector screen with an ancient burial site. Her speech intended to elicit mobilization.

She personalized the reason that led her to this profession. She came from Saint Thomas. She was not indigenous to the region. She specialized in allocating African countries. Caribbean islanders had their ethnicity stripped away. She explained that her African heritage had been diluted through forced interbreeding and rape, changing her family's complexion. My initial thoughts of her ambiguous heritage were indeed correct. I felt a sense of validation, but the reason behind it was tragic. She reiterated that she is a Saint Thomas national of African descent, a testament to her determination and resilience that instilled hope and respect.

Aliyah wanted to right the wrongs of slavery. She did so by preserving ancient burial sites.

Aliyah Smith's research, a tribute to her enslaved ancestors who arrived in Saint Thomas via the slave ship Society, is a powerful and emotionally weighty narrative. The ship carried 425 Africans to Saint Thomas, with one not reaching the island. As she shared this, I could see a collective realization dawning on the audience, uniting them in empathy for the emotional weight of her words.

She learned of the profession back in elementary school. It was a unique career choice. I believe archeology is an under-respected social science. Aliyah's ability to combine her charitable pursuits with her career was riveting. Her parents migrated to Canada when she was fourteen. She realized the opportunity her parents blessed her with. She focused on her education.

She took the appropriate prerequisites. Aliyah was on track to become an archeologist. She got her credentials from a university. Aliyah started by working as a professor's assistant. It opened up doors for her. She got hired at the university's archeology institute. Aliyah made her way up the ranks. Her superiority permitted her to work on personal pursuits. Aliyah began networking with black archeologists. She was an avid Black Lives Matter supporter. Aliyah went back to Saint Thomas. Her team dug up burial sites and preserved the remains. These sites are critical to black history. It was a black social rights initiative. I had never heard of a social rights initiative like this before.

I associated black rights with a lot of empowered and passionate protestors. I was intrigued that she did not follow the grain. In doing so, she is an impactful individual fighting for black equality. The entire auditorium erupted in adulation. I resonated with her. I have always had a philanthropic spirit. It was my dream to one day work in a profession where I could make a difference. I momentarily considered getting my credentials to become an archeologist. After her speech, I thought about her impact on the Black community. She was changing the Caribbean.

I thought about the concept of indigeneity. Saint Thomas had been her home for centuries. She was African.

She had lost her ties to her homeland. Her ethnicity had got stripped from her. I found that to be a horrific tragedy. I respected her. I returned to class. I reoccupied my mind with school matters. The question lingered in the background: Where do I come from? I was a blank canvas.

My ancestry left me full of questions. I needed to figure out where to begin my research. Why did no one keep track of records throughout the generations? There was a proven history of a diverse population in the region. The majority of the Lebanese populace claimed indigeneity. Genealogy is a powerful source of knowledge. I decided to challenge my genealogy. It meant prioritizing my ancestral history.

I thought I was Lebanese. I only knew my lineage in the 1890s. I felt moved by Aliyah Smith's speech. I went home and typed my surname, Jignyasu, into a website. The website kept historical ancestral records. The only drawback was the information tailored to European history. It had a minuscule Middle Eastern selection. Five results popped up. Three are unrelated to me. I need more than one result to provide me with information. I searched for more genealogical websites. A pre-made family tree would have been helpful. We did not have one. I thought about curating one. I needed to figure out where to begin. I lunged my body away from the computer. I sprinted into the living room.

My parents were watching television. Their statements backed up my research. My mom, Nadia, looked agitated.

"Yura, if it is not online, it is because no one in our family had access to the records. We have a large extended family. Someone would have done it. We come from Lebanon. Lebanon is a third-world country. There are no historical records of our family." I was not going down without a fight.

My resilience, a product of years of marginalization, has catalyzed personal growth. It has taught me that life doesn't offer opportunities; I must actively pursue my goals. With unwavering determination, I set my sights on my objectives. I took a deep breath, reaffirming my commitment to my journey.

"Mom, we need to overcome this barrier. We must find a roundabout solution. We need to be proactive."

Recognizing the barriers we faced due to a lack of knowledge, I refused to accept further marginalization of our family. A surge of energy overcame me, and my mindset allowed me to mobilize into action fully.

I got rebutted. My mother, Nadia, spoke, "We do not have access to records.

Our relatives would have that knowledge. The sheer fact that we do not have a family tree is telling. It is plausible that we have one that needs to be documented online. Otherwise, there is nothing to tell.

Genealogy is not the end of the world. Leave it alone." I found her comments to be malicious. I made a compelling argument. I thought my mother, Nadia, had put little effort into learning this subject. That would need to change. This form of education is enticing. It would allow my family to become well-informed self-advocates.

"Mom, the information I will acquire will change the world."

My mom did not understand why this was so important to me. I know the instability of the Middle East region has hurt so many families. Ancestry has the power to change the world. I am one person who will unwaveringly use my voice to ignite a positive change for thousands of people. I believe in the potential of my actions to bring hope and optimism to those affected.

"Yura, your grandparents were orphans. The records got tarnished. People in the village kept track mentally. If I had something to inform you about, I already would have. There is nothing to find. Our relatives would have that knowledge. You have yet to speak to anyone about this. One of our grandaunts would have done the entire Lebanese tree. I do not believe there is anything to tell. Sorry that the history is boring. You would like a more intrinsic backstory. That woman's story is about African slavery in the Caribbean. It does not apply to Lebanon. The majority of Lebanon is indigenous to the region. What could be so interesting that it must become uncovered?"

[I refrained from commenting. I began compiling the reasons this issue, with its complex layers and deep personal significance, meant so much to me. The restructuring of social order, recognizing past emigration patterns, and changing ancestry for the masses. I recognized that my mother did not fully comprehend the importance. I hoped she would change her mind about this in the future.

I disregarded what she said. I knew that being complacent was the worst thing to do in self-advocacy. I needed to ignore her harsh skepticism and retaliate with hard work. I knew I had to get a further backstory of our family's lineage. "I am going to know who my ancestors were." During childhood, our familial lineage had no value to me. My family bathed in their ignorance. Finding our roots proved to be too difficult. As I got older, I felt more sentimental. I knew I would be the first person in my family to find these roots.

Chapter 9: Elgin Marbles

Yura, I am vaguely familiar with ancient Islamic empires."
My mom paused for a moment before continuing. She My
mom stated, "There are national historical sites and
landmarks across Lebanon of architecture built during
these empires. I appreciated the insight. I will further
research these sites later". Having a Christian mother and
Muslim father meant there was a discourse about this
subject. My father, Malik, was more receptive to these
empires than my mother was. I side with my mother,
Aisha. I have extensively tried to empathize with my
father, Malik. It helped me gain a healthier perspective.
Therefore, I do not blame the descendants of the Ottoman
Empire. My best friend, Hamza, is an Ottoman. I hold no
animosity toward him. He can speak Turkish. He has
taught me a few words. To hate the Ottomans would mean
I hated Iran and Turkey.

"They have a high percentage of Turkic blood in them.
The largest ethnic subgroup in the Middle East is the
Ottomans. The same goes for Russia. I do recognize that
spewing hatred is racist. I do detest what resulted from the
empires. When my mother Aisha remarried later in life, she
married someone from Afghanistan. My stepfather, Abdul,
felt agitated about the religious trajectory that the country
went down. I learned a multitude of facts from that man.

Did you know that the Mughal Empire colonized Afghanistan? It was once a thriving cosmopolitan. They practiced Buddhism." That piqued my interest. I began listening more attentively.

I had elementary school friends from Afghanistan. They moderately practiced Islam. I wanted to acquire more insights into this topic. My father, Omar, resumed speaking. "The architecture backs this. Afghanistan once had a United Nations Educational, Scientific, and Cultural Organization World Heritage Site. This monument in the Bamiyan Valley, called Buddha of Bamyan, was eviscerated. The Taliban leader, Mullah Omar, became threatened by the statues. He did not want Buddha idolized. The only religions acceptable for worship were Islam and the Taliban." I shook my head in horror. I watched as he pulled out his cell phone from his pocket.

"Here is a picture of the statue. The other photo is of when it got annihilated."

I stood in horror. The statute is an essential artifact of history. It did not change the religious demographics of the region. The Taliban's one-sided mentality could not tolerate a minuscule presence of another religion on their soil. Afghanistan is 99.7 percent Muslim. The minority religions are Christians, Sikhs, Hindus, and Baha'i. Despite their religious persecution, these individuals continue to practice their faith, showing remarkable resilience. It's crucial that we, as a global community, raise awareness and extend our support to these persecuted individuals

"Dad, that is devastating. I do not understand. It is just an ancient statue. Why would they disintegrate an ancient artifact? It is their history. It does not deter them from their Islamic way of life."

I watched my mother and father's countenance change from neutral to concerned. She understands that the Taliban did this to silence their opposition. Oppositional figures often involve peaceful human rights activists: bloggers, lawyers, and protestors. These countries do not permit political discourse.

"I know, Yura. I want to fight extreme Islamic ideologies. I am just one man. Change starts small. Your mother and I knew we had the opportunity to raise two daughters to become strong, independent thinkers. That is what we did. There is always more room for progress. Afghanistan is not the only country committing these atrocities. It happened in Uralic Russia. The government demolished Shedrub Ling.

"Russian politics did not align with the symbol. It is the way dictators operate. Both monument eviscerations occurred in the 21st century. These were measures to ensure obedience. An inquiry into Buddhism was unacceptable. Doubting the leaders' capabilities could have been more beneficial. The destruction of these heritage sites did not go unnoticed. It received backlash and public outcries. The government persisted nonetheless. Democracy does not exist in violent dictatorships. The government aimed to destroy the symbol. Symbols invoke emotion. It promotes freedom of thought. It can dismantle oppressive regimes. These symbols challenge authority and prove to be a threat.

"Dictators will not take that chance. These symbols propagate the populace. They derive from prehistoric empires. The public must get this knowledge. These images remain on display.

"The Swastika originated from Buddhism and Hinduism. The original translation meant the promising footprints of the Buddha. Hitler adopted this symbol for his neo-Nazi party. The original symbol message got replaced. It is now a symbol for the alt-right. Most neo-Nazis adhere to Christianity. It appalls me. Many Jewish are of Iranian heritage. A lot of Jews now living in Israel are of Arabic descent. We need to focus on our similarities rather than differences.

"The Swastika is used to perpetuate hatred when it once was a symbol of purity. The Swastika is a violent symbol. It is the extermination of the Jewish population. These symbols mismatch religion. Buddhists and Hindus continue to use this symbol. It is a cultural shock to the Western world. When assessing Lebanese empires, focus on these symbols. Symbols show history. It is used to empower communities and goes against corrupt governments. Oppressive regimes want an uneducated population. They obtain this objective by spreading misinformation. The media promotes their agenda. After a prolonged period, people become accustomed.

"The government turns the populace against each other. They do not care about advancing as a society. This history involves the public. That is their ancestral lineage. Your genetics are a compilation of past generations. It goes back hundreds to thousands of years. It can date back to

500,000 years ago. Buddhism fell in the fourteenth century. Afghanistan was part of the Buddhist era. Now, due to the Islamic Empire, they get subjected to undue racism as a result. Islam is not well received. In my opinion, Buddhism is more tolerated. I do not understand the justification. Both commit violent crimes. Buddhists commit more crimes in East Asia. I have a theory about this.

"The isolated Far East Asian region is less prioritized. I think the distance dehumanizes people. Those living in Far East Asia are valued less. Islam carried out terrorist attacks in Christian nations. The major one was the 9/11 attack. Two hijacked planes crashed into the Twin Towers. New York City felt shaken. The episode is more nuanced than the public believes. The government could have averted the crash. The Federal Bureau of Investigation got alerted at 8.19 a.m. The plane crashed into the tower at 8.46 a.m. That is twenty-seven minutes to mobilize into action.

"The Federal Bureau of Investigation has a $3.339 billion budget. There is no excuse for their delayed reaction.

"The Federal Bureau of Investigation's job is to prevent terrorist attacks. The government knew this would be a reason to go to war. The government did not hijack the planes; the onus is on Al-Qaeda. It resulted in mass murders of ethnically diverse business people in New York City. They are a terrorist organization. The war in the Middle East did not even remove them from power. The Taliban has a high level of megalomania. I felt terrified that my children would be victimized by racism. We were innocent bystanders caught in the crossfire. I had never experienced the level of racism that I received on September 12. I felt sub-human. I had no involvement. I am a man.

"I held my head in shame. It was the first time I wished I could change my race. I called my mom, Aisha, and told her to remove her hijab. She was hesitant. Eventually, she did. It affected my family. Yura, I raised you to be an intellectual thinker. I gave you an honest portrayal of Allah. Do you remember? Here is a refresher. In the 500s, Muhammad proclaimed that he was God's messenger. The Saudi Arabian indigenous population labeled him a lunatic. The indigenous attempted to kill him many times. On one occasion, Muhammad hid from potential murderers when a spider formed a web. The web provided shielding. It saved his life. Muhammad went decades without recognition for being God's messenger.

"This colonization did not happen overnight. It took place within eight centuries. There is a lot of push and pull. We are not a monolithic group of people. Your prehistoric roots do not influence beliefs. Beliefs are an individualized choice. We work together to create a more liberated future. Individuals must fight oppressive governments. It is how people become united." I took a moment to digest what he was saying. A lot of that aligned with my preset ideological views. My sister, Elizabeth, came into my parents' bedroom.

Her action was an intrusion into our conversation. I would have allowed her to converse with our parents without infringing on her privacy. Nonetheless, Elizabeth made her presence known. The entire room became silent, permitting her to speak.

"I could hear you from my room. I want to add insight to the conversation." My immediate thought is that she is an intruder in this conversation.

We tend to disagree on multiple geo-political issues. My sister's opinions are controversial. I felt undetermined about whether she could provide me with any helpful information. My sister was transgender and Muslim. She did not want to assist my genealogical journey. She wanted to push Islam. Any critiques of Islam, she was there. She was their most adamant supporter. "There has been improvement since the Altai invasion. Religious believers have modernized in certain aspects. The Altai did infiltrate Africa and the Middle East. Europe invaded too. Europe committed heinous acts against Africans and Americans. They indoctrinated them into Christianity. Muslim governments are not monolithic.

"Governments range in severity. In Saudi Arabia, stoning still exists. It is not the only problem we face. Female mutilation exists in certain countries. I feel privileged to come from Lebanon. I am Muslim and transgender. Things are changing. I am a trailblazer. Moderate Muslims will fight for what is right. Attacking Islam is never appropriate. Islam needs restoration. The gay, lesbian, bi-sexual, transgender, queer, and 2Spirit community will get accepted eventually, inshallah. Gay men were prominent in ancient Islamic empires."

As someone with a transgender sister, I wish the Muslims in the 21st century felt willing to adapt and develop an inclusionary society where members of the lesbian, gay, bisexual, and transgender communities felt included. The contention bothered my family instrumentally, especially with Elizabeth's indoctrination of Islam.

I rebutted, "Who was gay in the prehistoric Islamic Empires?"

Elizabeth resumed speaking. "Al-Mutamid, Ibn Sahl, Mubarak and Muzaffar, Sultan Mahmud, Malik Al-Ashraf, Murad IV, and Muhammad Al-Amin, just to name a few."

The rulers determined that it was problematic. They changed the Quran. Religious leaders have informed me that it is permitted to have feelings for the same sex. People were Acting on these feelings is prohibited. Many spiritual leaders shame them as members of the lesbian, gay, bisexual, and transgender community. The condemnation to burn in hell is pervasive

Chapter 10: Venus of Willendorf

"The rulers determined that it was problematic. They changed the Quran. It is permitted to have feelings for the same sex. People were prohibited from acting on these feelings. Many religious leaders shame them, claiming we will burn in hell. The extremists have carried out violent acts, including murder. Modern Muslims accept them. It is a continuous battle. In religious countries, they get murdered. It occurs in Christianity too. Homosexuality is a sin.

"Trans-genders get murdered in Westernized nations too. Trans-genders are four times higher to be a victim of violence. Black trans-genders are most prone to getting murdered. Some people are more accepting than others. Religion has nothing to do with this.

"Feminism is the focal point. It is at the forefront of all religious confrontations. The extremists infringe on their beliefs about women. It gets worldwide humanitarian attention. Many countries do not allow women to work. Women fight for freedom of autonomy. In Saudi Arabia, they must have a male companion. Women are male property. Women want to be classified as human. The Quran's textual beliefs became outdated. There have been claims that Western religions are violent. They point to Hinduism and Buddhism for enlightenment.

"Islam is an Asian religion. Hindus and Buddhists practice their faith in the Western world. There is a discourse within those who practice Islam. There are three different types of Islam: Shia, Sunni, and Sufi. Sufi is the most peaceful form of Islam. Druze is similar to Islam. Christian and Jewish prophets are from Israel. In my opinion, Lebanon, Syria, Israel, Iraq, and Jordan should all be part of Europe.

"I converted to Sufi. Also, to Dad's point, the indigenous community no longer exists. The Middle East needs to accept that. You could still learn the Syriac language. There are United Nations Educational, Scientific, and Cultural Organization heritage sites in Lebanon from these empires. We are not in Afghanistan. Do not equate the Taliban with Islam. It is not an Islamic issue." Elizabeth stopped speaking. She looked content. I pondered Elizabeth's statements. They had validity. She is defensive of Islam. Elizabeth is also able to recognize its flaws. She was insightful. I did appreciate her liberal take on Islam.

I recognized that ideological discourse can invoke innovation and creativity. I respected Elizabeth's thoughts and provided a source of intellectual value. Elizabeth and I have engaged in these types of conversations frequently, and they have enhanced spiritual self-growth. I am grateful for the insightful discourse we have.

"Thank you for your contributions, guys. You did not have to assist me with my project. That is appreciated. It was an insightful morning." I needed to make a mental note. I learned a multitude of fascinating facts through this interaction. I quickly realized that that information was imperative to my research. I needed to write their main points on a notepad.

As I quickly exited their bedroom, a sense of urgency filled me. I entered my room, retrieved my backpack, and unzipped the main zipper. I took out my notepad and pen, ready to capture our profound discussions. The fear of missing critical vital pieces of information was a constant companion, heightening my anxiety. But as I re-entered their room and reverberated what I had written to them, their reassurance that I had not missed any crucial topic discussed was a soothing balm to my nerves. Their role in calming my nerves was significant, and I felt a deep sense of gratitude toward them.

My stepfather replied, "You're welcome, sweetie." We embraced in a family group hug. I felt the room full of familial love. It warmed my heart. I felt understood by my parents. I no longer felt alone. I left my parent's room.

Months later, my inquiries continued. They got enhanced. I had a passion for the topic. I felt enthralled by the historical unknowns. It got so bad that I brought it up every day. I wanted my friends and family to have the same level of passion. They were intrigued by the process. My interest in the topic far surpassed theirs. It filled my heart with wonder. My desire to partake in something larger than myself came to fruition. I left my bedroom. I went to the basement. I retrieved our family photo album. I opened the photo album looking for a racial indicator. I hoped the photos would give me information.

I am semi-educated, and this task seemed too big for my capabilities. I doubted myself. I needed to figure out where to start my research. I needed to get a better understanding of myself. I was staring at an empty barrel of information. I questioned whether I could find anything of value in the old artifacts in my parents' basement. They possess photographs and documents and have stored them for decades. I knew about the Paleolithic period. It was any time before 10,000 B.C. Humans have evolved throughout the centuries. The fundamental characteristics have stayed the same. Our body protects us from the elements. Homo sapiens were able to harness their environment.

Later, we developed a higher level of intelligence. Humans have changed. I have done extensive research into archaeology. I expected this image to match an isolated region. Morphology is a geographical occurrence. It occurs within the indigenous populations. It is the serial-founder effect. It is the direct link between genetics and geography. It changes a person's heterozygosity. I opened up my laptop. I searched for differentiating facial features in the browser. I clicked on a link. It said: Homogeneous environments result in a mixture. International relations occur, and they produce offspring. The ethnic mix is typical. Ethnic racial facial features overlap with the prehistoric empire that existed in the region.

These features exist within a subgroup of the community. Mixed-race individuals preserve their race by intermarrying with others who share a similar mixture. The percentage gets diluted in the process. with other mixed individuals. The indigeneity became compromised, and the percentage got diluted. It resulted in their unique heterozygosity. It is difficult to differentiate between the indigenous and foreign races. There are indicators shown in their facial appearances. Lebanon has accepted diversity as an indigeneity. It made the region more tolerant. It also spiked racism. Dark-skinned individuals get lumped into the same category as light-skins. It deters them from seeking help. Racism is prevalent in the Middle East and North Africa.

Dark-skinned individuals deal with racial micro-aggressions daily. Skin tone does not determine a person's location. Many indicators must be present. Deviating from the expected appearance could lower the quality of life. It needs to change. People need to identify their race. There needs to be more information given to the public. It does not provide an accurate depiction of the history. It has led to an unjustifiable over-claim of indigeneity. Indigeneity in Lebanon has diluted quite a bit. After the annexation of the Ottoman Empire, Lebanon continued to engage in interracial relationships. Lebanon is a diverse region. Some people's facial features are an indicator of the empire.

A sub-sect has prominent Asian features. Facial characteristics were an indicator of race. Asians mutated their cheekbone structure. It happens to 25% of the population. My grandparents had a high cheekbone structure. I examined the zygomatic bone. It could have been a result of ancestral variations. Mass migration was once common in Lebanon. It helped me categorize their facial characteristics. I jotted this tidbit of information onto a notepad. I needed to keep this information for later. I thought this was telling. It turned out to be a fluke. It made me assess the reasons for morphology. My grandmother had certain stereotypical Asian features.

When I was a child, I occasionally examined her. I marveled at her Asian-looking appearance. A large part of me wanted to come from Asia. I dismissed this. She descended from Lebanon. It was not a debatable issue. I did not understand how her Asian morphology came to be. Asians are similar to Europeans. A sub-sect of Asians has a white complexion. Therefore, they would qualify as white. It depends on their skin tone. That could have been my grandmother.

Their facial characteristics differentiate them. I needed to get a better understanding of this subject. It would help me understand my own family's morphology anomalies better.

Ancient genetics may prove why she had these features. Throughout history, the zygomatic bone has changed. It occurred in various isolated regions. Scientists hypothesize the reasoning. The two main factors are diet and climate. Far Eastern Asians adapted to the region's environment. It changed their facial structure. Far East Asians voyaged and settled in uncharted territories. The voyagers had Far Eastern morphology. Natural selection took its course. Their beauty standards were different. It influenced mating practices after getting a solid understanding of the topic. The research helped me realize that the Mamluks and Ottomans kept their original morphology and added European.

It is a strong indicator that my family came from the region. Far East Asian morphology is not that different from Middle Eastern. It is close by. I read that in the Middle East, a subgroup still looks Asian. It depends on their ancient mating habits. It occurred in some families. It is a mixture of European and Asian descent.

I pondered whether my grandmother could have these traits without being Far East Asian. I slowly realized that my grandmother could have come from Altai. If that were the case, my speech would have been correct. It could indicate that my fib was the truth. Many families in Lebanon have descended from the Altai. That admixture made the country beautiful. Far East Asians experienced isolation. Interrelationships with foreigners were also common. It altered their facial heterozygosity morphology.

Indigeneity is common in Lebanon. I felt uncertain about my heritage. Their morphology was an indicator. I questioned our indigeneity. I assumed that my family was indigenous. My parents claimed that they were Arabs. My research challenged this. Foreign mass migration impacts the population. It hinders the ability to showcase the isolated regions' heterozygosity. My father, Omar, had strawberry-blonde hair and blue eyes. His eyes resembled Far Eastern Asian ancestry. He was paler than me. We shared a similar skin tone. He could pass for a European man with Asian facial characteristics. My mother, Nadia, could pass for a biracial woman. She had Far Eastern Asian facial characteristics.

I know firsthand that people perceive my appearance as Mediterranean. It was proving to be too difficult a task.

The Ottomans changed Lebanon's ethnic race. The power dynamics favored the Europeans in the later years of the Ottoman Empire. The rulers were called Pasha. Pasha came from various regions across the globe. Admixture is crucial to a socially accepting society. Lack of education is our biggest pitfall. I needed to dedicate more to studying this topic. I honed in on my research. I created many accounts on genealogical websites. I thought I would find a leaf. I had my eye out for migration and birth records. I discovered that Lebanese people have similar names. I found this venture to be taxing.

Names were deceptive. I went down that rabbit hole many times. My relatives popped up on my screen—the information needed to be more varied. I felt myself getting frustrated. I needed to remedy my emotions. I ordered two separate ancestral DNA (deoxyribonucleic acid) kits online. The website explained the process. The laboratory technicians assess a person's genome's compatibility with a global region. The information was priceless. Yura Jignyasu was not going down without a fight. That was one of many things I planned to do.

Chapter 11: Sphinx of Hatshepsut

The morning was uneventful. I just needed to get used to the new foreign surroundings.

I must have gotten lost twelve times. I went to a college kiosk and asked an associate for help. A man named Nick provided me with a comprehensive map of the college campus. "The college campus sections are broken down alphabetically. On the tile floors, there is a marked letter." I looked at the ground. I noticed the letter C.

The symbol vindicated my suspicion that I was utterly lost. I shook my head in disarray. The campus appeared to be one giant unsolved puzzle I must solve quickly to stay caught up academically. The urgency of this task, pressing on me like a heavyweight, was not lost on me as I smiled embarrassingly at Nick.

"Thank you. If I am in section C, how can I get to section F?"

- "It is in chronological order. On the corner of the map, there is a campus compass. That should help you with your navigation process."

[I felt humiliated asking for help with something straightforward. I needed to cut myself some slack and remind myself that I was new to the campus and navigating the facilities would take time.

"Thank you, Nick." As I walked, I kept my head down. It enabled me to go under the radar. I stared at the tiles.

I found the calligraphy added to the ambiance of the college. It made the college accessible. I found that to be innovative. It helps the directionally challenged, like myself, find their way around campus. In every single class, the professor required an introduction. It involved limited academics. It was still draining. I felt exhausted. The day was full of newness. I am a creature of habit. I got through it. The day was coming to an end. I survived. I felt incredibly awkward all day. I wanted to revert to my research. It was my comfort zone. I phoned the Lebanese embassy. I dialed the number. A man answered, "Hello, how may I help you?"

I felt satisfied that my phone call did not immediately go to voicemail. It increased my chances of receiving a concrete result, and I felt one step closer to achieving my goal. I took a deep breath and mustered the courage to ask you my question.

"Hello. How can I access my genealogical records? I want to obtain the names of my late relatives?"

Immediately, I felt trepidation that I would be disappointed with the response. I did not want to be a pest to the staff at the local cemetery, so I hoped the man would understand my request. Momentarily, a soft-spoken gentleman replied.

"You must know the names and cemetery locations of the relatives. Without this information, I cannot assist you."

As I realized the potential for this to become a requirement, I felt a sense of dread. It was a significant barrier in my pursuit of information, but it only fueled my determination to overcome it, even if it meant enduring more strain. "I do not have this information. Is there any way around this?"

My face flushed with embarrassment, a stark reminder of the racial inequality I was facing. This was not just a barrier, but a personal experience of disenfranchisement that I had endured throughout my life, and was now determined to overcome.

"No, there is not. I am sorry. Is that all I can help you with?"

I expected this reply, but hearing those utterances felt beyond disheartening. I wanted to know if my objectives were obtainable. Those words knocked the wind right out of me. I needed to remind myself that this major setback would not deter me from pursuing this further.

I managed to muster out the word.

"Yes."

The one-word statement proved to be too much for me. I noticed a crack in my voice. My response was disproportionate to the situation. Determining my ancestral roots has dominated all arenas in my life.

"Have a good day, ma'am." I was at a dead end. I felt let down. I wanted to comfort myself. I ordered a spicy curry. I needed to go pick it up. It was a five-minute bus ride. I arrived at the restaurant and paid for my food. I planned to return home. I waited for the bus.

When the bus arrived, I got on. A racist man was sitting at the front of the bus. He made his views of the Middle East apparent.

I felt myself reverting to myself. I questioned whether it was because the men realized I was Arabic. I pondered my safety. I wanted to get off immediately. I felt sick to my stomach. I entered my house and ran to the restroom. My mother, Nadia, sensed that something was wrong. She followed me. I was looking in the bathroom mirror. I criticized my appearance. My mom, Nadia, noticed the pain in my eyes. "What happened, sweetie?"

[I attempted to be discreet, consciously trying to hide my feelings. I did not want to burden anyone with my issues. However, my body language may have inadvertently betrayed my distress. I took a deep breath, and I thought of fabricating a story. It was a tempting escape, but in the end, I chose to confide in her about the verbal harassment I experienced on my bus ride home, feeling a wave of relief wash over me.]

"I got called a terrorist on my way here." Being attacked by a stranger on the bus proved to be too much. I felt distressed. I questioned if I belonged in my own country. "Mom, should I move to Lebanon? There, I will get accepted."

My snarky side comment had a tinge of sarcasm and desire. Xenophobia and Islamophobia were spiraling out of control in Canada. I wondered how my mother would perceive my comment. She loved visiting Lebanon. I anticipated her response before she delivered it.

"You belong here. You belong here more than me. You were born here. You are a Canadian. One racist cannot take that away."

Her comment had merit. I had once received unwanted xenophobia and Islamophobic slurs from a new immigrant who came from Europe with a Christian theology. These experiences, having lived here all my life, have significantly shaped my perceptions. His birthright overpowers me substantially.

My mom, Nadia, made a cute remark. "They were jealous that you are Arabic. Not everyone gets to say that."

The words stung. I knew my family consisted of hard-working middle-class individuals who had tried to assimilate into Canadian culture to the best of their abilities. We did not deserve this injustice.

"Mom, it is not that easy. Modern-day racism is the sole divider among people. I get classified as other. It means that people think I am less. I do not try to provoke racism. Racism finds me."

"Yura, I understand. When I was a child, I was in the same dilemma. I tried to form friendships with the white kids. Friendships do form, but there is underlying racism. I tended to gravitate toward those in the same predicament. People of color understood me more. My Arabic friendships were more substantial." My mother, Nadia, was curious to know if her statement had been well received. I thought about her sentiments. We formed a tacit agreement. I sympathized with my mom, Nadia.

"Forming inclusive friendships was a difficult task. I was different. It is easy to feel you do not belong anywhere. Marginalized groups get subjected to racism. This results in economic disadvantages. I am an average woman. Growing up in Canada, I felt like an outcast. I was a

Lebanese ex-Muslim. I did not fit into my community. It left me with a skewed sense of self. I was on a continuous journey. I needed to find my place within society.

"It was due to my ethnicity. It is a dilemma for modernized Arabs. It is a continuous battle. It will impact upcoming generations. We can overcome it. You are stronger than the racists."

"Mom, I am experiencing an identity crisis. I could pass as a European individual. Thus, why could I not form friendships in the same way? At the same token, I embraced being a person of color. I experience hatred that goes unrecognized. My pain felt minimized. I get attacked for my religious association daily."

Being an Arab in a racist world proved to be too much. My mom, Nadia, noticed that I had disdain for being Arab. Europeans had everything. There was no justice. No inequality. My mom noticed that I was staring at my eye's epicanthic fold.

"Yura, you are a beautiful girl, sweetheart. There have been strong women feeling the way you do now. You will not be the first. You will not be the last. Every Arab woman has different facial characteristics. The Arab region spans most of Asia and North Africa. That is a large land mass with varying ethnic characteristics. That does not take away from your beauty. It adds to the diversity. It does not take away from your heritage. You are Lebanese. It is the culture you grew up with. I hope you learn to embrace your culture. I love you with all my heart. Does that not count for anything?" I smiled. I was on the brink of tears.

Her encouragement, affirming my humanitarian path, a journey I embarked on to bring positive change to the world, was a testament to her unwavering support. Despite the deep wounds inflicted by hurtful words, her love, a comforting and healing force, was always there. I treasured this moment, understanding my mother's role as my psychological bedrock. Her enduring support reassured me that I would readily offer the same support to her in a different circumstance.

My mom, Nadia, resumed speaking.

"I did my job to ensure you are confident. I cannot change the racist ideologies. Everyone has different views. Intransigence can be oppressive. I want you to feel equal in this world. I talked to my friend, Monika Lopez, about this. She said this was a common occurrence in South America. The majority of South Americans are white. There are minority groups: Black and Asian. Monika is a feminist. She stressed to me the unhealthy beauty standards of the region. Women feel insecure about their race if they are not white. Every racial group is Latina. The treatment among ethnic groups is not the same. It also occurs across the vast Middle Eastern region. You should know this more than anyone. You have studied the prehistoric migration habits."

[Her aggrandizing comments boosted my self-confidence, and I appreciated her kind words. I have learned the dangers of over-aggrandizing myself, which has led me to make a concerted effort to balance self-assuredness and humility

I had an immediate response. "This is what I have studied, recognizing the region. Regions in Lebanon experienced different migrations. It is an indicator of our heritage. It is in surnames. Surnames have meanings. In prehistoric empires, individuals named themselves after the location they came from. It is misleading. Once an individual settles in the region, a mixture with the indigenous is expected. They may indicate professions your ancestors had. Remember our past conversation in my bedroom about janissaries?" I paused for a moment.

[I had temporarily forgotten that the conversation had taken place. It took me a few minutes to access the memory. The lack of awareness made me feel nervous about the state of my mental faculties. I reassured myself that I had stored it in my long-term memory.

"I recall the conversation."

A sense of emotional ease overtook my entire body. I smiled with a sense of relief. My mother reciprocated by replicating my facial expression. She appeared to be formulating her following comments. I patiently and with great respect waited for her to state her valuable input, eagerly anticipating the new information I would gain. "That is good. Names showcase signs of slavery within the Islamic Empire. There are signs an individual was once destitute. A surname is a good indicator. Darwish meant a poor peasant or enslaved person. People with the name Darwish likely came from slavery. One of my relatives has the surname Darwish." My mom, Nadia, was incredibly insightful. I pondered whether my family endured slavery. Many families have descended from janissaries. That may be an avenue worthy of consideration.

[Janissaries alluded to the dark history of colonization. I retrieved my phone from my pocket and began casually browsing the internet. I clicked on the first credible article. It read that janissaries came from Christian communities. Burly men from the Altai region abducted isolated children. It's astonishing to think that these young adolescent boys, who experienced an unwilling induction into propaganda training camps, came from Christian communities. Under the watchful eye of their masters, these boys had a mixture of cavalry, militarized training, and Qur'anic studies. The article noted that the lower socio-economic indigenous population, envious of the Janissaries' training, willingly joined the camp. Upon completion of the training, the masters would question the adolescent boy about his beliefs in their Islamic and expansionist pursuits. Despite the overwhelming indoctrination, a few boys resisted the new ideological thinking. Disillusioned by the messaging, these resilient individuals were permitted to return home. As I finished skimming the article, I felt deep empathy for these boys. I closed the tab and put my phone back into my pocket, pondering the strength of their character. I stared at my mom.

"I know, Mom. I learned that we can assess Lebanese heritage through facial appearances. It often showcases ancient migrations. It is in their facial characteristics. Your facial traits do not match a geographical region. Many races got exposed to admixture throughout the centuries. This ethnic group is heterogeneous. The alternative group had their characteristics and traits isolated. It changes when migrants arrive.

"People may casually assess their family's heterozygosity. Being from Lebanon does not accurately portray heritage."

Being raised Lebanese instilled a profound emotional bond with the region. I understand that altering my ancestral lineage would not erase the past two decades of my life, during which I absorbed my heritage's customs, traditions, language, and religion.

"I told you. You do not want us to be Arabic. You have brought genealogy and history into it."

My mother has misunderstood my intentions. My Arab identity has been a guiding force through my formative years. My research is not just an academic pursuit but a vital element in my life, a personal journey that enriches and fortifies my identity. I am thankful for my upbringing in a marginalized community, which has endowed me with resilience and a deep empathy for those who have faced xenophobia and Islamophobia.

"That is not it. I got inspired by my grandma's death. I wanted to right the wrongs of her ancestors." When my grandmother passed away, I found myself becoming more sentimental. The absence of a family tree, a remembrance that could have preserved our family's history, became more pronounced. This realization led me to make the conscious decision to embark on an emotional journey of creating one, despite the daunting task ahead due to the significant gaps in our knowledge dating back generations.

However, my determination to see this through remains unwavering.

"I know. I am proud of you. I hope your research pays off."

"Mom, why do I feel my work is never credited? My research always needs to catch up. It is an uphill battle with no end in sight. Why couldn't I be smart?"

My guilt was immediate and overwhelming after I made a thoughtless comment to seek sympathy. Despite my own insecurities about my intelligence, I should have kept them to myself.

"You are smart, Yura. Whenever you do not feel competent, think about your beauty. Your appearance takes after me. I have always been prettier than you. You are pretty, nonetheless."

My smile was sarcastic. The past year has been a constant struggle with body dysmorphia, a battle that was sparked by the artificiality of the digital world. Social media filters have created unrealistic beauty standards, making my natural aesthetic seem inadequate.

I knew my mom, Nadia, was teasing. I smiled. My insecurities were at an all-time high. "We need to embrace our heritage. Yura, you are respected amongst the Middle Eastern community. I boast about you to my Arabic friends regularly. They are impressed with your endeavor."

Chapter 12: Kensington Runestone

"My friend, Ramzaya, made an interesting comment. You may be interested in it. She said that Lebanese racial composition differs amongst families. Many Lebanese individuals are from a different ethnic group other than Lebanon. They reside in Lebanon. Ramzaya claims Lebanese ancestry. Her ancestors originally descended from Georgia."

"Lebanese people are not homogeneous. There is no correct way to be Lebanese. You can forge your path. You are phenomenal. Yura, you have wisdom paired with knowledge. You could lead the Arabic population into a human rights movement. You can do amazing things."

Recently, I have realized the profound impact of words of affirmation as a love language. Carter has prioritized other scholastic obligatory duties over me, so he no longer serves me in this role. I am grateful to have my mother step in. Though not the same as those from a significant other, her words carry a unique emotional weight that I deeply value.

"Thank you, Mom. I appreciate your kindness. I will take your words into account."

I furthered my education through journals. I perused the previous Islamic empires in the region. The first empire of Lebanon happened when Syria conquered Lebanon. It was the Siege of Damascus. The language spoken was Syriac. It was an iconic time for the Levant Indigenous.

A foreign influence changed indigeneity in the Middle East. The Middle Eastern population wants to refocus on indigenous human rights. An example is the Moroccan Amazigh people. The Arabic population was invasive. It shifted as the Seljuk Turks, Mameluke, and Ottoman empires did. It was Altai's doing. They conquered the entire Middle East. These people swayed the world to see their vision. I felt the Altai's die-hard beliefs about Islam infringed on human rights. It is an unrecognized human rights violation. It occurred a long time ago. There is no appropriate course of action to resolve this. It was a vision that didn't have to see the light of day. It is up to the Middle East and North Africa to correct history.

I put the prehistoric empires of the Middle East in the back of my mind. I did not let this topic consume me 24/7. I embraced my college experience. I knew I would only go through my college experience once, at least at this age. I wanted to take advantage of this time. My life seemed exciting. The school was typical. I attended social gatherings. I went out on dates. I felt like your modern-day woman. I was an active member of campus clubs. My professor, Hanau Bravebird, mandated his students to partake in extracurricular activities. We were required to concentrate on human rights activism. I have rallied at the entryway of my college. I handed out charitable pamphlets. These pamphlets encouraged social involvement. I participated in volunteer initiatives. These were events held by my college. The college website had a section for volunteers. It listed the upcoming social events. An individual became required to sign up for these events.

I focused on becoming a luminary in my community. These charitable events drew me in. I volunteered with my classmates. We discussed international human rights. There are privileges to being European over Arabic. I wanted to fight for people of color. It is hard for Europeans to recognize privilege. One of these women went by the name Aoife. She was of Irish descent. She was passionate about history. Aoife aspired to get a job as a historian. She was business-oriented. She and I went to job fairs together. We both strived to work for the government. Aoife's interest in history dulled people. Not me. I found a kindred soul. A part of me thought she wanted to relive the 1800s.

Aoife and I once went to an ancient heritage site. We learned about how the European settlers lived. It was interesting. Aoife shocked me. She had made this experience more interactive. Aoife insights contributed to my knowledge. She knew more than the heritage site. Aoife told me about how her ancient relatives lived. She had in-depth knowledge. Aoife educated me about European settlements. She went as far back as the 1700s. Aoife had a family tree mapped out. She knew her ancestors in the 1400s. Aoife had images of these individuals in the 1600s. I felt envious. It is a racial disparity in archeology. There was more dug-up history in Ireland than in Lebanon.

I shared Aoife's interest in history. Aoife was more privileged than I. It was an injustice. Economic racism was apparent. It was not her fault. It needed to change. I talked to my other classmate's friend about this. Tina is of

European descent. Tina sided with Aoife. I did not understand how my European friends did not care about the Lebanese population's inequality. It is a human rights crisis. I decided to keep my European friends but needed to build a solid Arabic community. It would help me feel understood racially. Aoife and I met after classes to hang out. Aoife introduced me to her friend, Matilda. Matilda and I were both in world history. Before class, we spent two hours talking. The three of us shared a lot of similar interests.

Chapter 13: Ishtar Gate

We spent quality time together. We bonded over our love for history. I thought we would be good friends. I connected to Matilda's on various social accounts. I noticed extreme ideologies infiltrated her page. I became bothered. We walked to class together. She started disclosing her religiosity to me. She was part of the People's Temple 2.0. I saw the first revolutionary suicide. I watched a documentary series about it. Her ideologies meant she wanted to revive the Jim Jones cult. She said, "It was in homage to Jim Jones. His great-grandson started it. He is a sincere man. He knew what his great-grandpa did was wrong. Jim Jones was misrepresented in the media. He did not offer them a lethal punch. Guyana had an unregulated food and water system. Jim Jones went down as a murderer. There has been no further investigation into this. It has tormented Edward Jones."

Her gibberish jargon, which alluded to her mental instability, was part of a conversation I had with her. I knew her rhetoric contained fallacies, and I wanted to state my case to help her understand. However, I quickly realized she was a recruiter for a cult. Her behavior, with its manipulative undertones, made me wary. I did not want to have the same fate as Jim Jones's followers, so I was cautious in my interactions with her.

My internal dialogue piped up that Edward Jones had a superiority complex. Time would tell whether he was as dangerous. I did not want to find out for myself. Cults solve life's questions. Science was a better method. Matilda stated her case.

As I observed her mentally constructing her argument, I was acutely aware of her intent to sway me toward a different view of the cult. Her attempts at reassurance were futile, for I had firmly closed my mind to her manipulative tactics. My resolve to resist her persuasion was unwavering,

"Edward wants to clear Jim Jones's name. He wants the church to go back to Guyana. Edward has requested that his members get recruited. He wants numerous attendees. The attendees now tally to 1000. I have decided to go. It is a costly trip. I need to save money."

I saved money for living expenses after graduation so I would not go on a frivolous trip, especially one considered high-risk. I had a concrete plan for the future. Additionally, I wanted to avoid spending my time with people who would engage in childish antics.

I stood there in shock. I did not understand. Matilda did not seem suicidal. There were no signs of mental illness present. She seemed content. I did not know if she was masking it. I talked to Aoife about this. She felt concerned. We brought this up. Matilda got defensive. She gave me an ultimatum. Join the cult or cut ties with her. I needed to call the cops. I tried to pry out information about his whereabouts. Matilda remained silent. Regardless, I made a 911 call.

The dispatcher said Edward Jones had not committed a crime. It was legal for large groups to form. He had not committed a crime. There was no warrant to make an arrest. The cops were not willing to further investigate the cult. I thought that once the suicides began happening, the police would be slightly responsible. I knew that my safety was in jeopardy. I needed to remove myself from the situation. I felt petrified. I did not want any involvement with Aoife or Matilda. I needed to take appropriate safety precautions. I did not want to aggravate her. Matilda's affiliations made her a dangerous person. I knew that I needed to wean myself out of her life. I started avoiding her.

Our world history class lumps us together. I wanted to stay focused on my possible execution. In world history, I drew a picture of Matilda drinking a punch beside a graveyard. I can concentrate on the lectures better when I split up my attention. My professor told us we would have a test on Friday. That only gave me three days to study. I came anxious. "Today, we are breaking down Indigenous heritage." I was well-versed in the subject. My history professor was an animated character. Hanau BraveBird was able to encapsulate a room. That made me more engaged in the topic. He had riveting conversations. I hoped it would distract me from Matilda. I avoid making eye contact.

I thought my behavior seemed cold. She would sense something was wrong between us.

The professor began his lecture, "History showcased Europeans voyaging to archipelago islands. Voyagers settled in the region. Shetland and Iceland are prime examples. This documentation is in history. Canada got first occupied by Far East Asian voyagers. European colonizers followed it. As Europeans, we must understand the crimes against humanity that took place. Every year on May 5, my college pays homage to the victims of the residential schools. We must provide the Indigenous with reparations. They have a remarkable story about their arrival. They crossed the tundra from Siberia to Alaska.

"That thick sleet of ice bridged the gap between North America and Asia. The Far East Asians lived in harsh environments. There became a limited amount of protection against the elements."

I could not fathom living in such harsh environments. The newfound information captivated my attention, so I decided to expand my thinking about this topic. The formation of the earth has permitted the human population to grow exponentially, enabling humans to develop the industrial society that exists today.

My classmates looked inquisitive. Erica raised her hand. "I never knew that. How do you know?"

The teacher looked at her with sympathetic compassion, and his expression turned her face pink. I resonated with her embarrassment, so I paid close attention to the teacher's response to assist her with the ordeal.

The teacher grabbed a piece of chalk. "To grasp the cultural references, we must break down the root words. Ojib stems from Persia. If you doubt this, here is another Ojibwe term, Anishinabeg. Ani is rooted in a civilization in ancient Armenia. It is now in Turkey. Shina came from China and Japan. Beg came from Turkey. Have you heard of the Algonquin tribe?"

Chapter 14: Dead Sea Scrolls

"Can you guess what ethnicity the words derived from?" The students shook their heads.

As a Lebanese Canadian, I have always respected the Indigenous populations and the plethora of cultures. Changing my perception of the concept of indigeneity was mind-boggling. My curiosity began to pique up.

"Al derived from the Middle East. Gon is Japanese. Quin is from China." I felt intrigued by the class discussion. The professor's innovative teaching strategy, which provided us with new ways to learn and draw conclusions, has sparked my excitement as a lifelong learner

"There has been a concerted effort to Europeanize terminologies. Chippewa and Saulteaux have a French influence. Tribes have the intention of decolonizing Europe. The original intent became influenced by the Mamluks. They believed in Islam. The indigenous deities were the sun and the moon. It replicated Islam during medieval times. As time passed, astronomers learned about the galaxy. Science proved this was indubitable.

"The religious believers knew that God could not be the sun or moon. Religions had to shift their deities. It would have terminated religion. Islam changed. God is now an invisible deity. One question remained. How did the sun or moon talk to Allah? It did not occur to anyone but

Muhammad. He was a human who lived in the 500s. These ideologies infiltrated the entire Middle East. The Far East Asian community came to America practicing Islam." Parker looked appalled. He was a religious man. Parker was an evangelical Christian. He raised his hand. The professor called on him.

I felt hesitant to engage with Parker because of our rocky history. It became my mandatory obligation to maintain my composure throughout the class discussion. I decided to take a backseat in the debate. I choose to take part in a participatory, active listening role.

"I am in solidarity with other religions. I wanted to take a moment to condemn you for insinuating that Muhammad had hallucinations." Half the class agreed with Parker.

I respected his confidence in advocating his moral theology. However, I did not believe that chastising the teacher was the right approach.

"We do not have to take this. I am calling for a walkout." Five students followed Parker. The students walked out of the class.

The professor is in a place of authority. The students are not in a position to discredit the professor with aggressive vulgarity. I noticed it displayed in the intense tone of Parker's voice.

Hanau Bravebird seems perturbed. Shaken, he returned to his lecture, "Europeans arrived in North America. They indoctrinated the Far East Asians into Christianity into the population. South America had a different history. They believed in Hinduism. The

American Far East Asian religious practices altered from their original meaning.

"Vira is in Hindu and South American cultures. In Hinduism, Virashaivism means a devotee of Shiva. Viracocha is an adaptation of this belief. It is my theory. There is a significant overlap between religions. A lot of religious beliefs are indistinguishable. Pachamama is an excellent example. Taken from Sanskrit, this is a well-known Incan holiday. This celebration replicates the Jewish holiday Pascha. It is a celebration of fertility. The commonalities include the sacrifice of a lamb. Hinduism and Judaism overlap."

I felt intrigued by this topic. I raised my hand. "I would like to add some insight. Modern dictionaries claim words originated in Europe. Europe created words. They take credit for words that did not come from the region. These words came from Far East Asia. It is due to the mass migration of Asians to European countries."

I paused. During my statement, I noticed myself forming my conclusions along the way. I hoped my mom would understand my words and fully comprehend the intention. I considered restructuring my sentence structure and waited for her reply to see if that was necessary.

"That is right, Yura. Europe also whitewashed a lot of words. It happened to my ethnic community. I am a mixture of Ojibwe and Algonquin. I find it offensive that my surname is Bravebird. When I was younger, I thought it meant that I was as brave as the mighty falcon. When I got older, I realized it was all mumbo jumbo. Europeans have whitewashed our history. I needed more substantive knowledge to hold me over. My brother, Pilip, and I have spoken up against the false narrative of indigeneity.

"In my teen years, my inquiries into fact-based knowledge made me detest my name. It reminds me of a cartoon. I do not appreciate that my heritage is the Canadian mascot. We are an ethnicity for people who want to claim Canada as their heritage. It has little to do with the generational suffrage we face. It was traumatic. I appreciate the sympathy. However, people have crossed the line. Due to its peaceful nature, it is a safe ethnic group that Europeans enjoy touting. That is because it is all based on a false narrative. It has become one that Europeans are comfortable with. It does not showcase the ancient Seljuk Turk and Mamluk Empires that once existed.

"When the Europeans arrived, they changed the trajectory of those who resided in the Americas. It minimizes my pain. Europeans were disturbed that we were not expansionists. We co-existed in the pre-industrial revolution with Mother Nature. We lived the traditional nomadic life in Mongolia. The lifestyle is sustainable. We are dealing with a consumerist lifestyle. It is our biggest downfall. It is going to destroy the remaining nature reserves. It demeans my generational suffrage. We are not the Europeanized tribe that the media portrays. We are humans who have experienced one of the largest and worst genocides the world has ever seen. I want to humanize the first peoples of Canada.

"Our family has made the unanimous decision to fight for our human rights. I feel dedicated to this initiative. It is changing the trajectory of our heritage. It will help shape the younger generations." The students saw his emotional disposition. The entire class broke out into loud applause. I knew this was not easy for him; he believed it was for the greater good. My teacher nodded. "I am assigning a school paper. I am allowing students to choose a subject in history. Students became required to write a five-page thesis on it. It will be due on March 2. Any questions?"

I took out my notepad and wrote down the assignment and the due date. It was an academically stimulating challenge, and I hoped it would not feel draining. Nonetheless, I was determined to rise to the occasion and meet the teacher's demands.

George raised his hand. "What is the spacing needed?"

The teacher replied, "Double-spaced. Any more questions?" No one raised their hand. The class came to a close. I asked the professor if I could stay after class. I needed a quiet place to write the assignment.

He has previously permitted other students to use his classroom to complete their assignments. I perceived his answer to be yes well in advance. I accounted for unforeseeable circumstances. There was a short pause while I waited for his answer.

He said, "Okay."

A sweeping sense of relief overcame me. I rectified my hectic academic schedule by being well-prepared in advance. I ensured that the course load did not accumulate into an insurmountable stockpile of paperwork. My classmates shuffled out of the classroom.

My classmates left. When Matilda left, she asked me why I did not sit beside her. "Matilda, you are superior to me. It makes me feel insecure. I do not think we can be friends anymore. It takes a toll on my self-confidence." Matilda bought every line.

My foreboding premonition caused me to feel an unpleasant sensation in the pit of my stomach. I discreetly analyzed Matilda's body language, hoping my perception would be valid. The fear of my discernment deceiving me, a constant threat, loomed large.

"I am sorry. I didn't mean to. You could join the group too."

Having successfully invoked sympathy from her, I found her new emotions making her more susceptible to manipulation. I had no intention of joining this menacing cult, and the need to break the news to her in an amicable manner only added to my internal conflict.

"I am going to decline, Matilda. I am penniless. I could not contribute to your religion. Plus, I am a Muslim. I hope you understand."

Technically, these reasons were honest. Under no circumstances would I have taken part in utter insanity. I fully understand Matilda did not have her full mental faculties.

"I do. I will see you around."

When Matilda left the room, I took a gigantic exhalation. I remained in the classroom. I sat at my habitual desk. I took out a piece of paper from my binder. I opened my pencil case and selected a sharpened pencil. I started brainstorming ideas.

Chapter 15: Rosetta Stone

I wanted my essay to be innovative. I brainstormed thought-provoking subjects. The ideal topic would be one that stimulated my professor, Hanau Bravebird. My professor has his biases. My paper needed to suit my professor's ideological form of thinking. I knew that would put me at an advantage. My professor's ideology swayed his teaching style.

I knew his political affiliation. I made this realization through observation. Hanau was with the Liberal Party. He had a liberal pin in his backpack. Hanau did not say his political views. His teaching style backed his ideologies. The conservative students detested him. It was not the first time Parker and his cronies made multiple attempts to persecute the professor.

Hanau Bravebird is a cutting-edge professor. His ideologies are provocative. He allows students to cultivate their thoughts. Hanau Bravebird is not a dictator. Parker's cronies informed their parents of politics in the classroom. A conservative group rallied against him. My sister, Elizabeth, was an outright conservative.

Had she been in our class, she would have joined in. Elizabeth has excellent left-wing talking points. She does not align with the left. The conservative students labeled Hanau Bravebird as a provocateur. They intended to remove him as a professor. It was a headache for the college dean. The professor did everything correctly. Nothing warranted his termination. His ideologies matched mine. Hanau could dial back on controversial subjects. Overall, I found the classroom topics more riveting. The classroom felt inclusive. Every marginalized group became represented. I knew getting ostracized by his students was an awful ordeal for my professor. I wanted to make a statement that aligned with his beliefs. My writing needed to be meticulous. I chose my topic for the paper. I gathered my thoughts and began to write. Title: Inequalities in Canada. The resemblance in the Middle East. History repeats itself. It has since the dawn of civilization. It has been a recurring theme in Canada since the 1500s. Far-East Asian suffrage can easily be replaced with African.

The differentiating skin tones resulted from a subgroup mixing with Neanderthals. It lightens the skin tone. It was what has caused a deviation between white and black. When Europeans first arrived, they targeted the habitants of the region. In the late 1700s, Africans were forcibly taken from their homelands and shipped to the United States, South America, and the Caribbean. The enslaved Africans worked on the railways. Their malevolent European masters had explosives attached to them. It would prevent the disenfranchised worker from running away. The African community had barbaric lynching committed against them by the Europeans. The African community dreamed of living a better life. It was systematic oppression. Some Europeans knew their behavior was callous. John Lindsay had an illegitimate child with Maria Belle Lindsay in 1761. John's daughter was born into slavery. A human rights pioneer, John accepted his bi-racial child, Dido Elizabeth Belle. That made Dido Elizabeth Belle the first British aristocrat. London, England, was known for African slavery.

In the same period, Olaudah Equiano rose to prominence. Born in 1745, Olaudah Equiano was an iconic Nigerian. He endured multiple slavery attempts as a child. Olaudah tragically got captured at eleven years old. Olaudah was shipped to Barbados.

Interesting fact: Some countries in the Caribbean can trace the name back to a location in Africa. The Bahamas came from Baham village in Cameroon. Nigeria and Cameroon are bordering countries.

When Olaudah was twenty years old, Olaudah worked transporting goods from Georgia to the Caribbean. He had saved enough to purchase his freedom. While boarding a ship in Georgia, he almost got re-enslaved. In his later years of life, he moved to London, England. Olaudah joined the abolitionist movement. In 1783, he informed other abolitionists about the Zong massacre.

The Zong was an African slave ship in 1781. The vessel transported Africans to the Americas. The conditions on the boat were atrocious. It resulted in the Zong massacre, which took over 130 lives. In 1781, the captain of the Zong, Luke Collingwood, and his crew committed a financial crime. The captain and crew threw African captives overboard. They planned to file them as lost cargo. The ship would receive recompensation insurance. This court case occurred in 1783.

There are more notable heroic African saviors from that era. Harriet Tubman was one of the most profound activists of that time. She was a strong black feminist. Harriet Tubman freed herself and helped others escape from slavery. It was indisputable. The African treatment was horrendous. Many perished. The married African women were the victims of their European enslavers raping them. These women gave birth to illegitimate children. It made their African male spouse feel like they were not men. The black men were not allowed to look at a white woman.

White women often reported the men. These men paid with their lives. Later on in the movement, black men protested. They wanted the white men to see them as men. European Americans are at an economic advantage overall. Not every white person has financial security. America needs equity. Reparations are for those who suffered. Black suffrage continues to suffer from generational trauma as a result. It occurs today. People in multiracial relationships get scrutinized. Racial slurs are common. People believe the same races should date themselves. I have always found that notion racist. Humans are the same. Colonization is our differentiator.

The two races had moribund treatment. It did not occur in Canada. Black Americans built the underground railway. It led to Canada and the northern United States. Once they arrived, they experienced hostility. They had freed themselves from the shackles of slavery. The black community expected better treatment. They acquired harsh living arrangements. Their food and water did not have a regulatory system. The African community was prone to illness as a result. Many perished. They were victims of racist laws. The black experience in Canada has never been great. Marginalized groups got attacked. Cases often go unreported. Hatred silences people.

They are afraid of retaliation. The vulnerable are less likely to have access to resources. When they do report hate crimes, the victim expects to get vindicated. It rarely occurs. They have no choice; they must accept what is. It has detrimental mental health ramifications. Minority groups are susceptible to mental illness. In my opinion, people need to educate themselves on human rights. I had an epiphany when I was ten years old. I watched the news with my parents. One of the segments was on Black Lives Matter. It changed my view on racial inequalities in Canada. It was a social rights movement. Our technological devices have the opportunity for us to become activists.

The Black Lives Matter Movement began with one tweet. George Zimmerman shot a black teenager. He was tried for murder. He was acquitted. The impact was devastating for the black community. One caring black woman made a post about her heartbreak. Her name is Alicia Garza. She is an excellent luminary. Her post got reposted on different social media websites. Social activists coined the phrase. It began the slogan of the movement. I strive to do something as impactful as starting the Black Lives Matter movement. She is my role model. Alicia made a passionate call for social justice. The post started getting traction. Alicia Garza is your average woman. Now she is a hero. She called for worldwide action.

At one time, it became known in the black community. It has led to more social action within politics. In America, Black people get targeted by police. It is not the only problem black people face. One issue is systemic racism. Racism is inescapable. A person of color thinks about their race every day. It is out of fear that they will be subjected to racism. White people do not have the same dilemma. The only exception is religiosity. The world is in constant disarray. Our ideologies and appearances separate us. It leads to deaths, poverty, and decreased mortality. An issue is the portrayal of black men in the news. The news portrays a black murder victim as a thug.

The political affiliation of the media outlet will be the differentiating factor in the African portrayal. Racism in Canada is evident. Europeans versus other regions do not share the same experiences. Canada has a systemic problem with hushed racism. Canada has always favored the white race. Europe is the epicenter of whiteness. Christian Europeans are viewed as a superior human race. It leads to racial clashes. Europeans often feel attacked. People of color do not like to feel less than others. It does not just occur with race but also with religion. Muslims got perceived to be less. Their complexions matched those of Europeans. Judaism also opposed a threat. In Westernized countries, Christianity has infiltrated politics.

I am a Lebanese Canadian. We make up a large sect of the populace. I experience hatred. I did not do anything to provoke racism. Many people do not comprehend colonization. Lebanon had an Islamization in the 1000th century. It shows the ramifications of colonization. The

Islamic empires ruled the region for eight centuries. The same genocide occurred to the so-called Indigenous of Canada. They were Muslim Mongols. They lived under the Seljuk Turk and Mamluk empires. Countries became interconnected. Strife in Lebanon will involve Canada. The Canadian military is serving in the Middle East. It impacts racism in Canada. We were subjected to malicious hatred.

They had been mistreated since their arrival. Many Lebanese people were average farmers. Lebanon's prolific landscape made the country a perfect location to farm. Lebanon has endured manifold hardships. Lebanon is prone to economic crises. In the 19th century, the country was in languish. Famine had taken the lives of the economically disadvantaged. Lebanon no longer only gets food supplies from local farmers. Transported goods have assisted in resolving this issue.

Ottomans also sold vegetation. My grandfather's ancestral line guarded wheat. Wheat was a money-making commodity. Stealing wheat would result in monetary losses. The Ottomans took extra precautions.

Working for the Ottomans paid well. Goods were sold at seaports in Lebanon. The bazaar in Turkey was the biggest exporter. It became noticeable across the Middle East.

The Ottomans would lose power in the 1700s. The tides shifted. The Ottomans competed against other exporters. The Portuguese grew in the ranks. They were outselling the Ottomans. Monetary leverage started to falter. Russia had expansionist endeavors. To achieve this, Russia needed to annex the Ottoman Empire. Russia declared war on the Ottoman Empire. This battle was *Mehmet versus Vlad*. It was one that the Ottomans would lose. It occurred in the 1700s and again in the 1800s.

Russian men enlisted in the war. Jews would struggle once the Ottomans lost leadership. It is in Canadian politics. Muslims suffer with little attention. It has existed throughout the centuries. Europeans had a grudge against their treatment in the Ottoman Empire. They got mistreated. Europeans served as enslaved people. Serbians had the worst treatment and worked as underground tunnel diggers.

Chapter 16: Stonehenge

The conditions were harsh. Many perished. Regardless, the Ottomans considered themselves to be accepting. The Ottomans allowed Jewish people to join the Empire. Some accepted. They managed to maintain their religious values. They established themselves within the Empire.

They were often propitious businessmen. The Ottomans thought Jews got respected in the Empire. Jewish people made good business decisions. That generated monetary income, which they kept. The Ottomans did not control their profits. They had restrictive beneficiary laws. Janissaries could not pass down money to their heirs. Jewish people flourished under Asian control. The men exported styled kitchen accessories. The Middle East became known for its lavish designs. It was a money-making empire. The Middle Eastern indigenous population was not fond of Jews. They did not comprehend the Ottomans' acceptance. Jewish experienced abuse by the indigenous.

Under the Ottomans, hatred was tense but manageable. The two religions were able to cohabitate. Mosques and temples existed in the same country. Symbols of Judaism existed throughout the Arabic world. It is in Canada. Canada attempts to practice religious tolerance. Lebanon is more inclusive than other Middle Eastern countries.

Christians and Muslims practice their religion in Lebanon. Jews were once permitted to practice their religion. When Israel became a country, the Lebanese population erupted in violent backlash. The Jewish population gets prohibited from practicing their religion. Some Jews are not allowed to go to Lebanon.

Lebanon and Israel are neighboring enemy countries. The Jewish populace proclaimed they got mistreated by Arabs. Being Jewish in an Islamic region isolated them. Having two different ideologies caused conflict. Europeans shared the same sentiments as the Middle East. The Christians were indifferent to standoffishness toward other religions. In the Medieval Ages, Christian Europeans expelled the Jewish and Muslim populations. Judaism had once gotten more tolerated in the Arab nations than in European countries. Spain expelled the Jews in the 1400s. It occurred before they discovered South America. Spain is the violent perpetrator of multiple racial and religious genocides.

They also had a plethora of enslaved Africans that got taken to the Caribbean and South America. Spain has a poor track record of mistreating minority groups. Ottomans helped resettle the Jewish population after their expulsion. The Jews got resettled in Greece, Syria, and Turkey. It was not the worst event that happened to the Jews. The Holocaust had diminished most of their population. Arabic Muslims have never caused a Jewish genocide. Under Arabic rule, the Jewish people endured harsh living conditions. Life was not perfect in the Middle East. It was enough to enrage the Jews. "Hello, class. Today we are going to talk about janissaries.

"Janissaries were enslaved people in the Ottoman Empire. Christian people became janissaries through Ottoman raids in Africa, Europe, and Asia. Innocent bystanders became victimized. The enslaved people got sold at the Constantinople slave market. I will tailor today's lecture to specify the details of the Serbia and Montenegro tragedy. Serbians were one of the most mistreated groups in the Ottoman Empire. They got assigned the least glamorous job. These men worked as underground tunnel diggers. The fortification of Belgrade, Serbia, is beautiful. Many neighborhoods have underground tunnels. The community has gotten innovative and decided to use these tunnels as storage. They store food and wine. The gorgeous tapestry was the result of hard work. Digging tunnels is a dangerous job, as caves are prone to collapse. The Serbians dug tunnels that the Turkish Sultans requested. It was a warfare strategy. The Turks hoped this would allow them to go unnoticed in battle.

"The strategy backfired. The tactic got spoiled by a whistleblower. The plan got sabotaged. It killed a manifold of Serbian diggers. I found a video explaining the history well." He pulled down the class projector.

The excitement felt palpable throughout the room. Since elementary school, watching an educational movie during class has been my favorite scholastic activity. On these rare occasions, I get to let my mind fall dormant, and a wave of therapeutic relaxation overtakes my entire body.

"Can I volunteer to go get it from the class next room?" Sophie raised her hand. The class watched as Hanau Bravebird downloaded the video onto a Universal Serial Bus drive. It took a few minutes for the download to complete. He put the Universal Serial Bus drive into the projector.

I shifted my body to get into a comfortable position, which would enhance my overall enjoyment. I ultimately settled on placing my feet on the metal wire on my desk legs. My body sprawled out across my desk, and other students replicated my behavior.

The video began playing. I read the video captions. [When the Altai tribe emerged, they married Iranians. The meaning of Mamluk was suitable for their military tactics. Mamluk means slavery. The Mamluks kidnapped young boys. They were of Greek, Russian, and Asian heritage. There was one exception: Muslims. Ottomans did not enslave Muslims. These boys got taken from their homelands. They got placed in propaganda camps.]

[They were taught to fight. They had extensive equestrian training. Their masters crafted a brainwashing scheme. Once the boy seemed responsive to Islam, they asked a question. Do you believe in Islam? The majority said yes. A small minority group said no return to their homeland. A lot became interested in serving in the Mamluk empire. They got paid well.]

[The men often served as bodyguards in their fields. These men protected forts that are now historical sites. Some of them chose to work as diggers in Serbia. It was an innovative military tactic. The Islamic Empire focused on monetary profits. It helped them build forts and create a prosperous economy. Masters touted their wealth and lived a life of luxury. The Islamic Empire sold goods.]

What differentiated them was their styles. They got praised for their decorative textures. Enslaved people were able to prove themselves. They were able to rise through the ranks. It was beneficial. The enslaved people received monetary gains. The poor locals observed their treatment. They appeared to be treated well and made good money. The locals joined as recruits.]

I immediately disregarded informal recruitment, a practice that disrespected the plight of those taken captive and sold at Constantinople. This method of recruitment, often involving coercion and deception, led to the captives being deprived of basic human necessities on their voyage. Many perished before arriving, while others came on the brink of death. The ancient Islamic Empires committed a heinous human rights violation.

The enslaved people sent the money back home. The money helped build churches in the region. The men wanted to strengthen Christianity. Many of the teenage boys felt homesick. They wanted to return home after their service. It left them stranded in their new region. Some resided in Egypt, others in Syria. It was where they ran into trouble. Once they left, they were not allowed to return.]

[The government prohibited this. They were a corruptible influence. Christian countries held onto their beliefs. Women also were victims of the slave trade. The Mamluk Empire looked down on the locals. They did not want the locals to think they were the same. The Islamic

Empire wanted the public to view them with esteem. They kept their distance.]

The fact that the ancient infiltrators regarded themselves with reverence and the Indigenous population with condemnation left me feeling disillusioned. The colonization, a force that stripped away their national identity and customary practices and traditions, is a stark reminder of the enduring impact on the Indigenous population. It underscores the importance of remembering the past to understand the present and shape the future.

[The idea of losing respect in their hierarchy was devastating. The rule did not always get practiced in the Mamluk Empire. Ottomans purchased women as their brides. The female sex trade was born. Turkey was a sexual haven. They had women in chambers. Those women prepared to meet a man. Men did not settle. And their ultra-sexual lifestyle was a stark contrast to the prevailing sexual norms in the Middle East, where the Quarnic doctrine dictates that men and women must refrain from sexual intercourse until marriage. The promiscuity I witnessed was truly shocking, sparking a global discussion on Muslim sexual and reproductive rights among feminists.

[The women got assigned intercourse with the masters. Suleiman met a beautiful Ukrainian woman. She was intelligent and gathered military insights. Suleiman was smitten. It was the first time a sultan got married. She was an enslaved person who acquired power. She was the female Spartacus. Middle Eastern Ottoman children had an interesting family dynamic. Their mom endured slavery.]

Considering the potential for an unhealthy upbringing environment due to generational trauma from slavery, it's crucial that we question whether biologists and psychologists have adequately researched the psychological impact of past mass enslavement on the Middle Eastern community.

[Their dad was the master. The offspring was a mixture of the master and enslaved. It was a dichotomy. Men experienced victimization. Women did too. Women got taken during raids. They were captured and taken to Constantinople and sold at the slave market. Sometimes enslaved people bought their wives from the same country. They went to the slave market to select their wife. These women led semi-formal lives. They fulfilled the role of a housewife.]

[It diluted their race from Asian to European. It showcases the true history of the country. The conditions of their arrival were harsh. They survived. They had bids placed on them. They met their masters. They traveled by cattle cars to their new destination. It forever changed the trajectory of the Middle East, both positively and negatively.]

I pondered the ramifications the slave trade had on civil society in the Middle East. I contemplated whether it would have reshaped the region significantly had the slave trade been absent. Although this occurred long ago, I felt remorseful for the individuals who had endured this maltreatment. I am not disillusioned because modern-day slavery still runs rampant in developing countries across the globe.]

I found the video to be insightful. After class, I did not have anything to do. Once the video finished, I went home. I felt lonely. I needed friends. I did not know how I could find friends with my shared personality. Arab anarchists! I was a lone wolf. My luck was about to change. I walked into English class. We had an assignment. The professor assigned everyone a group. As soon as I got assigned to my group, I introduced myself. I, fortunately, met Fatima. She is an exceptionally unique character. Fatima had both of her arms sleeved. I thought her tattoos were beautiful. I assumed that she was Christian. That was inaccurate. Fatima is a liberated woman. She did not confine herself to her religion, although Muslim-born. After class, we talked about racial inequalities. I told her how brave it was for her to come out of the closet. We were both fed up with the treatment of women. We deserved to start our own women's movement. It was the way of the suffragette in the 1800s. Fatima was not your typical Muslim woman. She was a proud member of the lesbian, gay, bi-sexual, transgender, queer, 2-Spirit community. She had a girlfriend, Sophia Scott. Sophia was a European Christian woman.

The couple worked on inclusion within the lesbian community. I told Fatima about my sister. Fatima did not match Elizabeth's standards. I knew their personalities would clash. Sophia rejected Islam. She was still close to her parents. Fatima lived her entire life in Canada. Fatima's sister was bisexual. She became interested in becoming friends. After school, I went outside to wait for the bus. I noticed that she had a Harley motorcycle.

Chapter 17: Babylonian Map of the World

I felt shocked. Fatima was an empowered human rights activist. She was planning to remove the stigma of being Syrian. I knew that we were going to be close.

From then on, we often ate lunch together. I met Fatima's girlfriend. Sophia Gosling had a single older brother named Carter. I remember the first time we met. He had these piercing blue eyes. His eyes tantalized me. I could see my reflection. His hair was strawberry blonde. He had a chiseled jawline. It reshaped his face. I thought he could be a model. His chest was fit. I could not believe someone this hot was talking to me. I managed good composure. He told me he was studying to become a nurse. He saw me as an unobtainable vixen. I felt turned on. He began to show interest. He sat with a large group of friends at lunchtime. I grew tired of being the third wheel.

I started spending less time with Fatima and Sophia. I spent my time with Carter. We hung out after class. Carter showed me a picture of his ex-girlfriend. I felt intimidated. The girl was stunning. She had long, wavy hair and green eyes. Carter looked the same. He towered over her. His big hands were noticeable. In the photo, Carter wrapped his hands around his ex's waist in a clumsy way. It did not deter me. We studied together. Carter was academically inclined.

He helped me with my schoolwork. I found it sexy that he was multi-talented. I saw that as qualities of a long-term partner. We were both doing well in school. Today felt like no exception. I headed for world history.

I went to retrieve books from my locker. I passed the cafeteria. I noticed a television had turned on. The television program seemed familiar. I watched this television program with my parents. It caught my attention.

"Hello. I am Cindy Holiday with your latest news updates. Ladies and gentlemen, the moment has finally arrived. We have spotted extraterrestrial life. Last night, the government made this news available. The Aerospace International Committee reported on it. An identified planet one million light years away is habitable. Planet Sega! This planet is in a habitable zone. It was a remarkable find. Scientists have determined they have brain capacities.

"The astronauts listed the reasons for the delay. They utilized their monetary resources to research finding water. The expected certain periodic elements to be present. The scientists felt shocked that they were non-existent. Scientists were using elements as a guide. The aliens are an aberration. They required different bodily elements found on the periodic table. We did not expect them to be like us. The aliens pose a threat to humanity. We are curious to know if the extraterrestrials have a level of intelligence or if we can communicate. It was a remarkable project, led by Steven Heaver. He said that we need to refine our criteria for alien life.

"Humans must have access to water. The aliens drank calcium phosphate and calcium magnesium. Scientists at

Aerospace will continue to assess exoplanets. The prime minister got invited to an international conference. One hundred parliamentary leaders will form a plan. We will inform you of the story's developments. Stay tuned." I messaged Carter.

I needed to recompose myself. The class was about to start. I rushed to world history class.

I am prompt and often have plenty of time to mosey down to class. Watching the news breaking segment has stalled my short period of arriving at class on time. Thankfully, my newfound hustle and bustle prevented me from arriving late to class.

"Hello, class. Today we are going to be talking about the first people of Canada. They are dubbed Indigenous. Everyone in the class should know they are of Far East Asian heritage." I could tell my classmates felt intrigued by today's subject. My classmates enjoyed reminiscing about the prehistoric history of America. The professor resumed speaking, "Canadians need to acknowledge this history. Together, we must work toward healing the wounds caused by residential schools. The residential schools led to children perishing. It impacts me personally. I grew up believing I was of Ojibwe and Algonquin descent. These first-people tribes have attempted to reclaim their cultural heritage. It is through powwows, visual arts, and storytelling.

"When I was your age, I was an indigenous human rights activist. I have called out genocidal colonization. Indigenous people lost their culture. Canada is looking to make amends. The government has called out the atrocities.

Residential schools were established in Canada to assimilate Indigenous children into mainstream European culture. The government created residential schools with religious influences. The schools operated from the late 19th century until the 1990s. The children who attended these schools got forcibly removed from their families. The children got cut off from their communities.

"The child got subjected to physical, emotional, and sexual abuse. The residential school system was a dark chapter in Canadian history that had a profoundly negative impact on Indigenous peoples. The trauma inflicted on these children has had lasting effects on their lives as well as on their families and communities. The survivors have spoken out about their experiences in these schools, revealing the extent of the abuse. There is a growing awareness of the legacy of residential schools in Canada. There are efforts to address this legacy through initiatives such as truth and reconciliation commissions. Archeologists dug up ancient Indigenous graves.

"They intended to preserve indigenous heritage. The indigenous felt it was a violation of their rights. Their ancestors deserved the right to rest. I side with the archeologists. Colonization whitewashed the culture. Europeans infiltrated language. It altered their belief system. The public became indoctrinated into Christianity. It confused the population. They were still determining what their original beliefs were. Archeologists have worked to uncover the past and piece it together. There are still unknown answers. Archeologists have determined the Indigenous came from Far East Asia. That was a tremendous discovery. Indigeneity was a made-up concept. The theory got curated by racists unfamiliar with the region.

"When European settlers arrived, they thought America was India. The European government is required to comprehend history. It was a detrimental oversight. There are similarities between the races. The black Mongolians and Indians are the same. Black Mongolians conquered parts of India. It occurred in the Pacific Islands and Oceania. There are three races: White, Black, and Asian." I reflected on what the professor was saying. I am white. Lebanon got listed as a Caucasian country. People's religion changes their race. That is a conjured-up ideology. India is near the Middle East. People are more similar than different.

Corruptible governments do. My professor continued with his lecture, "When Europeans arrived, they thought they were superior. Europeans displayed psychological dilemmas. The brain suffers corruptible ideologies of power, greed, and violence. In the future, genetic engineering can remove these brain impairments. Until then, it will be a reoccurring issue. The Asians became victimized as a result. It is due to the amygdala. The amygdala will have a higher activation when an individual spots someone classified as different. The Far East Asians did not do anything wrong. America is situated closer to Far East Asia. Therefore, the location was ideal for Far East Asian voyagers.

"It was close to them. That is what resulted in their discovering the region. It made them the first inhabitants.

Europeans made similar discoveries. The Irish discovered Iceland. Irish Monks were the first inhabitants of Iceland. It occurred from the seventh to the ninth century. Iceland is 1191 nautical miles away from Ireland. That was remarkable. These individuals were renegades. It is like the Polynesians who found Oceania. They both arrived in far-distant lands by boat. Closer land discoveries in the United Kingdom also occurred. Shetland is an archipelago island. The Scots first inhabited the region in 3600–4200 BC.

"Shetland is 255.88 nautical miles away from mainland Scotland. Utilizing the land space is how we have advanced as a society. We grew as a populous. More inventions have gotten curated as a result. Humans have been habituating to undomesticated regions. These settlements date to the prehistoric era. Archeologists have determined Canada's earliest settlement. The Far East Asians first arrived in 500 BCE. New waves of immigrants came later. Chinese clothing elements date back to 1046 BC. Chinese traditional clothes got designed in the early 1800s. Chinese clothing was a concept. Adaptations have arisen since then. Indigenous is a Far East Asian culture."

Chapter 18: Quipu of Caral

"Asia influenced the Arab world and vice versa. Far East Asian and Indian men grew their hair long. They believed it showcased intelligence and nobility. Men with short hair got viewed as criminals. It was also a sign of slavery. It is viable information that can provide the American Indigenous with answers. It gave answers for their long hair. Most tribes made slight alterations to their ideologies. They attempted to pass on their history. In doing so, they displayed a unilateral front. Those efforts were in vain. The Europeans wanted to get rid of the indigeneity. The Spanish conquistadors burned books written by the Aztecs.

"It got ordered by the Catholic priests. It ensured that the practices did not continue. It is cultural erasure. Colonialism caused devastation. The community lacks resources and wants re-connection to its cultural heritage. Many indigenous communities face discrimination and poverty. They are working to preserve their cultures and languages and promote social justice. We must recognize the contributions that the disenfranchised Far East Asians make to our societies. We must work to create a more equitable world where all people can thrive regardless of their background or identity. Archeologist research uncovered their ethnicity. They dug up those ancient cemeteries.

"They determined the death toll of the residential schools. It is a very painful and healing measure for the ethnic group. Archaeology is a powerful tool we had in prehistoric eras. It could empower marginalized groups of people. I hope we can fix the hardships the tribes endure. South America has the most vulnerable population. They live in harsh conditions on reservations. These contribute to low mortality rates. It is the result of low-income jobs and poor living conditions. Their social life gets hindered by domestic violence and harsh racism. It is an endless cycle of poverty. Their tribe is dwindling in numbers. It is due to increased inter-marital relations.

"Their ethnicity will continue to shrink. The ones looking to marry within their same race have lower dating opportunities." Hanau abruptly stopped speaking. He took a sip of his bottled water. He resumed speaking, "You are going to be required to write an assignment. Your topic is solutions for South America. You are to make a compelling case. It will account for 15% of your grade. Have a great weekend, everyone." I left the class emotional. I live in Canada. South America is far from me. I feel powerless. I have a great desire to make a change in the world. I do not know what I could do to help them. I would need to learn more about this topic to make a positive change in their lives.

It will help me write an empowering essay. It was due at the end of the semester. In the meantime, I needed to become an avid observer of various South American media outlets. I planned to become more engaged in political affairs. My mind felt scattered. I was still determining which topic I should entertain. I needed to reorganize my thoughts. I needed to prioritize what I chose to engage in wisely.

In the meantime, I needed to become an avid observer of various South American media outlets. I planned to become more engaged in political affairs.

I took out my cell phone on my bus ride to my parents' house. I did an internet search on South American human rights issues. I got bombarded with tragedies. I felt helpless. The political atmosphere in South America is in a constant state of disarray. Brazilian housing is essentially inhabitable. An issue for those who live in the favelas is low sanitation. The systems need to be improved. They are inadequate or aging. Some communities have built sanitation systems illegally. The issue with building illegal sanitation is an incorrect system assembled. The lack of sanitation results in high mortality rates for the vulnerable population.

Infants, children, and senior citizens! The poor infrastructure of the favelas in South America makes them more susceptible to climate change disasters. Coastal regions are vulnerable to hurricanes and tsunamis. Their lack of security continues beyond there. Many South Americans deal with food insecurities. The inflation of food prices has resulted in food wars. People fight in grocery stores for food. South Americans struggle to provide their families with nutritious food.

Countries across South America blame corrupt governments for their poor quality of life. I opened a brainstorming application on my phone.

I jotted down my main points. I also copied and pasted the links to the websites I found. When I arrived home, I halted my school assignment. I had more fascinating topics to talk about. The extraterrestrials were a recurring theme in my mind. The extraterrestrials were a recurring theme in my mind. After class, I rushed home. I planned to discuss the discovery of aliens. My parents had already got informed. The atmosphere felt eerie. I could tell they felt powerless. The prime minister would handle it. It felt like an unsafe gambling wager.

I trusted the elected officials to look out for my best interests. My life hung in the balance. My parents did nothing to calm my nerves. I entered the kitchen. I decided to douse my woes with ice cream cake and chocolate milk. Why wasn't life simple? I had immense anxiety. I allowed emotions to fester. I felt worried about an alien invasion. Food was a source of comfort. My stepfather entered the kitchen. I noticed he had a fork in his hand. He made his way toward me. I sensed his motivations. He wanted to steal my ice cream cake. There is no chance I would allow that to happen. I must shield my food. He sat down at the table and tugged at my plate.

I noticed that he would not give in. I challenged him to an arm wrestling competition. The winner got the cake. We are well-matched. While we arm wrestled, we engaged in conversation.

"How do you feel about the aerospace finding?"

He seemed to approach the topic with a light-hearted touch, but I believe the discovery of alien life should be treated with utmost seriousness. These beings could potentially pose a threat to all of humanity, making it the most significant existential crisis we are currently confronting. My father, a man who typically exuded confidence and humor, approached the topic with an uncharacteristic seriousness.

He replied, "I am not in a position of authority. I am the supervisor at Rama Pama Superstore. This subject makes me uncomfortable. I want to talk about something else. I have some news about your genealogical endeavors. I gathered information about the city's genealogical process. The city tracks old death certificates that occurred here." I took a moment to digest what he said.

I appreciated that he took the time to invest in my interests. His support and interest in my passions have significantly shaped my identity. The thought brought a sincere smile to my face. My father immediately recognized that his statements had a positive impact on me. I took a moment to formulate a solid response properly.

"Were older generations buried here?" He nodded.

I appeared to be winning the arm wrestling competition. My dad Omar came up with a strategy to distract me. "Elizabeth is entering the room." I turned my head to check. She was not there. My stepdad Omar won. I felt resentful. It was an unfair battle. It was a beneficial social interaction. I knew where to start my research. I did not intend for that to go to waste. I planned to follow through. Tomorrow, I will go to the cemetery to visit my ancestors. I took it easy for the rest of the day. I watched comedic television for a few hours before I fell asleep. I woke up and did my morning routine. I left the house at 8:15 a.m. to catch the bus.

I took my backpack with me. Inside the bag, there was a notebook with a pen. The trip took me two bus transfers.

On the bus, I messaged Carter. I told him I would see him tomorrow. I watched a live stream of Lila and Anthony. They sat on a blanket under a maple tree. They ate their lunch together. In the video, they talked about their lives and hobbies together. Their conversation flowed easily from one topic to another. Lila had popped her earbuds in. Anthony asked her what she was listening to. She eloquently responded with, "International music. What do you suggest I listen to?" Anthony stated his suggestion.

Before he spoke, I had already sided with Lila. About sixty percent of the music I listen to comes from Africa, the Middle East, and Latin America. This diverse and energetic music, which you introduced me to, has been instrumental in cultivating inclusion and fostering my creativity and innovation. Nonetheless, I waited for Anthony to give his two cents.

"Hip-Hop." As a third-party observer, I was not surprised. Lila and Anthony had polarized interests. For example, she read and watched romantic comedies. He watched science fiction movies.

The couple got up and packed up. Lila and Anthony put their blankets in the picnic basket. Anthony suggested they go for a hike. Anthony often exhibited reckless behavior. I hoped he would mature once he embraced manhood. His ill-advised comment indicated he could not care for Lila correctly. Her learning disability puts her at a disadvantage, and she requires extra support

Lila spoke, "The attendant told us that there are bears."

"Lila, you cannot be scared of life? Chances are we will not see one." Lila took Anthony's hand. She gave a weary smile. Anthony seemed excited. They took in their surroundings. The couple saw a bear in the far distance. Lila got petrified. They slowly turned around. They made a concerted effort to be as silent as possible. The bear stayed back. We got a considerable distance away. The worst scenario came to fruition. She saw a baby bear cub. Tears began to roll down her face.

"What do we do, Anthony?" Anthony saw a road. The two sprinted for it. The two ran fast. It must have taken them five minutes before they reached the road. They got out safely. I was an observer. I felt terrified the entire time. I finally arrived at the cemetery. I made my way to the administration office. A lady named Candace was at the front office. She looked to be in her late seventies. She pulled out a paper of the landscape. She circled the section where my relatives were buried. I walked along the tombstones until I noticed the names of my relatives. Once I recognized the names, I paid my respects. I copied the words engraved on the tombstone into my notepad.

By the time I left, I had a total of six names. The following day, I went to a separate cemetery. When I arrived, I went to the front office. A lady by the name of Audrey answered. She gave me a pamphlet about the graveyard. She gave me a detailed description of how to get to the appropriate section. "You are in Section A. You want to get to Section F. Section F is behind the cremation wall." I left the office. The section was easy to find. I perused the names on the tombstones. I found two surnames. I noticed that my maternal grand-uncle. His tombstone read Othman. *Had we been Ottomans, we would not have been the only ones. Yet, that name is a clear indicator of our Islamic Empire affiliation.*

My family appeared to carry that title. The modern Levant showed vitriol toward the Ottomans. *We are the colonizers of that region.* I pondered the meaning's significance. *Were we in the Ottoman Empire?* I continued searching the tombstones. The graveyard signaled to me the presence of the Islamic Empire. The chances that I was indigenous were unlikely. I needed to consult my Great-Aunt Zena about this. She was an excellent resource. Zena was a Muslim.

Chapter 19: Trundholm Sun Chariot

She did not buy into the entire narrative. Zena wanted the youth to reshape the religion. We formed a close bond. I called Zena's number on my cell phone. "Hello, Zena. I do not want to bother you. We have a relative with the last name Basque Othman. Were you in the Ottoman Empire?"

"Hello, sweetie. Yes. I do believe we came from the Ottoman Empire." I immediately smiled. I remembered my awkward fib when I was in grade 11. I claimed that my grandmother was from Altai. *Was I right all along?* I began to blush. Zena continued providing insights.

"One of our ancient ancestors must have altered it from Ottoman to Othman. It is common practice to deviate from surnames. People self-designated surnames. Not everyone in our family calls themselves Othman. Your grandmother, Adele Basque, was born in Jdeideh. She was an Othman. Her dad decided she should not refer to herself as an Ottoman. It is up to the man in the family to determine their surname."

It was my breakthrough moment, a thrilling discovery that set my heart racing. I finally had my first major clue to help me solve my missing ancestral lineage. The surname bestowed me with a gift. It indicated that my ancestors came from the Ottoman Empire, a historical powerhouse that once spanned many continents. This revelation now felt like a solid foundation for me to start piecing together my family's history.

"Thank you so much, Zena. I got to go. I will see you soon. I love you very much."

"I love you too, Yura." I hung up on Zena. I found that to be an enlightening conversation. I could not wait to uncover more information. I got caught off guard. I did not realize my grandma was born in Jdeideh. That was an interesting tidbit of information. It felt unexpected. The majority of my classmates came from Beirut. I was from a tiny village in the mountains. It made me appear more impoverished. Beirut was more glamorous. It is more modernized.

Life in the mountains was more traditional. My friends who came from Beirut were Christians. I was Muslim. The village needed to become developed. It felt like walking around in a third-world country. It was not glamorous. I started placing my heritage together. It led me to realize we were Ottomans. Names have meanings. My ancestors gave themselves that name. It was an indicator. It was compelling evidence. It was a breakthrough in my case. On my way home, I allowed this information to sink in. It is a well-known fact that Ottomans existed in Lebanon. The Ottomans got to Lebanon through Syria. When the Ottomans lost power, they got ostracized.

Prior their power and wealth could combat it. We are an Islamized country. Many Ottomans had wives who came from slavery. They purchased these women at slave markets.

There was a high chance I came from the enslaved person and the enslaver. I found the information to be controversial. I felt victimized. I did not want this to isolate me from the indigenous of Lebanon. As far as I knew, I came from an impoverished line. I did not want this to backfire on me. It would be self-inflicted racism. I returned home. I showed my parents my findings.

Highlighting all the names I collected. I asked my parents who they were. My mother, Nadia, nodded.

I gave her one of my papers from my notepad. She made a comprehensive chart. She was unable to connect one of the names to our family. She scratched out the name. My mother, Nadia, handed me her chart. I rushed to my handheld tablet. I searched on the city website for their death certificate registry. I filled out the application. It was twenty-two dollars per death report. I pulled out my credit card and applied. Once I completed the process, I had to wait twelve to fifteen business days. I could focus on my other interests. By then, the government should have a conclusive answer on what to do with the astronautical scientific discovery of alien life.

In the meantime, I decided to take a power nap. An hour later, I found myself in the kitchen. I made myself an afternoon snack. My mother, Nadia, came into the room. She realized that I was eating her leftover lasagna. She appeared irked. My stepfather had a habit of eating my mom's leftovers. My mom, Nadia, has developed patience in this matter. Regardless, she looked at me with disdain. The disillusioned energy in the room was palpable. There are no utensils on the table. My mom, Nadia, appeared puzzled until she realized I was using my hands. In my mother's earlier years, she was in beauty pageants.

My table manners appalled her. My mother, Nadia, attempted to teach me how to be a woman to no avail. My mother, Nadia, utilized her meditation practices of deep breathing. I watched as my mother, Nadia, took noticeable inhalations and exhalations. She sat down on the seat parallel to me. "Yura, when you were eight years old, you asked me what the meaning of life was. When you were eight, you thought I had the answers to everything. I miss the heroic idolization. I attempted to answer your question, regardless. I replied to join the army. You rebutted, reminding me to be serious. You felt my disinterest in the matter. I sensed it infuriated you.

"A few hours later, you realized I did not know the answers. That is how I feel about the alien life living incongruently with us. I want to reassure you that it is going to be okay. There are a million questions I will always need to find the answers to. Together, we will overcome anything." Her kind words caused a tear to trickle down my throat. I tried to suppress it. I was not fond of the sensation; I did not want to cry unnecessarily. I recognized the privilege of having a supportive mom who took my aspirations seriously.

We embraced. "Thank you for the kind words." My mother, Nadia, checked her cell phone. I pondered what she was doing. I glanced over and noticed she was on Facebook. She was scrolling through her feed.

My mother's recent embrace of social media has led to some changes in our family dynamics. She humorously

148

pointed out the irony of our temporary disconnection due to digital connectivity. However, she also emphasized the shared experience of adapting to new technology, which made us feel more connected, and the benefits of widespread accessibility to informative websites and social media.

"Yura, I go on social media to connect with my friends," I cheerfully said. The widespread use of social media has infiltrated every age demographic across the globe. My mother, initially resistant to these platforms, became an anomaly. Only when her best friend Basma moved back to Lebanon did she agree to keep in contact via social media. I watched my mother form an addiction to checking her feed.

"We should connect online." My mom looked hesitant.

My mother, Nadia, utilized the platform to connect with her relatives. Some of these relatives were older and resided in Lebanon. They were the perfect candidates to pry information out of. My mom, Nadia, uncovered that her cousin Amir had taken an ancestral deoxyribonucleic acid test. She found it surprising that he took the test. She was curious about the results. My mom, Nadia, told me she saw an image of his results. She forwarded the photo to me. It said that he was from the Balkans. European! I immediately thought it could be a mix-up. Lebanon is very close to Europe. We also could have migrated from Europe to Lebanon. Later on, I realized that his deoxyribonucleic acid overlapped with his mother's results.

I found that to be an intriguing fact. My other cousin, Zara, took the test. It came back as Russian and Georgian.

There is an argument that this strengthened Amir's results. Amir is European. Europeans have infiltrated Georgian society. It is in Georgian architecture. Georgia was the first place to adopt Christianity. It is due to the countless European Christian missionaries who went to Georgia. It is a plausible theory. It is not a definitive answer. Many people from Georgia are indigenous to the region. We will always have answers. Russians were of European and Asian ancestry. I was under the impression that my family was Lebanese. I knew Russia once had a presence in Lebanon.

I began organizing my thoughts. I went to the computer. I put the image into a Word document. Besides the photo, I wrote all the relevant information about Russian influence in Lebanon. The Russian occupation of Beirut was significant in the early 17th century. In 1915, during World War I, Russian forces fought in Beirut. It was part of a larger strategy by the Allies to gain control over key strategic locations in the Middle East and cut off Ottoman supply lines. Their presence had a profound impact on Beirut. It led to increased tensions between Russia and the Ottoman Empire. It ultimately contributed to the collapse of the Ottoman Empire after World War I.

The occupation impacted Lebanon's political landscape, as it helped to solidify French influence in the country. Despite its significance, the Russian occupation of Beirut gets overlooked in discussions of Middle Eastern history. Nevertheless, it highlights the complex geopolitical dynamics during World War I and their lasting impact on regional politics. It is my family's genetic makeup. I did not know this at birth. Arabic people feel disenfranchised. We do not have the same equality as Europeans. It has been our downfall as an ethnic group. After the Islamic Revolution, society silenced knowledge. It prohibited free thinking. I frequented genealogy websites.

It requires brain capacity. It was lunchtime. I went to the kitchen where my mom, Nadia, was. I sat in the chair opposite to her. I requested that she inform me of every member of her family tree. She obliged. It took around fifteen minutes. My mom, Nadia, listed the majority of her relatives. She did her best. She could have been better informed. She got stuck with my great-grandparents. I thanked her for her time. She did not have to help me, yet she did. It was my project.

Chapter 20: Basse Yutz Flagons

I was going to see it through. I opened a genealogy application. The format was open-ended. It allowed individuals to add their families. It is a search engine for family genealogical records. It is a racially inclusive website. Any race could add information to the site. I typed the names into a family tree website. I connected with my family. Once I finished, I continued to add unconnected people. It became a hobby. I started going to burial sites and adding information.

I allocated cemeteries in foreign regions that I had yet to hear of. I engaged with professionals over email. I emphasized the importance of economic poverty. It is critical to equality. The genealogists acquiesced. I realized that this tragedy also happened in Canada. I wanted their forgotten history restored. It became my mission. I went to two different cemeteries. The tombstone had no relation to me.

I brought some paper and a pencil with me. I stood by my ancestors' graves. I wrote my ancestors' names. I had six pages' worth of surnames by the time I left. I uploaded the information to burial websites. I felt heroic. I still needed to include my older Lebanese history. The website informed me how to access records. In Lebanon, Mukhtar's records track birth and death records.

These records are tracked separately in every village. The word did not sound Arabic. I researched this. It derives from Uzbekistan. Timur, a notable individual from the Mongol Empire, was born in Uzbekistan. Timur was born into the Turkicized Barlas tribe. He was from Uzbekistan.

His tribe meant he was loyal to the Mongol Empire. Timur was not Mongolian. He was still determining whether the Mongolians would accept his leadership. Timur sought respect from the Mongolians. It swayed his decision about choosing his bride. He married a Mongolian woman. It paid off. He led the Mongolians with great power. That made him more powerful in the Middle East. It strengthened the colonization of the region. Timur had megalomania. He ruled the Mongol Empire, leaving an irrefutable mark on the Middle East. He was a notorious leader. He kept a pyramid of skulls. His military campaigns killed seventeen million people. That accounted for 5% of the world's population.

Timur is known for the bloodshed he caused. Timur became idolized alongside Genghis Khan. Malicious leaders got celebrated. Ubashi needs to get noticed. Ubashi saved the Oirat tribe. It needs to change. People need to pay homage to history correctly. Prehistoric civilizations make up the totality of an individual in the 21st century. I felt intrigued by the website 'Lebanese Mukhtars Records.' It claimed to specialize in Middle Eastern genealogy. I clicked on the website. I felt impressed with the layout. It was easy to navigate. It required a monthly payment plan. Before I paid, I needed to check the legitimacy. The website checked out.

I had bought a monthly subscription on an ancestral website. It gave me access to Mukhtar's records. The website had a wider variety of Christian than Islamic records. People born Muslim had access to a civil registry. I felt impressed that the company managed to compile all this information.

I instantly messaged my sister. We both rejoiced. She asked me if I had any compelling findings to share with her.

A few minutes later, I got a text from Lila.

The text message notification brought a smile to my face. I had recently realized that receiving a text message from Lila would never feel like talking to her in person. I went into my cell phone message application and retrieved the text message.

"Elizabeth told me that you found an interesting website. I hope the website produces favorable results."

I appreciated her kind words and the effort she put into her initial message. However, her vagueness in the message informed me I was required to further my research to have more content to share with Lila. I needed to form a short and sweet response. I paused for a moment and then began quickly typing.

"Thank you, Lila. Finding this website has rejuvenated me."

My cordial response was direct, leaving little opportunity for Lila to misconstrue the message. I was eager to contribute valuable insight to the conversation, as I value your perspective and believe it will enrich our discussion. However, I needed help finding the right words. I re-read my message, hoping to improve it and add meaning to our discussion. My reply felt like a conversation ender, so I thought the conversation would end abruptly. I am a friendly individual who actively engages through text messages, and I was looking forward to continuing our conversation. However, I was mistaken, and a few moments later, I saw text bubbles emerge and disappear two times before I received another text message notification from Lila.

Lila had a polite response.

"That is great."

"Thank you. I am more dedicated to my research. Lila, do you remember when I halted my research? I felt gutted. Despite my plateau, I resumed my search. It is a continuous battle."

"After our grandmother died, it crushed me. I knew I had to see this through for my grandmother." I knew my words would invoke sympathy and concern that I had not overcome the passing of my grandmother. I intended to share my purpose with Lila. I hoped that my words would not be misconstrued. Her reply would indicate her perception of my comment.

"You should tell your mother. I am sure she would be beyond proud of you, the way Elizabeth is."

"I appreciate that, Lila! I will let her know if I am successful. I am going to my room. I am exhausted. I have been on the move for the past two days. I will see you later."

It felt like a deeply bittersweet farewell, a moment heavy with complex emotions. I sincerely appreciated our meaningful conversation. Conversations with Lila often feel therapeutic. I remember my mother saying that all good things must come to an end. I entered the bathroom across the hall, grabbed my toothbrush, and slowly began stroking my teeth. Then, I returned to my bedroom.

I got into bed and thought about making my community proud. Most Arabs do not realize they got colonized.

The Middle East gets referred to as colonizers by Africans. Many Africans speak Arabic and practice Islam. The Middle East got victimized by colonization. In Lebanon, it changed the language spoken. It altered the Syrian way of life. The Middle East was once the epicenter of colonization. It occurred between the years 1000 and 1800. Far East Asians colonized Africa and the Middle East. It is the heart of African social rights. It is what Aliyah Smith was preaching. She wanted to uncover Saint Thomas's lineage. Colonization occurred before she got taken to the Caribbean. Africans have an entitlement to this information. I needed to publicize my findings.

It should be well-known to the public. Africa claims to be home to hundreds of indigenous tribes. How much of the population was indigenous to Africa? The European invasion of African heritage has diluted their race. The history of Far East Asia still needs to be remembered. It is a human rights crisis. Most Africans have European and Asian ancestry. It is going on in Lebanon with no recognition. Lebanon has had its cultural indigeneity stolen. It is a historical erasure. Once records get destroyed, they cannot get recovered. Those who were once Ottomans do not have any recognition of this. It is unfortunate. People need to comprehend who they are. It dates back centuries.

Individuals do not know how to heal. I spent my time immersed in prehistoric empires. I did not only have a passion for ancestry. I cannot think of anything more enchanting than empowering my community. The only other thing that could top it is being in love with Carter. I lay in bed. I visualize his body being on top of mine. I thought of his sensual capabilities. His big hands came in handy. I began to tingle. I sent him a text.

My self-confidence reached an all-time high, and then it automatically plateaued. I realized I had a decreased probability of receiving a text message because I desperately wanted Carter to. In secondary school, Lila and I made a pact to have the mentality to seize the day. We divulged the importance of taking the opportunity to behave like sexual women everywhere the moment presents itself. My bodily sensations told me to act upon the pact. Moments where I have set my sights on reaching my sexual prowess tend to remind me that I am an awkward, quirky girl. I decided to silence my trepidation and forge ahead with my plan to send a flirty text message. I pulled out my cell phone, opened the message application, and began typing.

"Hey, sexy, are you doing anything?"
After I sent it, I immediately felt flustered. My face felt hot, and I imagined it was bright red. This bold assertion was outside of my character. I wondered if Carter would exhibit reciprocal intentions. It would permit me to

do that again in the future. Simultaneously, I had anxiety about his reaction. I hoped he would not patronize me by agonizingly teasing me. My request felt deeply embarrassing. My overconfidence increased my risk of him poking fun at me. I put the pillow over my head and let out a scream. WHY AM I SO AWKWARD? I waited impatiently for his response. I notice text message bubbles emerge on my cell phone.]

I felt sexually frustrated. I hoped that my sensations would not have to be imaginary soon.

Carter responded. I recognized the importance of sexual intercourse in our relationship. Carter and I both required a certain amount of physical contact in a physical week; when we did not receive our required amount, we both began to feel agitated.

"I am coming over." I lunged to my dresser and retrieved my newly bought lingerie. When I tried it on, I succumbed to a wave of body dysmorphia. The positioning of the outfit highlighted my body fat. I felt hideous. I wanted to incite Carter, not repulse him. I stared at myself in the mirror and wanted to cry. I retrieved my Huda Kattan makeup and began contouring my face and breasts. I spent half an hour completing my makeup. I forgot about my body insecurities once I felt satisfied with my results. I looked at myself in the mirror and felt beautiful.

Our relationship was a slow build. We engaged in sexual intercourse after a month of dating. Sexual activity strengthened our relationship.

We had a cute courting experience. We went to dinners, bowling, movies, and the arcade. The tension between us built. I experienced a high level of sexual attraction based on his physicality. I realized that my love language was acts of service and receiving gifts. We had built a relationship based on communication. We understood what the other person required to be in a healthy relationship. Carter showered me with gifts and admiration. Every morning, I felt excited to get up. I received good morning texts. The texts had a $20 gift card attached to Steve's Cup. I had not paid for my coffee in months. A real gentleman never lets a woman pay.

Carter must have wired me over $500 for my shopping expenditures. I have never felt more beautiful in my entire life. I bought a Balenciaga purse that was on sale online. Carter took me to a five-star restaurant. He drove me to school. We bonded during this time. We got frisky between classes. It included heavy public displays of affection. We were into public displays of affection. School limited our sexual activity. It was illegal to have sex in public. We needed to find a way around this. We snuck into the library and had sex in between the stacks. I knew that my classmates were studying in the library. I had to be quiet. It was an adrenaline rush.

If my classmates knew we were engaging in sexual intercourse, we were not aware. My classmates did not say anything. I had fears about getting in trouble. His edgy side made me nervous. It also excited me. I found my rebellious side coming out more. I went the nine yards to keep him sexually aroused. I made an appointment with my family doctor. I had a vaginal ring put in. It permitted Carter to go raw. We were sexually compatible. I have been with men where there was no chemistry. The sexual satisfaction was not there. That was not the case with Carter. I could not go long without some form of physical contact. The relationship lasted five months.

It was a whirlwind romance. I thought about getting engaged. I had always yearned to be a bride one day. I tried to hint at marriage. I felt afraid. Carter might not be ready for marriage. Occasionally, when marriage gets proposed too early, it terminates the relationship. That was my biggest fear. I would not be able to handle that. Things took a turn for the sour. He told me he wanted to pause our relationship. It was my fear that came to fruition. I did not know how I was going to live without Carter. I felt lost. I had grown accustomed to him. I felt safe in his arms. I was in a complete freefall. I needed other people to come to help me pick up the pieces.

Chapter 21: The Parthenon Sculptures

I went home. My stepfather, Omar, decided to renovate the living room. I was experiencing the worst heartbreak of my life. I wanted to be with my family during this time. My stepfather, Omar, hired a construction worker. He was to redo the fireplace. My parents opted for electrical. My stepfather ordered a television for the mantle. The construction worker hung up the television screen. This television was twice the size of the first one my parents previously owned. The television needed programming to operate. My parents called a technician company to assist them. When my mom, Nadia, called, the technician company gave her their earliest availability.

My parents acquiesced to the payment terms. I had been sobbing in my room for weeks. My breakup stifled my genealogical research. I did not know that this encounter meant I would get reignited about this pursuit. The television technician arrived. His name was Aslan. He was a racially ambiguous man. Aslan was knowledgeable about technical support. His synergy highlighted his heterozygosity. Aslan's features deviated from stereotypical Arab facial features and appeared more Far East Asian. His mannerisms were Middle Eastern. Later in the visit, he stated his heritage. Aslan was an Ottoman

Turk. His pride was outspoken. I had an understanding of the Ottomans.

I knew that I descended from the Ottomans from my cemetery visit. His ethnicity backed up my knowledge. It puts my mind at ease. It confirmed all my research had been accurate. It was my first encounter with an Ottoman. My interest in Arab subgroups grew. Arabic history was coming alive. Indigenous groups who rail against the Ottomans claim he is not Turkish. He is.

When the earthquake hit, he felt devastated. It was the earthquake that hit Turkey in 2023. It killed over 500,000 people. Aslan blamed the government for those deaths. He thought corruption led to poor infrastructure. I knew that poor infrastructure was a Turkish human rights violation.

He planned to send money back to his country. It was his charitable attempt to rectify the situation. We need to remember Ottomans are people. An individual does not have a say in this.

It gets predetermined for them at birth. The technician detests getting told he is not from Turkey is harmful. His family has not lived in Far East Asia for centuries. Turkey is his homeland. It is in his facial characteristics. He is your average Muslim man. Aslan educated people about his heritage. It got passed down by his parents. Not every Ottoman got that luxury. That is something I want to change. Ignorant people classify all Middle Easterners as indigenous.

People need to develop more interest in this salient topic. Alsan's girlfriend was from the Cree tribe. He seemed encapsulated in her. When he spoke about his girlfriend, he beamed with pride. Her name is Aiyana. She worked as a social worker in her community. I found that to be a cute coupling. I have done extensive research on indigeneity. I wanted to grasp why individuals learned about ancient cultures. People desire to reconnect with their race. Aiyana appeared to be one of these people. Some of these practices must get revamped. The world needs to change its beliefs to suit modern times. It is not appropriate to dismiss the work of ancient scholars.

Their contributions were beyond their time. Plato's work in philosophy has survived over 2,400 years. His literature became recognized by students in higher education. Indigenous individuals like to think of their ancestors as scholars. Their ideologies were almost identical to those of Far East Asia. Their intelligence was unequivocal. They were nomadic tribes that farmed the land. Each tribe formed its language. It is identical to the Mongolian way of life. Understanding who they were is healing. In some aspects, I respect Aiyana. Liberal scientists have made an example of the indigenous environmental way of life. They refer to this as sustainability.

The tribes took what they needed from the land. They did not harness the land. Industrial civilization has changed our environment. The human mind has developed since the caveman era. Greed became a detrimental psychological trait. Scientists felt concerned about our consumer lifestyle. Climate change is a looming threat. Human rights activists are trying to avoid these apocalyptic events. It would wipe out humanity. This revolution is taking place now. People should reconsider the ancient ways of sustainability. The technician left. My parents had plans with their friends. I sat on the couch alone for a few minutes before I went to the wine cabinet. I got a little tipsy before I passed out. I decided to set my genealogical research project aside for now. I needed to relax.

My cousin, Lila, had planned to visit me today. We were once attached 24/7. Lila expressed to me that our relationship took a negative toll on her personality. She felt she molded herself to become more like me. I empathize with Lila. It was not my intention to stifle her individuality.

I knew that Lila was experiencing an identity crisis. She had got compared to me. I had personally witnessed Lila mimicking my mannerisms. I knew the comparisons were hard on her. In our last year of high school, she decided we needed to create distance between us. Lila decided to go to a different college. Her decision gave me anxiety. I equally relied on her companionship.

I attempted to hide my emotions. I did not want anyone to see that I was struggling. It made my integration into college more difficult. Lila handled it better than I did. I managed to survive my first semester. Lila and I made a pact to reconnect whenever possible. I sat and watched television. While I waited for her, I reminisced about our childhood. Lila struggled growing up. Academics were not her strong suit. I remember our formative years. Lila needed to get tested for a learning disability. Lila got required to take an aptitude test. We got separated for a week. It was hard on me. I reluctantly went to class. My mom, Nadia, noticed I exhibited more passive aggression every day before school.

I felt jealous that Lila got to skip school for a week. She got diagnosed with Asperger syndrome. Her father put on a front for her. Afterward, he cried. I found this out through family gossip. He felt it was his fault. I knew that it crushed Lila inside. She began falling behind in school. A malicious teacher said she would end up destitute. Despite her disability, Lila loved learning subjects in school. She had taken an interest in science. Her grades needed to match her interest. She was prone to failure. Lila found comfort in it. As her cousin, I felt helpless. When I was ten, I decided to be proactive. I did some research to help Lila resolve these problems.

I thought that together we would be unstoppable. I entered the word Asperger syndrome into the computer. I printed out the article for her. The author was understanding and unbiased. The journal had valuable recommendations. Lila should inform the general population of her condition. She needed to promote an inclusive environment. They could accommodate them if they knew of her limitations. It emphasized anti-discrimination laws. The supreme court ruled that discrimination was illegal. It included mental capacities. The author said that judgment was the worst symptom. It runs rampant in society. It is inescapable. Fear of judgment prevents people from seeking help.

It makes their disability worse. We live in a competitive world. Students make comparisons with their peers. Individuals compete for partners and employees.

When individuals cannot keep up, they get overlooked. Individuals with disabilities are prone to low self-worth. Families and friends need to act as allies. We need to promote acceptance. We want everyone to stay caught up. Lila had a supportive dad and immediate family. Lila has overcome her hurdles. Now she needed to work on the refinement. Lila is full of promise and determination. I once read an ancient proverb: Those who have overcome adversity are profound. It applied to Lila. She saw us as a team.

I was a ten-year-old, not a psychologist. It humanized me. I was on her side. Lila appreciated my assistance. She perused the articles I sent her. We would discuss how Lila could build off this information. I noticed my contributions made a difference. I compiled more news articles. I followed the advice of the specialist, Hana Taylor. She received her Bachelor of Arts in Early Childhood Education. She was well-versed in the topic. Hana explained the brain-development process well. She said the infant's brain develops during the first three weeks.

Lila spent the first week of her life in squalor. Defying the impossible, she managed to survive.

Lila got put on life support. Lila was on the brink of death. Her brain began to decay. It was unknown at the time that this would cause brain deformities. That was not her only deterrent. Her mother smoked throughout her pregnancy. The formative years are critical. They determine an individual's level of success throughout life.

Chapter 22: Ram in the Thicket

The first stage is the outline of the neural system. I developed this at four. My multisensory and perceptual systems were in effect. It was when my mom, Nadia, noticed Lila had a cognitive delay. My mom, Nadia, took her to see an occupational therapist.

Once she returned, she would talk about therapy. Lila told me about the activities she did. She enjoyed going to occupational therapy. She went monthly. Her parents saw improvement.

Lila was a determined individual. We got older, and our brains continued to develop. I formed my memory and decision-making systems. My mom, Nadia, noticed a growth in my emotional intelligence. Lila was making strides. Eventually, she was in parallel with her peers.

The therapies were a success. In our teens, we developed our personalities. Lila now lives with a manageable condition. She has taken the liberty to become a lifelong learner.

Lila is now of average to above-average intelligence. This prodigious outcome was the result of hard work. Lila turned out to be stunning. She is an academically inclined individual.

Her teachers adored her, and the boys chased after her. Lila still faces challenges. One of those challenges was her inability to be on time. I checked my watch. I had been waiting for her for over an hour. I finally heard a knock at my door. I opened the door. Lila appeared disheveled. She showed concern through her facial expressions. Lila seemed exhausted. It was not an appropriate welcome. I expected a happy individual. An apology for making me wait, none of which occurred.

Lila stared at the sectional couch and laid down. She positioned her body to face the television. I did not want her to feel uncomfortable. I laid down. I placed my head against hers. Lila told me how shallow her classmates were. "Yura, Barris College is proving itself to be a wonderful campus. I do not know why a manifold of my classmates is malicious toward those who exhibit aberrations. I already feel different due to my Asperger syndrome. Why must people point it out?"

I empathize with Lila. Aspergers is a significant barrier she has had to overcome. The symptoms protruded into her daily life. I recognized the privilege I had of being neurotypical. I resonated with the quirks associated with being a neurodivergent. My ability to understand her issues was crucial in forming a stronger bond, emphasizing the importance of empathy in our relationship.

"Lila, people are superficial. They only look at the surface level. You are so much more than your disability." I knew having Asperger Syndrome took a toll on her self-confidence.

"Lila, I tried to help you overcome this insecurity. We went to therapy. Do you remember?" Lila stopped to think about this. Her mind seemed to wander momentarily. I wondered what she was thinking about. She resurfaced and began adding insight into our conversation.

Despite her learning disability, I have always found her commentary imperative to enhance my self-growth. Besides her intellect, Lila has had to overcome significant life difficulties, and her persistence and resilience are character traits I have always admired. It has shaped her mentality.

"I remember, Yura. I told the therapist that I had deviated from my mom, Noor. She had an academically inclined brain. I never thought I would add up to her. My mother, Noor, attended Kingdom University. She graduated with her Master's in Art. I took after my father, Marković. My father, Marković, only got his high school diploma. Despite his education, he was the better parent. I have always been jealous of my mom, Noor.

"Everything came easy to her. Her parenting style was horrific. It is not fair. I suffered from neglect. I needed a maternal presence. There were none. My mom, Noor, spent the required maternity leave with me alongside my father, Marković. He was in between jobs that year. In infancy, my mom, Noor, could have made a difference. The first three years of life are critical. Children learn by observation. That is how they grasp the appropriate mannerisms. It is a small overview of their life to come. I felt disjointed. I have reminisced about this period before."

Her ordeal was atrocious. Growing up alongside her, I was beyond privileged while she suffered tremendously. I have always had unnecessary guilt about that. But I've come to understand that it was not my fault. I was a young child and could not have rectified the situation. My parents did not have the financial capability to support anyone besides their two children. This journey of understanding has led me to conclude that it is an injustice in life and a catalyst for personal growth.

"Lila, that was a horrific misfortune. Neurobiology develops from zero to three. The formative years are from birth to year eight. It was one of the most chaotic periods of your life. You experienced poor emotional support and neglect. It was parental abuse. It makes you more prone to hardships. Noor will not go down as Mother of the Year."

Lila had a look of guilt on her face. I felt Lila thought she was the malicious one instead of her mother. Lila was being honest. She needed to realize that it was okay to vent. We were in a safe space. No one could hear what we were saying. "Luckily, my father, Marković, stepped in. He acted in both roles. I respect him. She suffered with her mental health. My mother, Noor, got raped at ten years old. She was also in a domestic abuse relationship. She was sixteen, and it was her first boyfriend."

Noor's suffrage was traumatizing; however, she did not have to project the generational trauma onto Lila. She could ensure that Lila grew up in a healthy environment. She negated her parental obligations. I have always found Noor's behaviors inexcusable. I found myself getting agitated.

"No, Lila. The therapist told you that it was not an excuse. Your mother exhibited poor behavior. It traumatized you throughout your life."

I could tell Lila found solace in my reassuring rhetoric. Lila had always blamed herself for not being the daughter her mother wished she had. She had put in tremendous efforts to become an exemplary adult, despite her learning disability, to show her mother she was and is worthy of love. All her actions went unnoticed. It made me sympathize with Lila tremendously.

"I know. The therapist made me dig deep into my memory. It was a painful session."

I have never enjoyed going to therapy; after the conversation, I tend to replay the sessions on repeat until the next session. It became detrimental to my emotional well-being. However, through this experience, I've gained a deeper understanding of myself and my needs. I concluded that I was not reaping the benefits of therapy but rather having a decline in my cognition. I know therapy has worked excellently for Lila; everyone responds to treatment differently.

"Lila, do you remember what you told the therapist? You were five years old, listening to profanity. Your mom fed you food with no nutritional value. She did not value your health. I even recalled her dropping you off at our house. You got left on our doorsteps."

Recalling the memory of witnessing blatant child abuse traumatized me. I could not fathom the psychological pain Lila must have felt. Dark memories like these are not fleeting. They tend to linger in the mind, either dormant or protruding, but never entirely disappear. Her parents did not have an ounce of compassion for her, nor could they be bothered by their obligatory paternal duties.

"I know, Yura. I got abandoned. It hurt my feelings that no one wanted to care for me. I was a forgotten child. I wish I was you, Yura. You experienced adornment. I felt like an unwanted nuisance. I wanted to scream so many times. I found solace in the pain. I was different. It was out of my control. For the majority of my life, I got rejected. The rejection came from my family and classmates."

"Lila, your father took care of you as an infant. You observed his mannerisms. You were a sponge for your surroundings. That was a skewed reality."

I felt the urge to retrieve my phone and research environmental influences shaping minds during the formative years. I knew the research would vindicate my insight into my casual conversation with Lila. However, I trusted Lila's knowledge and refrained from doing so, waiting for her to give her natural input. There was a short pause before Lila replied.

"Skewed. Tell me about it, Yura. It is putting it lightly. My Father Marković has a mental illness and autism. I viewed his behavior as acceptable. One example was when he spoke in a loud tone. My dad, Marković, talked at a high volume. He got perceived to be yelling.

"My father's influence led me to do the same. His entire family spoke loudly. I felt I received the short end of the stick. I adored him, and my hatred for my mom, Noor, grew. I still have a relationship with my mom, Noor. That shows my maturity. My dad, Marković, is smitten with her. Those two are in a loving, inter-abled relationship. My parents maintained a healthy relationship for thirty years. I do not know if I got Asperger syndrome because of my dad, Marković. He has an undiagnosed learning disability. He did not want judgment for his disability. Had he gotten a diagnosis, his symptoms would have improved. It also impacted my great-grandfather.

"Our family believes he suffered from Asperger syndrome. He had no formal diagnosis for this. A century ago, Asperger syndrome was not a diagnosis. His behavioral patterning mimicked autism. People who knew him thought he was strange. He never went to the doctor. He would have never gone for something so trivial. Doctor visitation fees were expensive in Bosnia and Herzegovina. It is our family speculation. My mother, Noor, told me about my great-grandfather. It was her attempt at being a good parent. We engaged in conversations infrequently. My mother, Noor, is shy and reserved. I have those traits too. It is a commonality we share. Most of my personality traits are identical to my father, Marković. It was because my mother Noor did not bond with me."

I hated my Aunt Noor for her callousness. When I was younger, she attempted to bond with me because I had preferable traits a daughter should possess. I did not realize it was because Lila suffered from Aspergers. Noor and I went to the spa on multiple occasions, excluding Lila. As a teenager, I went to their house and noticed Lila had forgotten to put away her journal. Her journal entry read that she hated herself and she wished she could eradicate her developmental disability. She mentioned her jealousy of my spa days with her aunt Noor. I felt a tremendous amount of guilt. Her aunt used me as a prop to hurt Lila.

"I thought that the therapy went well, Lila. You left with a lot of healthy takeaways. Do you remember what the psychologist told you? I do. Since you have been a fetus, you have been on a trajectory. Lila, your parents have dictated your success from a young age. Good parenting is critical for a prosperous life. In your case, paternal genetics were more dominant. Your mother did not do anything to assist you. She resulted in you developing a worse condition. Your psychological blueprint became altered. You latch onto men because you respect your father.

"Your father took on the traditional mother role. When it came to your maternal influences, there were none. Your mother was not a presence in your life. That would have benefited you. It would assist you in developing neuro-typical behaviors. It is not a healthy family dynamic. Your mother continued with her altruistic lifestyle. It puts you at a disadvantage throughout life. Psychologists debate nature versus nurture. It did not matter. It does not apply to you. You have experienced both. Lila, you experienced complications during childbirth. You received parental abuse. Lila, remember you are a complete person. The therapist suggested you look into the impacts of parental abuse."

After Lila's therapy session, I was deeply concerned about her well-being. I knew she might struggle with her daily responsibilities, so I decided to take action. I spent a significant amount of time researching parental abuse and trauma, trying to understand what she might be going through. I learned that the brain and the intestinal tract play a crucial role in managing stress, and I compiled a document with resources she could use when feeling overwhelmed.

"I know, Yura. The therapist told me how I could self-advocate. You did extensive research for me as a result. We went to the library. I took out a book on the impacts of abuse. I remember feeling drained. Yura, I am grateful you were there throughout the session. Sharing my insecurities and vulnerabilities is difficult. I was thankful for the advice."

Chapter 23: Scythian Golden Comb

"It took courage for me to go to therapy. I received solid advice that I intended to follow. I went to the library. I spoke to one of the librarians. Linda.

"She appeared to be of Indian descent, with henna tattoos. She was a wise individual. Linda gave a thoughtful response. 'Psychology books are typically already checked out. These books focus on mental issues. It is important to focus on mental well-being. I recommend a book on the importance of self-love. Everyone deserves that.' I went and retrieved the book. *There Is Only One You.*"

Lila paused and then resumed speaking, "I remember that you nodded in agreement with the decision. I had already believed in that ideology. I expected a new emotional growth development in my personality." Lila was in a healthy relationship with Anthony.

That did not mean she did not struggle to make friends. People tended to think she was strange. It turned Lila into a perfectionist. It took a toll on her self-esteem. She took it out on her physical appearance. Lila looked like me. Hearing her talk about her insecurities was difficult. It would trigger self-hatred within myself. That was not the road I want to be going down. Our similarities were uncanny. I also liked our personalities. We both embraced our individuality.

In doing so, we had fun. It is safe to say I was a strange person growing up. It followed me into adulthood. "Do you remember your meltdown at Breeze Shop? You were seven years old."

Lila nodded. "You wanted a chocolate bar. I did, too. Lila, do you remember your meltdown? You were so upset that you could not get a chocolate bar. I did not share the same meltdown feelings. I faked one so we both could get chocolate bars. You being autistic has benefited me." Lila chuckled.

We both outgrew our desire to eat chocolate bars. Our palates expanded, and our taste buds became more sophisticated. Our childhood innocence when we craved chocolate bars made me miss my formative years. Life, with all its complexities and nuances, became more apparent as we grew older. Lila's body language indicated that she reciprocated the fondness that I felt.

"Lila, that is not the only perk to being your cousin. You have contributed to my knowledge. Who knows more about philosophy than you? You have wisdom that no one can take away from you. Autism enhances you as a person. You can see many different perspectives. I have changed my ideologies because of you. You have debated with me on several occasions. I grew as a person knowing you." Lila appeared to be blushing.

She deserved credit where credit was due. Lila's presence has shifted my perspective on various issues and helped me become well-rounded. Her Aspergers made me a more compassionate and understanding person when dealing with people who have cognitive impairments.

"When I asked my parents questions about life, I felt like an annoying nuisance. My parents resorted to a higher power. I would not be an atheist without you, Lila." She smiled in embarrassment. Lila respected those who believed in a deity; however, dissecting the theology felt incompatible with her ideology. She shared her information with me, and I concurred. We formed a unilateral consensus to live without the presence of organized religion.

"Yura, that was mutual. I appreciated your depth. I am agnostic. I am always open to debate and discussion. I am taking the same program at my college. Our ideologies match. It was hard on me to go to a separate school from you, Yura. I am glad I went. It has been good for my self-growth. You have contributed to turning me into a woman. Thank you. The more I spoke to you, the more I felt accepted. I felt like an equal.

"I noticed I utilized my brain power. I looked up to you. More than that, Yura, I wanted to be you. You gave me an identity crisis. Our parents told us that we were Lebanese. You had to challenge that. You learned the entire history of Lebanon. Yura, you learned of the Middle Eastern Islamic empires. It enhanced my education as an Arabic woman. Thank you."

I felt elated. Tears welled up in my eyes, and a tear trickled down the back of my tongue. Her comment validated all my efforts. I have divulged into past generations to help understand the present day. I hoped it would become a beacon of hope for empowering marginalized and disenfranchised people. Lila's words were a positive encouragement. I paused, letting my heightened emotions subside, feeling a sense of validation that filled me with hope for the future.

"Lila, the two of us will conquer the world. I adore you. We should do an exercise to boost you up. We will not let your college classmates bring you down. We will overcome this together. Lila, think of all your accomplishments. We will take turns listing your strengths. You go first."

"Yura, that is unnecessary, but I will play along. I wanted to take control of my life. To do so, I needed a better understanding of my condition. I learned how to overcome my educational barriers. My educational process becomes propitious through repetition. I absorbed nuanced information. I did not think this would have been possible. It has helped me overcome my challenges."

Lila's insight is awe-inspiring. It's a clear sign of her dedicated self-growth journey, which will undoubtedly guide her toward career success. Her plans to kick start her career after college testify to her readiness. Elizabeth and I have always had our unwavering support and profound belief in Lila's capabilities, a belief that we deeply value and appreciate, and that won't change as she embarks on her next significant chapter.

"Yes. I am immensely proud of you for that, Lila. These are the parameters of your intelligence. You took the initiative to become a self-advocate. You sought out knowledge."

Education is an individual's most powerful tool, regardless of academic abilities. But when it comes to developmental disabilities, the journey is arduous. The individual must put in double the effort of a non-disabled person. I admire the determination not to give up. I have witnessed Lila's journey, where she has not just overcome but blossomed despite life's challenges. Her progress gives me hope she can have a brighter future.

"I know, Yura. When I absorb information, I pretend I am an empty canvas. It allowed me to be an active learner. I made an effort to store my knowledge in my long-term memory. I found myself being able to retrieve complex information from my mind. I put in hard work. It would not have been possible."

"Lila, I remember when you were a child. You got viewed as incompetent. Now people look to you for knowledge."

Lila's determination was her most significant asset. She had a clear vision of what she deserved and refused to settle for anything less, setting a high standard for herself. Despite people with malicious intentions trying to put her in her place, she disregarded their discouragement and consistently rose to the occasion. I have determined that Lila has the mentality to fall seven times and get up eight.

"I met my psychologist through you, Yura. Since then, my therapist has referred to me as an inspiration. I noticed that I am on par with my classmates at college. In elementary school, I did not think higher education would be on the cards. I have defied my learning disability."

I have met many people without a developmental disability who do not have the tenacity to pursue education and strive for excellence in the same capacity Lila does.

She is the underdog, and her mentality is undeterred. She will become victorious. As a neurotypical, I have come to admire the strength displayed by specific individuals classified by having a neurodivergent diagnosis. Their unique perspectives and approaches are not just a testament but a vital part of the value of neurodiversity in our society. They are not just different, but they are integral to our society.

"You have a lot to be proud of yourself for, Lila."

"Thanks; it would mean nothing without having someone to share those wins with. I managed to find Anthony. I remember that moment. That was my life achievement. I was sitting in English class. The teacher said that new students would be joining. I felt uninterested. How could a new student capture my interest? He walked in. My heart started pounding. Anthony was wearing a tight black shirt. I could see his muscles through his clothes. I could not believe how attractive he was. He looked insecure. He was awkward. I thought he was charming. After class, I mustered the courage to talk to him. I attempted to flirt. It may have been so pathetic that he did not notice.

"He told me he had Asperger syndrome. I could not believe we had the same learning disability. It was the best moment in my life. The more our relationship evolved, the more we had in common. He asked me out. We began cultivating our relationship. I no longer felt alone. We have been guiding each other through hardships. Anthony understood me. I became an unstoppable woman."

Anthony has become Lila's primary support, a role her psychologically absent parents failed to fulfill. His support is a cornerstone of Lila's well-being. However, Lila needs to strive for independence and self-sufficiency. This journey toward self-reliance is necessary and holds the potential for significant personal growth.

"You have the same potential as those without disabilities, Lila. You never expected to have a healthy, long-term relationship. I am so happy for you."

As Lila's best friend and cousin, I have embraced Anthony into our family with open arms. She introduced him to her parents on one occasion. The meeting was palpably tense and uncomfortable. Her parent's standoffish behavior clearly showed their indifference toward Lila. Anthony primarily interacted with Lila and, to a lesser extent, Elizabeth and myself.

"I know, Yura. Growing up was a painful experience. I did not fit in with anyone. That is the reason I clung to you, Yura."

You can cling to me anytime." Although I am Lila's cousin, I have more innate motherly instincts around her than a peer. As a young child, I witnessed her struggle tremendously and wanted to assist her however I could. This experience shifted the roles in our relationships, but it also revealed our resilience.

"You can cling to me anytime."

"I enjoyed hanging out with you today, Yura. It rejuvenated me. It felt more like therapy. I gotta go. I only came down for the day. Anthony misses me."

The short duration prohibited me from dissecting the validity of her statements about her current state of healthy being. I needed to take her at face value. We longed for more time to participate in interactive activities. I was not too fond of the strain the distance had put on our relationship. Next time, I must convince her to visit for a few days.

"I enjoyed your visit. I miss you already."

A lingering sadness crept over my entire body. The parting farewells, a bitter pill to swallow, sparked a fierce internal debate. Was their visit genuinely worth it? I debated whether the visit had merit, and in the end, I could not deny its value. Had Lila not spent the afternoon with me, the sadness would not be present now. Yet, amid this conflict, I couldn't deny the profound value of healthy family reunions, a treasure we must cherish and nurture.

"You will see me in a few months. Anthony felt upset, he did not get to see you."

I always found Anthony to be incredibly well-mannered and polite. His presence changes the relationship dynamics. Lila and I would not have been able to delve into childhood like we did now. I appreciated our girl's time. I hoped Lila would decide to visit more often. Our bonding time is a cherished part of my life, and I value it greatly.

"He should have come down with you. He is always welcome."

Lila smiled. "I will let him know." She seemed eager to return to Anthony, who had become her favorite person, replacing me. Initially, I felt a mild sense of irritation. But I knew I had to accept that this was the normal progression of life, the ebb and flow of emotions. She stood up from the couch and grabbed her purse from the floor. We walked toward the front door, her departing nonverbal remarks a reminder of life's changes.

"I will let him know. Thanks. Bye."

Feeling the need to lift the heaviness of our temporary parting, I made a spontaneous decision. Last night, as I casually browsed through my social media feed, a few classmates decided to go bar hopping. Without much thought, I decided to join them. I was comforted by the fact that I knew most of the attendees, but there would also be new faces to encounter.

"Bye, Lila." I felt sad watching Lila leave. I immediately felt lonely. My friends need help to provide the championship she provides me with. It has to do with our similarities. Our personalities complement each other. In the morning, I got up from my daybed.

I made my way to the kitchen. I attempted to get rid of my disorientation. It was the negative impact of drinking too much tequila. To remedy this situation, I foraged for food. I opened the fridge, and I noticed my sister standing there. "How is my big shot sister? Mom wanted to know when payment was due for the spring semester at college."

I had written the payment date on my agenda and kept it in my campus locker for safekeeping. I would have to retrieve the information first thing tomorrow morning. Right now, I need to buy myself time to avoid getting into trouble by not providing the correct answer.

"Hello, Elizabeth. I am fine. Tell Mom that I will handle it. The education I learned in world history is priceless. How was hormone therapy?" I hope my answer to the semester payment was sufficient. I wanted to change the topic to something more present, like Elizabeth's hormone therapy. Hormone therapy provided Elizabeth with spectacular medical procedures. These procedures have relieved Elizabeth's psychological distress and improved our family dynamics.

"Okay, Yura. I will tell Mom. Hormone therapy was okay. The doctor is impressed. My body handled the implantation well. In a few months, the transition will be complete. It is exciting for me. I cannot wait to be a woman."

After the initial shock of her transition, our entire family is on board and wants her to transition fully. Our collective acceptance and unwavering support for her journey is a testament to our love for her. I felt elated; I would finally have a sister. When my mother was pregnant with her second child, I hoped it was a girl. I was indifferent to having a baby brother. I remember telling Elizabeth that, and she blushed. I love being her support system.

"That is amazing, Elizabeth."

My remark was supportive and concise. One of Elizabeth's top love languages is words of affirmation; we overlap. I try to encourage her wherever applicable. She has praised my thoughtfulness on multiple occasions. We have a positive discourse, which helps us foster a sisterly bond.

"Thank you. After hormone therapy, I went to Shawarma Vera. There is leftover shawarma if you are interested." I nodded. I went to the fridge to retrieve the leftovers. Elizabeth engaged in a conversation with me.

185

I hoped her presence in the room would not make me feel forced to share the leftover Shawarma with her. There was a minuscule amount left inside the styrofoam container. I stared at the half-eaten rice, chicken, and utterly untouched tabbouleh. I felt preoccupied with grabbing my cutlery. However, I passively listened to her well-thought-out question, and my internal struggle to respect her right to ask was evident in my every move.

"How is your genealogy project going?"

Elizabeth's seemingly simple question has a nuanced answer integral to my significant project. It opens up various avenues for further exploration. I have pondered how best to respond and have decided to share some of my insights with her. I recognize Elizabeth's question as essential and of great value to my project. Answering the question may assist me in gaining introspection and retrospection, but more importantly, it has the potential to impact the project's direction significantly.

I gave a well-thought-out response. "It is an educational process. It is more than I bargained for. Our ancestry morphed during the Seljuk, Mameluke, and Ottoman Empire periods. The migration tracking history needs to be improved. Our ancestors are the forgotten ones."

The notion that the entire Middle East has yet to dissect this topic thoroughly felt unfathomable. The weight of this topic lies in how foreign influences in the region help strengthen the Middle East and Northern Africa. The potential impact of recognizing the Islamic

Empires and migration history, which could be immense in solving the Middle East, cannot be overstated.

"You should become a professor of history, Yura. Your contributions should not go unnoticed."

"Thank you, Elizabeth. I appreciate that. I am going to the mall later, would you like to come?"

When I reached adolescence, I learned I preferred shopping with others. Occasionally, I required a second opinion when debating making a purchase. It helped me avert impulse buys. Having Elizabeth as my companion made the experience more enjoyable, removing the obligatory tasking aspects of shopping.

Elizabeth replied, "Yes. I have been searching for a new skirt. I want to make an impression. I am hoping to find an appropriate male suitor. I am so nervous about the possibility of dating. I never met a Muslim man willing to date a transgender."

The exclusionary practices have hurt me from being a secondhand witness to the discrimination faced by the Muslim community. I do not understand how she can overcome these barriers while maintaining her faith in Allah. I wished I believed in something that much.

"Elizabeth, you are prettier than I am."

Chapter 24: The Shivaji Sword

"All that plastic surgery does not go unnoticed. Men think you are attractive. Of course, someone will want to date you. I will do everything in my power to help you. I will meet you in my car. Okay?" Elizabeth nodded. I went outside, got into the car, and turned the engine on.

Elizabeth came outside. I screamed, "Girl, get in!" She did. I turned on the radio and played the top-charted songs. We sang along. We arrived, and I parked my car in the garage.

We went to the store, Fashion Red. I went through the racks of clothes. I found three cute tops and one dress. Elizabeth found a conservative long skirt. We headed to the changing rooms. One of the tops I tried on needed to be more significant. I felt iffy about one of the tops. I tried on the dress, but it did not suit my body. I decided to only go with one item. I met Elizabeth outside the changing room. She was waiting for me. Elizabeth decided to buy the skirt. We had semi-success shopping.

We decided to return home. In the car, we decided to make a coffee stop. We ordered four decaf coffees. Two were for our parents. We were planning to surprise them. Once we got home, Elizabeth went to her room. I overheard her speaking on the telephone. She talked to Sabrina Mohamad. Elizabeth met her at the Youth Mosque Group.

It happens every Thursday. It was for individuals aged twelve to seventeen years old. The facilitators taught the children how to read the Quran. Elizabeth often felt isolated. Sabrina went out of her way to include her. My stepfather referred to Sabrina as her inclusive Muslim friend. Her beliefs in Islam were moderate.

She had a sweet older brother named Ahmed. He was single. I knew that Elizabeth had a crush on him. He treated her more like a friend. On one occasion, Elizabeth found out he had a date. It was hard for Elizabeth. Her energy was off-putting. I gave her space. In the evening, she came out of her room to eat. I could tell that she had cried about the situation. I felt helpless. I tried to communicate that I was also single. She did not seem to care. Elizabeth did not engage in conversation. She wanted to be invisible. I tried not to be insensitive. I wanted to soothe her pain. I ordered pizza and desserts to comfort her. It took thirty minutes to arrive. I offered Elizabeth some food.

Elizabeth accepted. She seemed more content. It worked. Elizabeth ate one slice. I had two. Afterward, we both ate a cookie. We felt full. I needed her to open up. I thought her bottling her emotions would damage her mental health. I cracked a joke. "I think you are upset that you cannot date yourself." Elizabeth used to be named Ahmed. His facial features matched hers when she was younger. She smiled.

She appeared to be glowing. I have watched my sister Elizabeth transition from a young boy into a beautiful, sophisticated woman. My family and I have yearned for the day a nice man would feel compelled to pursue her romantically. I could not believe the day had finally arrived; my entire family felt beyond satisfied.

"I was always cute. I have good taste. Yura, imagine you were once a man. You would never have been that attractive. You should not be speaking." We both laughed. It was solid bonding time. I suggested watching a few episodes on the television. She agreed.

Elizabeth was more preoccupied with his date than with the show. She could not concentrate and eventually went to her room. The wait was antagonizing. After the date, Sabrina called Elizabeth. Sabrina told her that Ahmed was not compatible with his date. He did not like that his date was a mentally ill single mom. The two decided to end the date halfway through.

I could sense the relief on her face. Elizabeth was a seventeen-year-old girl who had never dated.

The majority of her classmates were in relationships or had been in them. Elizabeth was waiting for a serious partner. Elizabeth wanted to be a dream woman. She did everything to appeal to men.

Elizabeth wondered if a man could look past her transgenderism. We shared a lot of commonalities. She passed as a woman to strangers. It was her decision who knew.

My thoughts wandered for hours. I decided to buckle down. It meant I could no longer get distracted by my thoughts. I needed to put my focus on something productive. I was going back to school in two days. My mother, Nadia, had sat me down in grade 11. It was a typical coming-of-age parental discussion. She told me I was reaching adulthood. It meant I needed to start acting like a mature adult. Her words vividly resurfaced. "Yura, do not reminisce about your childhood."

I took her advice. I needed to get to class. I took a bus to the college campus. I walked to world history class.

"Hello, class. I want everyone to welcome our new student, Leah Asher. I am Professor Hanau Bravebird. I hope you find my classes insightful. The Seljuk Turks were an influential group. They emerged from Central Asia during the 10th century. They were nomadic people who migrated to the Middle East. They established an Islamic empire. It lasted for several centuries. Under Seljuk Turks' leadership, they seized Persia and Iraq. The Seljuk Turks expanded their territories to include Anatolia.

"The Seljuk Turks were known for their military prowess and innovative tactics, which allowed them to defeat larger armies. One of the most significant contributions of the Seljuk Turks was their promotion of Islamic culture. They sponsored a manifold of scholars and built numerous madrasas (Islamic schools) throughout their empire. The Seljuk Empire eventually declined due to internal conflicts and external pressures from other powers. The Mamluk Empire replaced the Seljuk Turks. The Mamluk dynasty ruled Egypt and Syria from the 13th to the 16th century. The Mamluks were slave soldiers brought to Egypt by the Ayyubid sultanate in the late 12th century.

"The Mamluk military trained the soldiers from a young age in horsemanship and archery. The Mamluks successfully repelled numerous invasions. Turkish architecture saw a shift toward more elaborate and intricate designs, with an emphasis on geometric patterns and calligraphy. The unique architectural style blended elements from different cultures and civilizations.

"Under Mamluk's rule, Egypt became the center of trade and culture. The Mamluks also built impressive architectural structures such as mosques, madrasas, and mausoleums that still stand today. Two notable examples of Mamluk architecture in Turkey are the Karamanoglu Mosque and the Aladdin Mosque.

"The Mamluks faced internal struggles toward the end of their reign. Corruption and infighting weakened their hold on power. The Mamluk dynasty clashed with the Ottoman Empire. The Ottoman Empire overthrew the Mamluk Empire in 1517. The Ottoman Empire lasted from 1516 to 1918. At this time, Lebanon changed politically and economically. The Ottomans were a new ruling class within Lebanon. The Ottomans appointed elites to govern Lebanon. They played a crucial role in shaping Lebanese society and culture. Lebanon grew in trade and commerce industries. In the Ottoman Empire, Lebanon established several commercial centers in Beirut and other cities that facilitated trade with other parts of the world.

"The developments brought many challenges to Lebanon. The country suffered from political instability, economic decline, and social unrest. The impacts continue to shape modern-day Lebanon." It would be a dream for Lebanon to have the same social privileges that Europe has. Unfortunately, the prehistoric empires have ensured our fate. The class came to a close. I went home. I created a mental navigation map of my parents' neighborhood. I was always well aware of my surroundings.

I understood the dangers lurking around every corner. As a child, my father instilled these safety measures by constantly exposing me to the news. The cases of child kidnappings and abductions gave me night terrors. His malicious method worked, and I began developing an awareness of my surroundings. My parents and I implemented a safety strategy to limit the danger I felt exposed to.

I walked to my parents' home. I noticed Mia was at her house. I knocked on her door. She answered, "Yura. I need your help. I am seeing Thomas tomorrow. I do not know what to wear." She pulled out multiple outfits from her closet. I felt bombarded with her superficiality. I mentally classified her crisis as a nuisance. "Yura, what do you think?"

There was a moment when I felt the urge to come up with a response that might have come across as pretentious, all to keep our friendship intact. I hid my irritation, but then it hit me. The most effective way to change my perspective on the issue was to connect with her. This realization, a significant moment in my life, that understanding her viewpoint was essential to changing my own was a profound experience. I could relate to her use of clothes and makeup to stir emotions, although not as intensely as she did.

"Mia, he will think you are pretty in any outfit."

I felt proud of myself for displaying the maturity to answer an obnoxious question. I immediately noticed that it brought Mia a smile. As a child, I would have most likely fumbled the entire situation and lost Mia's friendship. I recognized my growth progression.

"You only say that because you are dating that slob, Carter. Thomas is a man of class." My cheeks were hot. I gave a fiery response to her callous remark.

Mia's overbearing self-centeredness, which she seemed oblivious to, had built up my irritation. Her actions curbed my impulsive reaction instincts and hurt my feelings. She made a direct attack on my boyfriend, which was a clear indication of her belief that she was superior to me. This situation, however, was a catalyst for my personal growth, making me realize the need to stand up for myself.

"Excuse you?" Mia got defensive.

Her emotions were oppositional. I had never seen this petty side of Mia before. Before this incident, I would have described her as polite and well-mannered. She said and did all the right things. She maintained a good rapport with everyone, which helped her maintain popularity. I was seeing a new side to Mia, and if she kept it up, I felt our friendship could soon be in serious jeopardy.

"Yura. Do you see a significant difference between us? You got Carter. Good for you. You were never on par with me." I stood there in shock. My heart palpitations were through the roof.

[I would never utter those statements to someone I hated. The worst part was that I considered Mia to be my friend. During our friendship, there were moments when I thought she was prettier than me. Those thoughts did not consume me. I was not too fond of civil society's urge to pit women against women. I always believed women should help bring each other up.

"Thomas and my appearance meet the criteria for a fashion magazine. Yura, you could fix your face with plastic surgery. Going to the gym would not hurt either."

I felt my eyes become watery. I reverted to myself. My inner self-esteem got shattered. I did not understand why I was letting Mia get away with this. I went home and cried. I decided that Mia was taking her internalized anger out on me. I did not deserve that. I did not know if I wanted to continue to be her friend. I decided Mia had an off day. I went to bed. The next morning, I woke up.

Chapter 25: The Bronze Statue of Artemis and a Deer

I needed to get ready for school. I arrived on campus and rushed to world history. "Hello, class. Let's get into the lecture. Today I am going to continue debunking American indigeneity.

"Our roots originally descended from Far East Asia. Far East Asians crossed the tundra to the Americas. They came from Yakutia. It is the farthest province in Russia. They became the first inhabitants of Canada. The Far East Asians took their ideologies with them. These individuals were part of the Seljuk Turk and Mamluk dynasties. Asians entered uncharted territories, promoting Islam. Genghis Khan influenced these tribes. It is in their surnames and culture. North Americans believed in medieval Islam. Their heritage was a variation of ancient Asian culture. The tribes attempted to mimic the culture. It does not go unnoticed. The Mamluk was an Islamic slave army in the Middle East.

"In North America, mukluks are seal boats. They are also a form of Inuit art. Far-East Asia culture is noticeable in their headpieces. Some headpieces are identical. Other indigenous headpieces are adaptations. The resemblance is uncanny. I noticed the recurring theme during the NoDAPL protest. One protester took to an online video platform. Her name was Alasie. She was an environmentalist. Alasie talked about the harsh brutalities she faced. She said that men with batons were attacking nurses. The nurses performed sacred prayers to heal the injured. That was how they reconnected with their culture. Alasie referred to this as the Kalmias. The word caught me off guard.

"It is an Islamic ideology. It is the worship of Allah. The indigenous practices indicate this ancient religion. Living in prehistoric Americas meant history got handed down through generations. Asian heritage became altered. It also happened to North Americans. When history gets rewritten, it becomes forgotten. It is due to misinformation. In this political climate, that is controversial. It is far from their only issue. Archeologists are nervous that the Indigenous would face backlash for their ancient way of life. It has prevented the community from getting informed about their prehistoric history. Their barbaric traditions became known all across the globe.

"In the Middle East and Europe, they practiced child sacrifice. It gets called out to attack the indigenous communities of the Americas. These were the practices of the medieval ages. Class dismissed." It was finally winter break. It meant three weeks of vacation. It was a bittersweet moment for Elizabeth and me. Elizabeth loved school. She went to a high school that had a specialized writing program. I shared similar sentiments. I found college was helping me grow. My ideologies had expanded substantially since I first attended. The only problem was that I was apart from Lila. I knew that I could not go much longer without seeing her. I had made plans months ago to see Lila during Winter Break.

After my last class, I took a local bus to the Z.T.O. charter bus station. I waited at the station for fifteen minutes before my bus departed. I felt excited to see Lila. My long-distance travel would equate to a positive visit. After hours of being on the charter bus, I reached my destination. I then walked to Lila's apartment. Eventually, I arrived at her one-bedroom apartment complex. I knocked on the door. Lila answered. I entered her apartment complex. In the living room, Lila bought two beige couches. One couch was placed along the window. The other faced the television. The room felt spacious. An island separated the living room and kitchen. The kitchen had amenities.

Anthony walked into the living room. I felt excited to see him. Nothing could have encapsulated my attention like young love. I loved love. My extracurricular activities include watching romantic comedies. I expected love to be in the air. The opposite occurred. Lila and Anthony were the antithesis of a romantic couple. The energy did not replicate what they were like as high school sweethearts. They were lovey-dovey in high school. I wondered if they were having relationship problems. Lila looked catatonic. I saw a few passive-aggressive exchanges with her boyfriend. My inquiry became heightened. Where was the relationship heading? Anthony's eyes appeared lifeless.

I wanted to help. I thought about orchestrating a couples counseling session. The atmosphere was somber. I pulled Lila to the side. I asked her what was going on. She shrugged me off. I knew that the situation was dire. I reiterated a sentiment that my mother, Nadia, once told me.

"Lila, we put on a facade to pretend we are not suffering. So, we neglect our inner selves. Do you remember when Elizabeth came out as trans-gendered? She tried to bottle up her feelings. When Elizabeth was six, my mom, Nadia, caught her cross-dressing. The therapist told my mother, Nadia, that Elizabeth was masking her emotions. The therapist told my mom, Nadia, how serious this was.

"Her son, Ahmed, was a woman and needed her. Transgender individuals are prone to suicide. My mother, Nadia, decided she could not let that happen to her child. Right now, I am worried about your mental state, Lila. You mask problems the same way Elizabeth does. Lila, your mental health will deteriorate. My sister, Elizabeth, is forthcoming with her individuality. I am proud. She is a propitious businesswoman. Elizabeth is a best-selling author. Being her sister, I bought every book. I have a shelf of her books sitting in my closet. Her success came as no surprise. Elizabeth spent the majority of her time writing. It had been her psychological support. Elizabeth honed in on her writing abilities.

"Her high school grade 10 English teacher noticed her exceptionalism. Elizabeth got nominated to take part in a writing competition. Write for the world! My sister received adulation from our parents. I felt envious. I wanted recognition for my abilities. I wish I had been nominated to enter the writing competition. It would have helped me stand out in my college admissions. The idea of getting rejected felt haunting. It took Elizabeth a month to submit it. Elizabeth was braggadocios during this time. When she finished, she ran into my room. Elizabeth became overcome with emotions. We walked over to our post office box. She said a prayer over the envelope and slid it in.

"Elizabeth had an agonizing three-month wait before she received the results. Elizabeth got a letter with her response. Our family gathered around the table. She came in third out of two hundred. She felt dissatisfied. Our parents reassured her. Elizabeth learned to be content with the results. I knew I would never surpass her accomplishments. That was a humbling moment. Elizabeth has a bright future. It all stemmed from her having the courage to speak up." I would never utter those statements to someone I hated. The worst part was that I considered Mia to be my friend. During our friendship, there were moments when I thought she was prettier than me. Those thoughts did not consume me. I was not too fond of civil society's urge to pit women against women. I always believed women should help bring each other up.

I have thought extensively about the ramifications if Elizabeth had not dared to tell her immediate family that she wanted to transition from male to female. We would have lost her to suicide. It would have destroyed my family. We want to avert this fate in as many humans as possible. Elizabeth became fully embraced. Life does not have to be excruciatingly painful,

Family support is crucial in this journey, and we must all strive to provide it. The positive impact of family support on the mental health and well-being of individuals like Elizabeth is tremendous. It can make the difference between life and death.

After a long pause, Lila broke her silence. "Anthony found out he got adopted at two years old. Anthony only found out last month. He has resorted to misusing alcohol.

"Anthony experienced uncontrollable rage and threw his family's photo album out of a five-story window. It resulted in the police coming to our apartment. The landlord gave us one month to pay the damages. The alternative is getting evicted. It amounts to five hundred dollars."

Lila was nervous that they would not be able to afford it. Lila always looked up to me. She wanted my help in finding his biological parents.

Lila, who has made significant progress, has depended on me for most of her life. She perceives herself as inadequate and often needs to rely on others. I have been emphasizing the importance of self-sufficiency and self-efficacy to her. Lila's insecurities are challenging, and I am dedicated to helping her overcome them.

My assistance in understanding Anthony's childhood would be limited. Lila would be able to give herself entirely to this endeavor, and it would produce higher-quality results than I could get in this matter. I never met Anthony's adoptive parents. Besides, I barely knew Anthony and felt sorry for his predicament. The weight of my blatant indifference to Anthony became crystal

clear in my mind. Given its complexity, I knew Lila could handle this matter better than I could.

"Yura, you are my go-to for genealogy inquiries."

"Lila, this is outside my jurisdiction. It is your initiative. What have you done so far?"

Lila looked nervous. She gave me an emotional response. I spoke to his adoptive parents on the telephone.

"I managed to pry out the names of his possible biological parents. The adoptive parents received those names at the orphanage. They needed to be sure of the name's validity. I told Anthony right away. It sparked his inquisition. He wanted to know for sure. I took charge. I purchased a biological kit. Anthony needs infinite answers. Yura, I invited you here tonight because it was the same night to help me with this. Anthony's suspected parents are coming over. I do not want to be alone." I stared at Lila blankly. I felt used. I thought Lila invited me here because she missed me. Unsure of how to feel, I sat on the couch and turned on the television. I anticipated the visit.

There was a knock at the door. I could sense panic in the room. Strangers are about to enter the apartment. I watched a true crime docuseries about how murders operate. They seek out secluded areas to engage in heinous acts. Lila held Anthony's hand, and they opened the door. They said their greetings. I noticed the emotional toll it had on them. The suspected biological parents made their way to the small kitchen island. After a while, I decided to help. I sat down on a bar stool. I opened the kit and read the instructions. The suspected biological parents seemed uncomfortable with the situation. I told them the requirements. They took the tube from my hand. They spit into it.

Chapter 26: The Hope Diamond

Anthony did the same. They made small talk. It was lighthearted. They mainly talked about the cold winter that we were experiencing. The suspected parents were eager to leave. They did so in an abrupt fashion. Anthony's monotonous face was isolating. I could sense that this drained him.

Anthony was going to need to take a moment to process this. I took their decomposition to the garbage chute. I returned to notice the two of them embracing. I decided it was time for my departure. I pulled Lila aside. I told her that it was getting late. I whispered that she could reach out if she had concerns about Anthony. I said my final goodbyes. I took the biological kit with me.

I agreed to put it in the post office box. In the elevator, I thought about the experience. I read the deoxyribonucleic acid kit box. Once the agency received the kit, they would assess the saliva. It took a month for the recipient to receive the answers. Lila was an impatient individual. She would fill me in on the results. I made the decision not to fixate on this.

It was between Lila and Anthony. I found my presence in this situation to be unnecessary. I felt sorry for Lila. The irony is that I am single while she is in a long-term relationship. Her relationship was solid, with the occasional hiccup. A part of me envied Lila. Watching Anthony search for his familial roots was interesting.

I had almost completed my genealogy journey. I was also supposed to receive my ancestral results next week. I exited the main entrance of the apartment. I needed to walk fifteen minutes to catch a terminal bus. I purchased my ticket from the attendant. I scoured the room. The majority sat with their young families. I sat down on an empty tulip chair. I realized that my excessive staring was making people uncomfortable. I did not know where to place my eyes. I looked down. I thought about how jealous I was that Lila had a long-term boyfriend. I had not been on a date since I broke up with Carter. I thought about dating life back on the college campus.

I made a non-binding pact with myself. I would make a concerted effort to go out on dates. Seeing romantic couples exacerbated my loneliness. In my psychology class, the professor discussed Maslow's Hierarchy of Needs. I needed to reach self-actualization. I would need more than my academic accolades. My emotional well-being was teetering. I needed to put myself first.

I decided to make use of the S.R.Z. Charter bus station cafeteria. I purchased a vegetarian wrap sandwich. At the cashier's post, there were newspapers. I picked one up. I flipped the pages. I read about astronautical extraterrestrial developments.

The astronauts at the Aerospace Agency had laid out the next course of action. I ate my meal. It took thirty minutes before they announced my departure. It is an hour-long bus trip. I spent the majority of the time peering out the window. Once the bus reached its final destination, I departed. I dialed a taxi service. I gave the taxi driver the address. I knocked on the door, and my mother, Nadia, answered. I felt elated to see her, and we embraced. My Stepfather Omar piped up.

I followed his echo to greet him. We spent the next few minutes engaging in friendly banter. Omar wanted to know how my college experience was going. I responded with an ever-so-typical answer.

"It is going okay." He could tell that I did not want to go into further discussion about this. Omar made the conscious decision not to press me. The atmosphere felt awkward.

To break the energy, I went to grab a pudding cup from the fridge. My little sister, Elizabeth, entered the room. She is getting ready to leave. Elizabeth was going to get hormone therapy. She had almost transitioned. My parents spent a hefty fee getting rid of her male genitals. She told me she was going to become a trans-Muslim-Arab activist. Elizabeth planned to pick up shawarma for us afterward.

I told her not to order anything for me. My Father Omar was going to be taking her. I had just arrived. We were now saying our goodbyes. Awful timing! We are the furthest thing from the typical Lebanese family. My parents do not adhere to traditional ideologies. My sister became indoctrinated into Islam by our uncle, Hassan. Hassan tried to convince Elizabeth that being transgender is a sin. Elizabeth still needed to transition. He was half successful. Elizabeth now believes in Islam. I became an atheist. His conversion did not work on me. I got swayed by modernized media. One talk show host explained how the idea of God was a preposterous theory.

My mother, Nadia, told me she invited her neighbor over. I needed to make myself scarce. I did not come to my parent's house to be a nuisance. My mother, Nadia, said Mia, my neighbor, was home. I should spend time with her. I was well acquainted with Mia. She was your typical prom queen. I remember meeting her in the tenth grade. We attended science class together. I called to see if she wanted to hang out. Mia and her boyfriend already had plans. They were going clubbing. I was welcome to tag along. I accepted. I needed to get ready. I went into my old childhood bedroom. I prepared my outfit. I pulled out a sleek black low-cut dress.

I went into the bathroom and placed my hair products on the counter. It took me half an hour to do my hair. I went into Elizabeth's room. I took her makeup. I got dolled up and walked over. Mia was in a lacy, short red dress. She looked stunning, which was no surprise. Mia is a Swedish Barbie doll. Once at the mall, a modeling agent noticed her. Mia is 5'10" with almost no facial blemishes. She had always been a relationship girl. In high school, she had an off-and-on relationship with Lucas Martin. He is a mix of Greek and African origins. They separated when he came out as gay. I once bumped into him at the mall with his partner.

Shocked, I knew his boyfriend, Marvin Taylor. We had gone to the same elementary school. He struggled in school. Marvin had dyslexia. I felt sorry for him. He was the only African in the class. Marvin had a learning disability. When I saw them together, it was sweet. They appeared to be smitten. Lucas told me that he wanted to catch up. I said okay. There was no rift between Mia and Lucas. She moved on, too. She was dating a European. Following her breakup, we had a girls' night out. Mia allowed me to choose the restaurant. I picked a Spanish place. Little did Mia know that her single status was about to change. As we arrived, I noticed the restaurant had re-branded.

At the entryway, I spoke to the host, "I regularly come to this restaurant. The name change caught me off guard. What resulted in the name change?"

I frequently engage with the hosts and servers in casual conversation. This friendly behavior, which I learned from my parents, has become a common courtesy for me. Replicating my parents ' behaviors has not only assisted in morphing my personality but also created a strong connection with them. The rebranding of the restaurant's image truly caught me off guard. It piqued my interest.

He replied, "New management." A European family purchased the restaurant. The host guided us to a table. We sat down. I browsed the menu. The server appeared. He engaged with us. "Is there anything I can get for you?"

I spoke, "We would like to start with a nacho platter." He jotted it down. I glanced over at him. I read his name tag. The server is named Thomas McKerracher. He appeared to be around our age. I noticed he caught several ladies' attention in the restaurant. I was never a fan of arrogant studs.

Mia did not share the same sentiments. It caused an alarm to go off in my mind. Thomas entertains ladies' fantasies by wearing tight clothes. That was his gimmick. I realized that Mia was blushing. I hushed my derogatory comments. The chemistry between the two was undeniable. My eyes rolled to the back of my head. Mia rushed to the restroom to fix her makeup. I tried to get a read on Thomas. Mia returned. I noticed she altered her top to show her cleavage. Mia was pulling out all the stops to get Thomas's attention. He noticed. He was polite and did not mention it.

The chemistry was heating up as the evening progressed. Thomas brought us our main course meal.

I spoke to him. On the wall, hung a television with a soccer game playing. I asked what team he was rooting for. The conversation started flowing between us. Mia introduced herself with a soft and seductive voice. Mia said that she always roots for Canada. Her demeanor had changed. Her voice hit another octave. I am in their way. I ducked out to the lady's room. I was still determining when I could resurface.

Chapter 27: The Dropa Stones

I was still determining when I could resurface. I clocked my time spent in the restroom. Fifteen minutes! During the fifteen minutes, I rummaged through my purse. I found a deck of cards and stacked them along the windowsill.

I played a game of solitaire. I had two winning hands and lost one. While I played, two women entered to use the facilities. I sensed that my presence made them uncomfortable. It was the price of being a good friend. When I returned, I asked her how the conversation went. Her expression said it all. Mia held a small piece of paper with cellular digits. It was an auspicious night out. My new friendship dynamics got laid out. I was going to be the third wheel. I could not become infatuated with Mia's relationship. I had my own school life. I needed to focus on graduation. Seeing Mia was inescapable. She was my next-door neighbor. I needed to have a social life.

Mia was my convenient option. I hung out with the couple. Thomas and Mia's sexual chemistry was superficial. They could have dug into more profound topics, such as world affairs. Mia and Thomas kept conversations light. They focused on having fun. Both Mia and Thomas are attractive. I felt like an unattractive friend tagging along. It had a detrimental impact on my self-esteem. It was no fault of their own. It was my internal battle. I did not have any male suitors. Dating in college proved to be too difficult. Carter had immersed himself in academics. Everyone else already had a significant other. I felt like a nuisance. I swiped on dating websites.

I got matches, but we needed to be compatible for various reasons. I felt insecure every day. I would scrutinize my facial features. I debated unfriending Mia. Comparisons were detrimental to my mental health. I weighed the pros and cons of this decision. I realized that all my social activities needed to benefit me. It caused me to remind myself that every time I hung out with the couple, I had fun. I projected my self-hatred. I needed to showcase my intelligence around Mia and Thomas. I did not have this issue with my other friends. My jealousy reverted when they felt intimidated. It was due to guilt. I needed to make Mia and Thomas feel inferior to shine.

Mia and Thomas only got their high school diplomas. Mia was more interested in makeup than studying. She got a job as a makeup artist. Mia had a steady income. The couple was interested in moving in together. I thought it would be too soon. They had only been dating for two months. I knew upon graduating from college. I would have to move back to my parents' house. I felt worried about paying my student loans. I pondered whether her decision to work after high school paid off. I wondered when my life would begin. We managed to look past our differences. I got invited to go clubbing with them. Today was no exception.

Partying with Mia and Thomas was a good time. The parties involved good music, Latin dancing, and alcohol.

Mia had thrown parties. She attends parties more often than throws them. The easiest way was to go to a club. I enjoyed the lively and energetic atmosphere. Mia went to clubs where party music gets people dancing. The type of music is usually upbeat and catchy. The club's Mia Goes had a Latin feel. The decorations and lighting made it a festive atmosphere. Mia is extroverted and outgoing. I am a mixture of an introvert and an extrovert. I seek out social interactions and connections with others. I needed to get ready. I needed to be at her house in fifteen minutes.

I went into my closet and selected sexy clubwear. I rang Mia's doorbell, and she answered. We headed to the club. Once we arrived, there was blaring Latin music. We both took turns dancing with Thomas. Thomas ordered shots of alcohol for us. We must have three rounds. A few hours later, we left. I called a taxi to pick us up. In the morning, I went to my college campus. I walked into world history class. Hanau Bravebird had hung up a poster of a genealogical convention that would take place at the college auditorium in two weeks. I stared at the event advertisement. It caught his attention. Hanau approached me. I spoke to him. "That is cool."

My calm demeanor alluded to my indifference to the event. Professor Bravebird stared at me intently. I attempted to analyze his non-communicative language. I hoped my interpretation would be correct. Regardless, he would verbalize his ultimate conclusion to me momentarily.

"Yes, it is Yura. The people who will be speaking are your classmates. We have some sensational students whose work must be highlighted. I believe that you are one of those students, Yura."

I stood there stunned by the complimentary words uttered to me. This grand event appeared beyond me. I typically attend these events as a spectator. I respected my professor, Hanau Bravebird. I held him to a high caliber, and he indirectly told me that respect was mutual.

I blushed. "I am in charge of who speaks at the event. I feel confident adding your name to the list of speakers." I felt humbled.

For as long as I can remember, I've harbored a deep-seated dream to deliver a TedTalk. This upcoming event could be the catalyst that finally propels me to the next level as a public speaker. My admiration for public speaking has been a constant battle. I've always wanted to be a part of it, but my anxiety has been a formidable obstacle.

"Yura, this would allow you to speak for racial groups." His words sank in.

Hanau was persistent. He convinced me to sign up. I verbalized my consent. "Okay. I will do it." He smiled. Hanau went into his work calendar and checked the schedule. He assigned me a time slot. I received a notification of the event. It is in a measly two weeks. I knew about this event before today.

I did not think I would be a part of the event. I could not believe that I was extraordinary. It gave me a sense of crippling anxiety. I went home from school. I went to my room. My room has a vibrant color scheme. I looked out my window. I needed to clear my mind. I went to my window to let the stuffy air out of my childhood bedroom. I felt the breezy wind. It made the room chilly.

I decided to leave the window open regardless. I felt my mind begin to relax. I took a sip of water. I felt refreshed. I blasted my favorite tunes on my computer. I looked through the window to notice that Thomas was at Mia's house. They appeared to be having an intense conversation. I got intrigued.

I noticed that her window was open. I attempted to listen in on their conversation. "I told my brother, Sammy, that you are friends with a trans-gendered person. Sammy thinks that is repulsive. He wants you to end the friendship. He said that her existence goes against the Bible."

Mia stared at him. Through her gaze, she tried to indicate that the Bible has beautiful scriptures. However, it cannot tell someone who would rather die by suicide than live another day in the wrong gender not to seek out gender reconstruction surgery. After a few moments, she spoke, negating any mention of Elizabeth being transgender.

"Thomas, I need friends. I have never hung out with Elizabeth. You cannot blame her for existing."

Mia's tolerance for transgender people came from forming solid friendships with gay men. These men swayed Mia to conclude that transphobia was not okay. Mia stared at Thomas with discontent. Thomas needed to back off slightly from hurting members of the lesbian, gay, bisexual, and transgender community.

"Mia, we need to uphold an image. We embody our conservative ideologies. Yura wants to be us."

"I know. Yura has been jealous of me since I met her. If you want, I can end the friendship."

Yura and Mia's friendship was not without challenges, but they always looked forward to positive changes. Initially formed by proximity, their bond endured moments of isolation where they longed for companionship. They both considered ending their friendship, but the anticipation of a better future kept them going. They knew their relationship would change once they moved out of their parent's house and were hopeful it would improve. This transition would remove the toxic jealousy often arising when rival girls compete.

"I will tell Sammy that this is temporary." I shut my window. I let out a gigantic scream. I felt enraged.

I could not contain the tears that rolled down my eyes. My internal child piped up.

I always knew that having a transgender sister would come back to haunt me. I momentarily felt angry at Elizabeth. My anger quickly subsided. I listed the reasons I loved Elizabeth. I was at an impasse. I debated my friendship choice. I questioned whether they were bad people. Thomas had control over Mia. I was not sure how healthy their relationship was.

Thomas centered around his belief in Jesus Christ. I also thought Islamophobia was a factor. Thomas acted like he enjoyed being friends with me. I genuinely thought we were friends. Our family is an aberration from the typical Muslim family.

It is a funny dichotomy. The majority of classmates would never be in this situation.

On the news, Islamic believers far surpassed Christian extremists. Christians berate Muslims for not accepting the gay, lesbian, bi-Sexual, transgender, 2Spirit community. It is a testament to how modern my family is. I wanted to tell someone about what I had overheard. I grabbed my cellular phone and dialed a number to the distress center. They answered.

"Hello, I am a volunteer operator. Are you okay?" Hearing the compassionate voice on the other end of the telephone felt bittersweet. My mother taught me to manage and mitigate my emotions and handle situations without relying on others. The college I was attending emphasized the importance of seeking psychological support when dealing with distressing events. It was the first time I had prioritized my well-being and reached out for help, inspiring me to take care of myself. I felt apprehensive but informed the social worker of what had happened.

"Hello. I overheard someone discriminating against me for having a transgender sister. I consider these people friends. What am I supposed to do?"

"I am sorry that happened to you. You do not need to continue your friendship. You could look past this. People are entitled to have different beliefs. If the situation escalates, I may consider getting new friends."

The social worker operator helped me reach the conclusion I had debated on multiple occasions: Mia's presence does not serve me. It has, at times, significantly hindered my psychological well-being. I knew our relationship would dissolve once I graduated college, so I decided not to start unnecessary conflict. I planned to wait, then take control of my life and cut her off completely.

"Thank you for your help. I will take your advice. Thank you. Goodbye." I proceeded to distract myself by checking their social media accounts. Mia had posted "I am feeling cheeky" with Thomas McKerracher.

I cannot believe that she had no remorse. Mia accepted Lucas when he came out as gay.

I remembered her telling me how proud of him she was. The Mia I once knew would have thought it was courageous.

The friend I once had changed. I did not know this new girl. I noticed that my cheeks were getting hot. I thought Mia was a nice person. Mia had lied to Thomas. Mia had once spent time with Elizabeth. I observed Mia getting along with Elizabeth.

Chapter 28: The London Hammer

The two bonded over television shows they liked to watch. I froze. I felt enraged once again. I wondered if Mia was still in her room. I pierced into Mia's window. She was still in her room. Mia was adjusting her appearance. Thomas re-entered the room. I overheard the conversation once again. "It is okay that you are friends with Yura. I forbid you from having any social engagement with Elizabeth. Mia, from now on, I will monitor your friendships."

Mia nodded. The McKerracher brothers had twisted ideologies that got embedded in Christianity. I knew plenty of Muslims who would side with them. I knew that her relationship was toxic. I wished we had never gone to the Spanish restaurant that night. Mia has been altering herself to fit in his world. I did not like who she became. I wanted to switch my focus. I knew this energy was damaging to my mental health. The McKerracher ideologies disturbed me. I adored that Elizabeth was in the gay, lesbian, bi-sexual, transgender, queer and 2 Spirit community. She took the experience from me through her religiosity. It could have been more enjoyable. I called Carter.

"Hey."

"Hello. Yura, what is up?"

His tone matched mine, yet I still felt seduced by his voice. Our relationship had begun to fizzle out, and I could not handle it. I have made countless efforts to save it, pouring my heart and soul into it; however, he has not reciprocated my initiatives . I decided to press on with our conversation regardless.

"I thought I would call to see how you were. Also, Mia decided to trash Elizabeth."

"I am sorry, Yura. I have always supported her transition."

His words caused a tear to trickle in my throat. His inclusiveness to the lesbian, gay, bisexual, and transgender community is the reason we met and later fell in love. He reminded me that our relationship was worth saving. I felt mobilized to try to up my flirtatious antics.

In a seductive voice, I said, "Thanks, Carter. Do you want to come over?"

"I cannot, Yura. I have to study. If I fail this assignment, my education will be for nothing. Yura, entertain yourself. I am not your boyfriend anymore. I suggest calling Lila. She would be a better support system than I will be able to." Carter's words cut like knives.

His words vindicated my deepest fear. This phone call was the worst decision I could have made for my overall mental well-being. I could no longer depend on him as my emotional support system. I began to utter and fumble. I decided to make an empowering statement.

"Carter, when we broke up, it hurt. Carter, you said you would be there for me. It was a lie."

"Do not take your battle with Mia out on me." I hung up.

I was fuming at Carter. I felt like I lost two friends at the same time. I watched television for a few hours before passing out. In the morning, I needed to get ready for school. On the bus ride, I gave serious consideration to my friendships. I weighed the decision to continue my friendship with Mia. I could not allow anyone to demean my family. I decided to cut ties with Mia. I felt proud of that decision. It meant I had stood up for myself.

I would no longer fixate on Thomas and Mia. I felt elated. I did not want them to occupy my mind. I needed to re-prioritize my thoughts.

I became dedicated to refocusing my energy on myself. I spent my time attempting to reach self-actualization. It required me to partake in activities that make me happy. The next day, my professor called me up to his desk. "Yura, I was wondering if you had made any progress with your speech." I looked shy and did not answer. I closed my eyes. I felt ashamed that I had made little progress. In front of my professor, I stood there bewildered. I went home. I attempted to rewrite my speech. I deleted several mediocre drafts. Minutes became hours. I had yet to make progress.

The droplets took formation in my eye ducts. I felt like a failure.

Elizabeth had come in third in a writing competition in high school. I could not write a public speech in college. I tried to boost my confidence. No one would be critiquing my writing. My judge would be the audience. All my hard work had become delegitimized. I had spent months coming up with an impactful speech. I could find things in my academic journals. I could incorporate it into my writing. I worried about plagiarism. My parents attempted to reaffirm me. My mother, Nadia, knocked on the door. I spoke. "Come in." My mother, Nadia, noticed that I was writing my speech. My distress was visible on my face. My mother, Nadia, appeared concerned.

"Yura, how is your speech going?" I got choked up.

The emotions that I had bottled up for a prolonged period erupted. I tried to contain my feelings. I refrained from speaking to maintain my composure. My mother immediately recognized my distress. She put her hand on my shoulder as a sign of psychological support. I appreciated the sweet gesture.

My mother, Nadia, spoke, "Oh, sweetie. I know you have the capability. You have always been a talented student. I know your grandmother will be with you through the entire process and on the day of the presentation." It backfired. It led me to want to succeed even more for my grandmother. I viewed myself as her legacy. I needed to meet those expectations. It meant my speech had to be exemplary. I crumbled up another rough draft. Writing my speech was a long-drawn-out process. When I wrote, I found myself at a loss for words. I needed to take charge of this speech. I needed to be the one in control. I am an educated individual.

My heart began experiencing palpitations. I was unsure whether it would lead to a panic attack. I needed to calm my nerves. I remembered a practice my therapist taught me. The five senses anxiety activity. I scavenged around the room. I focused on my visual surroundings. I was in the living room. I stared at the fireplace. I took several deep breaths. I could smell the fire burning. It was therapeutic. I needed to enhance my experience. I got up from my couch and moved toward the fireplace. I rested my hand on the glass. I felt the hot energy touch the back of my palm. There was a sensation coursing through my body. I listened to the paper log burning. I felt myself becoming calmer.

I made my way into the kitchen. I opened the kitchen cabinet and grabbed a glass. I turned on the kitchen faucet. I ran my hand over the hot water. I filled up my cup. I retrieved a teabag. I went to the living room. I watched television. I knew that I was capable of delivering a good speech. I needed to develop self-confidence. The biggest event of my life was coming up. It required a great deal of preparation. I needed to figure out where to begin. I searched online.

I read articles and watched videos. These platforms allowed anyone to become a celebrity. I was prone to watching shallow skits that required limited brain capacity. It is a time warp.

I could not go down that rabbit hole. I needed to hone in on my research. I needed to be serious. I sought out videos that were jam-packed with insightful information. I stumbled across archaeology videos. I noticed an archaeologist posted videos online. These were educational. The videos focused on teaching the public. I was absorbing the knowledge. Some videos focused on what I already knew. There were nuggets of new information. I perused an article on the latest discoveries in archaeology. In Lebanon, they uncovered a cemetery. There were three hundred individuals buried. The team of archaeologists was going to assess the remains.

It was going to piece history together. It has affected a village in Lebanon. A local newsreader covered their responses. I watched the video. It had English subtitles. The Lebanese community became intrigued by the discovery. They wanted justice for their relatives. It was the knowledge that I have been craving. This source of information was critical. I saved the video. I took pieces of their sentiments for my speech. I needed to continue with my stroke of luck. Similar events were happening in South America. Archaeologists had preserved a skull. The government decided to put the brain in a museum. It was to honor the genocide that occurred.

Some indigenous people thought it was inhumane. They believed their ancestors deserved to rest. Protesters clashed. The demonstrations were small. Scientists correctly piece history together. The Americans once had their history burned by Europeans. The Europeans committed a cultural erasure. Europeans wanted to disarm the community. It has changed as archeology evolved. This profession uncovered these prehistoric civilizations. The archeological pursuit is beautiful. It does not show the human side of ancestry. I found heartfelt ancestral videos.

I saw an adopted girl take the test. I watched an African American receive his results.

I found the learning to be enlightening. These videos were going to give the speech juice. It is all part of my personal growth. I had received resistance from my religious Islamic uncles in the past. Hassan stated that my knowledge delegitimizes Allah. I knew I needed to set aside the ill-talkers. I wanted to seek out knowledge. It was a task most Arabs failed to do. It was presentation day. I entered the grand auditorium. The room was empty. I stared at the stage, flabbergasted that

I would be presenting. The college auditorium was able to pack hundreds of guests. I felt unworthy. I ascended the stairs. I was center stage. I looked onward into the abyss.

In hours, this room would be full of attendees. I took in my surroundings. I looked at the rows of theater chairs. I said part of my speech.

Chapter 29: Mummy of Katebet

An observer watching me would think I had won a Nobel Peace Prize. I left the auditorium. I went to the cafeteria for a few hours. I needed to visualize myself delivering a good speech. I popped on music from my phone and ate dinner. I noticed people recognized me from the posters. Hours passed, and I needed to make my way to the auditorium. I entered through the back doors.

I mentally prepared for my speech. I peered through the thick silk-red curtains.

I saw a jam-packed theater. The master of ceremonies rushed to the stage. He appeared to be of Far Eastern Asian descent. This man did not display all the stereotypical features. His eyes had an epicanthic fold. The Masters of Ceremonies had blonde hair. I stood backstage with the other five speakers. My internal anxieties crept up on me. My life felt surreal. I am an average college student. I did not belong here. I watched the master of ceremonies being center stage. He appeared to be a grand statue. He was introducing me. It did not seem appropriate. It should have been the other way around. The light switch workers ramped up the audience.

The switchboard attendant did a sweep of the entire auditorium. The lights fixated on the microphone. "Welcome to the Starlight event. I am Lui Chan. I am proud to present an impressive group of people. These individuals have impressive resumes. They have made an impact in their community. It is through their remarkable human rights initiatives. I hope you leave here tonight deeply impacted by these individuals." I felt humbled. Lila entered backstage with an access card. She noticed that I was hyperventilating. Lila attempted to calm me down.

I appreciated her kind gesture. Lila's unwavering support has always been a lifeline for me, especially in times of need. I knew I would never forget this moment. It will become a memory of our beautiful bonding moment. It is a testament to the deep emotional connection Lila and I

share, which I will always hold dear.

"No one deserves to be here more than you, Yura. You made ground-breaking findings in Lebanese genealogy. You are an inspiration. You are the key to uncovering your Arabic heritage." Her words were sweet. I think of multiple archeological and historian professionals better equipped to impart this knowledge to a large auditorium filled with young learners. I am a student who is interested in this topic. When I started this journey, I never imagined that I, a mere student, would be the one giving a speech about my scientific research.

"Thanks, Lila." I smiled. We stood in silence. A stage man told Lila that she must take her seat in VIP. Her invitation came from me, the guest speaker. Lila got placed in Section B. I knew where to search for her when I got on stage. It made her a top priority. It made Lila feel important, too. Lila tapped on my shoulder. She assured me it would be okay. I could stare at her throughout my presentation.

Lila was a safe person. She is my biggest supporter. Lila made a prompt exit. When Lila left, I focused my attention elsewhere. I eavesdropped on guest speakers rehearsing.

I heard the Master of Ceremonies have a conversation with a speaker. Her name was Lola Hodan. She is biracial, half African, half European. Her charitable pursuits caught the attention of the Dean. It resulted in a gravitational pull among several professors. Lola Hodan took the stage. "Hello. I am Lola Hodan. I am a bi-racial woman. My mother, Karima, comes from Somalia. My father, Fionn, comes from England. I have spent two years studying archaeology. I have an understanding of past civilizations. I want to give you my backstory of what led me here tonight. I volunteered at an old nursing home in high school. My job was to entertain the residents.

"One of the seniors became interested in creating her family tree. I decided to help her. I signed the resident up on an ancestral website. We managed to compile her records for the 1700s. At the time, I only knew my grandparents' names. It intrigued my curiosity. I went home and asked my parents if we had a family tree. I received more information. I learned my dad's great-grandparents' names. That was not going to suffice. I need to utilize the information I just acquired. I signed myself up for an ancestral website. I learned that my ancestors struggled under the Ajuran Empire. It did not help that they had eight children together. Somalia's military is Mamluk. "Mamluks are enslaved people from foreign regions. My Somalian family managed to hold onto their Christian faith. My family story is bleak. At one point in history, the government tried to deprive us of food. Online, I perused my village's history. I felt mortified. I am surprised that my family did not die of famine. The fact that we survived was a miracle. I questioned my indigeneity in Somalia. I pulled out a document from my oldest known relative. I am going to read an excerpt from his journal.

January 5th 1894,

Dear Aisha Hodan,

My sweet grandmother, Aisha, this is my farewell letter. My immediate family's financial stability is in peril. For the last month and a half, our conversations have centered around food security, which has negatively affected us. I turned 19 on December 14, 1893, and must provide for my wife and infant. Since puberty, I have worked guarding crops for a wealthy family's farm. I can no longer depend on this career for economic stability. Their family business is now facing bankruptcy. The family is now facing bankruptcy.

Large oligarchs have monopolized the farming industry and engaged in shady business dealings. The general public views these corporations as reputable for providing inexpensive goods. Last year, my older brother decided to seek better employment opportunities in Lebanon and encouraged me to follow suit. I felt apprehensive but ultimately decided it may ensure my family has economic prosperity and the necessities for survival. Do not worry; I will not forget my mixture of

Muslim and Christian religious roots. According to my brother, Lebanon is an ethnically inclusive region, with Christianity and Islam being the two dominant religions in the area. My younger brother has reached the same conclusion. Ten young men and their families have decided to voyage to Lebanon via a ship. The ship leaves later tonight.

Do not worry; I will not forget my mixture of Muslim and Christian religious roots. According tomy brother, Lebanon is an ethnically inclusive region, with Christianity and Islam being the two dominant religions in the area. My younger brother has reached the same conclusion. Ten young men and their families have decided to voyage to Lebanon via a ship. The ship leaves later tonight.

Leaving Somalia feels bittersweet. I am an empowered young black man taking charge of his fate. My sweet Aisha Hodan, please know that I grew up in Somalia. I never intended to leave, but it was a forced decision based on our current financial predicament.

Mohomad Hodon
January 5th 1894,

Dear Aisha Hodan

My sweet Aisha Hodan, I may return to Somalia sooner than I initially expected. Our family left to escape the harsh treachery of the Ajuran Empire. The Ottoman Empire has proven to be worse. The Ottoman Empire is starving the Christian population. Do not worry; my family is okay. We have assimilated into the Muslim community.

Nonetheless, I have not forgotten about my Christian roots. I have witnessed the implications of

the famine on the Christian community. It is a mass genocide aimed at killing Armenians. My former boss, who descends from Armenian, lost ten relatives in this current famine. My family has made the conscientious decision to move to Egypt.

We hope it provides the experience of living in Africa with better economic prosperities. Once we arrive, I will send you another postcard. I think about you often and love you immensely.

· Mohomad Hodon

"I felt touched reading the letters. It heightened my curiosity about my heritage. I needed to immerse myself in this topic. I decided to take an ancestral deoxyribonucleic acid test. It took a month to arrive. During that time, I did extensive research. I read about prehistoric empires in the Middle East. I had a better understanding of who I was. The deoxyribonucleic acid arrived. I spit my saliva into a tube. I was anticipating the results. My results arrived. It was the moment that I had been waiting for. I was 34% Cameron, 20% Iraqi, 20% Albanian, 10% Levant, 12% Namibian and 6% United Kingdom. The ancestral kit contains biometric information.

"They have samples of deoxyribonucleic acid from across the globe. It is an indicator of the genotype of your region. It overlaps with other regional demographics. This results in oversights. There are miscalculations. Each human is a new variation. They have different genotypes. They may not have the same genotype as their parents. Genotypes occur at random. They got connected to our ancient ancestry. You may have the same genotype as a prehistoric relative. It is an indicator of their race. Heritage got lost in this process. Your deoxyribonucleic acid kit results do not determine your ethnicity.

"The biometric data must depict someone's ancestral roots when altered. Misinformation occurs. Individuals believe that deoxyribonucleic acid tests are accurate. It is partly reliable. Deoxyribonucleic acid tests provide helpful information nonetheless. What does one do when there is no information? I want to share this indispensable knowledge with my generation. Being unable to provide the answers would be disheartening. The more I thought about it, the more frustrated I got. Does my ethnicity mean I am not entitled to records? Is it an issue of privilege? I felt myself wanting to quit many times.

"Has anyone here ever felt like that? I am going to take a moment to quiet those voices. I am reminding you that there are solutions. You may not get all the answers. You will enhance your knowledge. You will get a better sense of yourself. There are now solutions to this. I created my own ancestral deoxyribonucleic acid kit company. The samples are only applicable to people of black heritage. We have taken 200 samples.

"All of which are of African deoxyribonucleic acid. I am here to bridge the gap of equality. My company has fifteen paid employees. All the employees are of African and Namibian heritage.

"These individuals were on the brink of poverty. It has gone back into the community. The impact has been tremendous. The project helps to rebuild the community. My business has generated over forty-five thousand dollars. That concludes my speech." She received a standing ovation. I heard thunderous applause. She exited the stage. Following an act like that left me feeling unremarkable. I remembered when I attempted to start a non-profit. Unsure of how to mourn, I registered a charity in my grandfather's honor. The charity quickly got dismantled and fell. He had already passed away.

Chapter 30: Sophilos Vase

The Master of Ceremonies took the stage. Lui Chan spoke in a tone that pumped up the audience. "Up next, Rachel Cabal." She walked up the stairs. Rachel was center stage

I admired and wished to emulate her insurmountable confidence. She stared into the auditorium and managed to energize the gathered crowd. I assumed she had taken public speaking classes. It would have floored me to learn those were her innate skill sets.

She began speaking, "Hello. I am going to talk about the validity of the deoxyribonucleic acid tests. I would like to have an in-depth look at these tests. I have assessed the level of credibility. The ancestry test is a tube with instructions. A person gets asked to spit into a medical test tube. The individual is required to seal it immaculately. Tampered medical test tubes are useless. This tube gets sent back to a laboratory. The saliva gets scrutinized by genealogists.

"The conclusive findings mark a calculation that estimates ethnic percentages. The test assesses the saliva through microarray technology. It is an autosomal test. Genealogists have differentiated over 700,000 samples. Genealogists have classified the root of origin for each of the saliva samples. The ancestral deoxyribonucleic acid test collects microdata from the Y-DNA (paternal bloodline).

The MT-DNA (maternal line) is also collected. The autosomal test may consist of temporary data from a hundred years ago to 50,000 years ago. Your ethnicity predates the last known ancestor in your family line. An individual only inherits some genotypes.

"Every child deviates from the original prototype. These results differ between generations. The results are that of biometric data. That led the scientists to such a conclusion. The genealogist assesses around 650,000 to 700,000 biometric data. Online, individuals can browse their ancestral root percentages. It locates relatives. There are critics of the ancestral test's validity. Activists post their critiques on various online outlets. The skeptics state that one test taken by one company will limit the chances of accuracy. I am a skeptical individual. My mom, Zara, and I received ancestral roots from Russia. I took two tests with my mother, Zara. The tests came back the same.

"The tests were spot-on. I began believing the results. A voice of doubt began echoing. I once felt that these tests were nonfactual. I parsed the information. I wanted to determine whether the test was accurate or a swing in the dark. I realized it is both. The ancestral test showcases a small percentage of a person's heritage. The test is fact-based. I researched my results. My ancestry percentage of my ethnicity broke down into fractions. I considered the possibility of a miscalculation. The ancestral deoxyribonucleic acid kit is an estimate of indigeneity.

"There are underestimates. There are overestimates. The ancestry deoxyribonucleic acid test does pinpoint countries. The percentage of my Arabic heritage was minuscule. I was less than 15% Lebanese. I learned the truth about genetics. Ethnicity does not get passed down. An individual only receives the dominant blood haplogroups. The recessive haplogroups become dismissed.

"Sometimes these haplogroups resurface in later generations. In families, some people have a higher blood quantum than other members. Genetics occur at random. It is out of a genealogist's jurisdiction. It is an inaccurate portrayal of ancestry. The companies take the proper practices and protocols. They assessed people from each region. The genealogist noted the slight variations between the countries.

"Their small sample is used as a guide when they look for benchmarked criteria. The world is far more nuanced than the genealogical research leads you to believe. There are so many anomalies on the world map. The genealogist does not account for those. In North Caucasus, Russia alone, there are two anomalies: Astrakhan and Kalmykia. Astrakhan once had a large influx of Indian migrants to the region. The Indians looked to do business trading with the Middle East. Russia designated one location where they could live. Astrakhan! Astrakhan borders Kalmykia. Kalmykia is a Mongolian Buddhist province in Russia. It is the result of the Oirat tribe enduring the tragic Dzungaria genocide.

"The tribe sought a haven in Russia. My ancestry stated that I was from North Caucasus, Russia. I know that there is significant overlap between the Indigenous, Mongolian, and Indians in the region. The test stated I am indigenous to the area. It is a disservice. It does not show a depiction of my ancestral lineage. That is something the ancestry companies need to change. Their samplings is limited. It gives the individual receiving the ancestry results from a false impression of their race. These companies need to produce the correct conclusions for their customers. The genealogists must grasp a deeper understanding of regions. They must seek out a larger sample.

"It would increase the ancestral test accuracy. The entire globe has experienced mass migration. The majority of people are multiracial without realizing it. My ancestors displayed Far East Asian characteristics with no explanation. These characteristics reflect different ethnicities that were once in the region. It is in the North Caucasus. It would affect the Russian neighboring countries to an extent. This oversight leads people to inaccuracies. It would require hard-working geographers to assess the regions properly. The majority of the population is oblivious to this. My ancestral test educated me on who my ancestors were. They were renegades, soldiers, and enslaved people.

"Learning about my history has been stative. I had to heal from unknown slavery. I became affected by this newfound knowledge. Not only were they enslaved people, but they were also masters. I needed a few months to digest the information. Scientists will never reach a perfect method. The best way for the tests to improve is to get a comprehensive geographical understanding of the regional demographics. Many regions have unrecognized settlements. These settlers came in the medieval ages. The

Middle East combines indigenous, Far East Asia, and Europe. Thank you. It has been an honor to speak to you." Rachel Cabal exited the stage.

The Master of Ceremonies returned. "Thank you. Rachel. Up next is Willow Traces."

Our family formed a bond with the Traces family, and Gavin, Willow Traces's older brother, played a significant role in our lives. As Elizabeth's pediatrician, he became a figure of admiration for her. Gavin's resilience and determination were instilled in Elizabeth and inspired us all. His influence on Elizabeth's life is a testament to his character, a character we deeply respect and appreciate. We are all the better for it. Thanks to Gavin's positive influence, my family felt reassured that Elizabeth's future was bright.

Willow Traces entered the stage. "Hello. I am here to share my story. My mom survived the Kafala system. My mom, Amira, still exhibits Far East Asian characteristics from the Altai region. These facial traits are noticeable in Lebanon. A subgroup with Asian features is more prone to poverty.

"My mom, Amira, had an extended family. They were unable to support her. At six years old, my mom decided she would have to find employment. No legitimized agencies employed six-year-olds. My mother, Amira, met a family willing to allow her to be their maid.

"She did not have any other option. My mom accepted the job. She left her family. My mom settled in. That first week, she experienced domestic abuse. It was a common occurrence. Also, my grandmother received irregular

236

paychecks. They did not pay well. My mother was a child housemaid who received regular beatings. She was treated like a second-class citizen. Her sleeping arrangements felt inhumane. My mom was required to sleep on the floor in a barn. The rats bit her during the night. My mother, Amira, does not know when her birthday is. She teeters between the tenth and thirteenth of August.

"Before my grandmother passed, she told us her birth year. The tracking system in Lebanon is a pitiful process. I came from a line of impoverished individuals. They received low to inadequate life care. As she got older, she was nervous she would not get married. My mother, Amira, felt anxious. She feared no one would find her attractive. She received word that a man wanted to marry her. He served as a bodyguard. He was close to her. This man was a distant relative. My mom acquiesced. Our family has been in Lebanon for centuries. My mom is not indigenous. She is a foreigner from Lebanon. Facial features give people privilege.

"Individuals who look alike receive better treatment. She was not a part of the classic Kafala system. My family has lived in Lebanon for centuries. Poverty was the reason for her modern-day slavery. She was not the only foreigner to experience Kafala. Lebanon is enslaving ethnic minorities. It is not the traditional form of slavery. It is a human rights crisis. The Lebanese population tends to discount subgroups. The Lebanese equate subgroups as the same or different, there is no in-between. Subgroups require an in-between. That is racist rhetoric. My mother,

237

Amira, is equally Lebanese. That is the only country she knows. Our family has been there for generations.

"Her heritage got lost somewhere down the line. What if my mom had been a black woman? Regardless, our family lived in Lebanon for generations. I am not indigenous.

"In the same way, a black woman from that region is not. There are no exceptions. My mom, Amira, received psychological support for this. She did not find her answers. My mother did not know what led to her poor treatment. She struggled, her characteristics are aberrations. She wanted to gain an understanding of her cognition. Being her daughter, I had an interest in genealogy. It occurred when I realized I was different. My mom bought an ancestral kit for me.

Chapter 31: Great Sphinx of Giza

"The results shocked me. I was 20% Mongolian. That meant my mom, Amira, was biracial. Her treatment became a racial hate crime. We need more pride in Arabic subgroups. They should not get looked down on for not being indigenous. It sparked me to become a genealogy activist. The Arabic community is under-represented. I want to serve the underprivileged. I enrolled in an online course. It taught free lessons on the Lebanese Empire. I started piecing the history together. An individual has the opportunity to be a self-advocate. It helps those who get mistreated. My mom, Amira, was not the only victim. The Ottoman Empire enslaved individuals. Janissaries!

"The Ottomans also committed the horrific Armenian Genocide. I felt turmoil when I found out I was an Ottoman. I experienced shame and guilt. What my ancestors did is not my fault. I did not do anything. Eventually, I embraced that my mom, Amira, came from Altai. Many Middle Easterners have Altai ancestry. Diversity is common in Lebanon. Far East Asian is not the only race that made their presence seen in the region. Europeans voyaged to Lebanon. Foreigners settled in the Middle East. African slavery was a blight on the Ottoman Empire. African slavery occurred to a lesser degree within the Islamic

Empire. You can get overwhelmed by the information. Take it step-by-step.

"Being a third-party spectator, you think you would know this. Many families did a poor job tracking. They wanted their children to be from the region. Misinformation will not change history. It is a disservice to the new generations. No kept tracked records are historical erasures. It is common. It happened to my family. There are ways around it. The most effective way is to get educated. The best knowledge is from family-tracked history. They are stronger individuals for it.

"The Indigenous and non-Indigenous are equally important. We are the genetic makeup of Lebanon. The Middle East is not the only exception. It happened all across the globe.

"They received low to inadequate forms of treatment. My parents were both fed up with their treatment. They decided to find a better life elsewhere. That is my time. Thank you for listening." She left the stage.

I thoroughly enjoyed the recited speech performance. Standing alongside these acclaimed public speakers made me feel important. At the beginning of the semester, I never imagined that I would have earned my spot at this event.]

The Master of Ceremonies, Lui Chan, returned. "Thank you, Willow Traces. It was an honor to hear your story. Up next is the marvelous Selena Hibo."

The auditorium erupted in applause. My intrigue heightened, and the anticipation about the upcoming impassioned speech became insurmountable. Selena appeared confident and a tad nervous about her upcoming speech.

Selena Hibo walked up the stairs. She appeared nervous. Selena tapped on the microphone. "Hello. I am here to give you a depiction of life in the Beqaa Valley. Here is a rundown. Various civilizations inhabited the Beqaa Valley in Lebanon for thousands of years. It gets traced back to the Phoenician era.

"The valley was a salient trade route between the Mediterranean coast and the inland regions, which made it a strategic location for the Mamluk and Ottoman Empires. There are castles of the Islamic Empire's presence. These are cultural heritage sites. The buildings once had been filled to the brim with foreigners. During the Roman period, the Beqaa Valley. It is known as Heliopolis. It was home to one of the largest temples dedicated to the sun god. In the Islamic Empire, it was a salient agricultural center due to its fertile soil and abundant water resources.

"Life in the mountains once flourished under the Islamic Empires. Now the quality of life is harsh.

"The population felt displeased with their presence. The Roman Empire played a significant role in the history of Lebanon. The region was initially under the control of the Seleucid Empire until it was conquered by the Romans in 64 BC. The Romans established several cities in Lebanon.

"It became a salient center for trade and culture. Under Roman rule, Lebanon experienced a period of prosperity and stability. The Romans built roads, aqueducts, and other infrastructure that helped to develop the economy. They also introduced their language and culture to Lebanon, which had a lasting impact on its society. However, Roman rule was not without its challenges.

"There were frequent uprisings by local tribes who resisted Roman authority. The Empire faced external threats from neighboring powers, such as Persia. The Beqaa Valley gets subjugated to inequalities. These disparities led to a lower quality of life. The dissimilarity to Beirut leads to worse standards of living. They have an increased early immortality rate. It is unacceptable. The electrical circuits go in and out of service. In more developed countries, this happens less. It is also an issue with Lebanese development. There needs to be more amenities. There are a limited number of restaurants. Humans lose their identity due to these hardships. Beirut, founded in the third millennium BC, shares a different story.

"Many empires ruled in Beirut throughout its history. During the Phoenician era, Beirut was a major center for trade and commerce in the Mediterranean region. It was also a salient cultural hub that produced some of the greatest philosophers and scholars of ancient times. In the Roman era, Beirut became a thriving metropolis with magnificent architecture and infrastructure. It makes the region more hospitable. My contribution is informing people of the prehistoric empires in Lebanon. Thank you for listening to my speech. I hope you have a great rest of your night." Selena walked off the stage.

The Master of Ceremonies, Lui Chan, walked up to the microphone. "Thank you, Selena. Your information is valuable. Up next is Becca Zakaria."

I watched her develop temporary stage fright for a moment. Becca understood this was her moment, and she was required to overcome any trepidation she was experiencing. She appeared frantic and frazzled. Her behavior surprised me. She exuded confidence and had spoken to an auditorium like this one before.

I watched her develop temporary stage fright for a moment. Becca understood this was her moment, and she was required to overcome any trepidation she was experiencing. She appeared frantic and frazzled. Her behavior surprised me. She exuded confidence and had spoken to an auditorium like this one before

Becca walked to the stage. "Hello. I am here to share my story. My grandparents came to Canada along with his brothers. They packed up their belongings and left. My grandmother traveled by boat. It was a week-long journey. They made a pit spot in Italy. Eventually, they arrived in Halifax. They moved to Ottawa. Her new profession would be a housewife. She tended to the house and children. My grandfather sought employment. It was the typical newcomer to Canada story. They brought their traditions and culture to Canada.

"They were strict, traditional parents. Yet they pushed the boundaries of tolerance. It went beyond that of the generations prior. The restrictions placed on me were damaging. My sisters and I met Arabic male suitors. They came to our house, requesting my hand in marriage. These were relatives or family friends. Two of my sisters got betrothed to family relatives. I took a different path. It led to heartbreak and despair. One afternoon, my brother was in the hospital. He was removing his hemorrhoids. I met the man next to him. Jimmy! I did not know that it was my future spouse. Following that, there were months of courtship. Jimmy was begging me to go out.

"Eventually, I accepted. We had a secret, blossoming romance. I paid on every single date. Jimmy paid for nothing. There were many red flags. I felt scared of becoming left with no alternative. I hushed the voice of internalized skepticism. Jimmy made fortified promises of a better life. The man was hiding an epoch-making secret. Jimmy did not work. He could not read or write due to autism. I got left in the dark. I entered the next stage of our relationship. Engagement! There was an issue because he was Christian. I was Muslim. Neither of us practiced. Our parents were the problem. Both of us were raised religiously. Jimmy got baptized in the Lutheran Protestant Church.

"I attended the mosque. I stopped going at eighteen. My parents raised funds to build the first mosque in Ottawa. It was a big deal. The fact I rejected Islam is scandalous. That is not something most Muslims could say. I was a liberated woman. It is an ancient religion. I wanted to marry someone who did not practice Islam. The toad was not charming. I went along with it nonetheless. I did not have a choice. When it came to marriage, it was coercion. My boyfriend threatened to expose me to my dad, Gaddafi. My dad, Gaddafi, could not find out about my secret rendezvous. My father, Gaddafi, was prone to extreme bouts of rage. I did not want to be his target.

"I introduced the two. My father, Gaddafi, acquiesced to marriage under set terms. The union would take place as long as Jimmy converted. Jimmy signed a paper with the Imam. His signature changed his religion. It made him a Muslim. After the wedding, the secrets he was hiding came to light. I saw the man in full view. He was illiterate, lazy, and a liar. He was a mixture of mentally ill and autistic. I feel judgmental. The marriage should have never taken place. Later in our relationship, my father, Gaddafi, died. I made a wrong decision in the thick of mourning. I decided to have a child. I wanted to fulfill his dying wish. I was fertile. The process went smoothly.

"It changed when I delivered the baby. There was a series of misfortunate events. It altered my life. It started with the umbilical cord around her neck.

Chapter 32: Antikythera Mechanism

"It was not the only complication. I hadn't fed my child for three days, which led to dehydration. The nurse realized that the baby was in severe starvation. My baby got rushed onto life support. I felt mortified. I just met my baby. Chances were, I was going to need to say goodbye. Luckily Sabrina pulled through. My child was diagnosed with autism. It did not help that my husband was autistic. My husband had more dominant genomes. Sabrina got enrolled in a school with extra accommodations.

"She performed lower than her classmates. Sabrina has been tutoring and has made great strides. I am immensely proud of her. Sabrina will develop into a delayed adult. I want to be an advocate for my daughter. Being Lebanese with special needs is challenging. I want to show my daughter that her heritage is beautiful. I am here to tell you my story. I am honored to be here as a luminary. I want to use my voice as a catalyst to serve the disenfranchised. Understanding our heritage strengthens us. We deserve an answer for all our hardships. Together, we can overcome it. I want to thank the audience for listening. Have a great rest of your night." She left the stage.

Becca received a standing ovation. I felt impressed by her speech. There were moments when I felt emotional. Becca had experienced such hardships. She had a positive outlook. Becca seemed overwhelmed by what had just occurred. Backstage, the people continued to congratulate her for her excellent performance. Becca managed to move the entire auditorium.

It would impact the audience once they left. The speech would be remembered. That was the whole point of this event. We hope that the residue of our sermons will have long-lasting positive impacts on their lives. Becca managed to obtain that. That was the power of a strong public speaker.

I hoped the content was mundane. I would have loathed missing important aspirational segments. The speakers are enlightening. Their stories have become imprinted on my mind. The information I have learned tonight will likely stick with me for a prolonged duration

I made a quick bathroom break. I left my seat by the makeup table. I missed the first part of one of the speeches

I hoped the content was mundane. I would have loathed missing important aspirational segments. The speakers are enlightening. Their stories have become imprinted on my mind. The information I have learned tonight will likely stick with me for a prolonged duration..

I returned. "Hello, my name is Kabir Gupta. My father, Rohan, is a descendant of the Mughal Empire. He is from Astrakhan. My mother, Ayita, is an Indigenous individual from the Cree tribe. Being bi-racial proved challenging at times. Attending this college has been a tremendously eye-opening experience. I want to thank Hanau Bravebird. He recommended that I speak at this event. I am beyond grateful to be here. Hanau Bravebird is not just my professor. He became my mentor. Hanau has helped my personal growth. I wanted to give that man a shout-out.

"At the beginning of the semester, I wanted to understand how I connected to my Indigenous roots. I tend to feel more Indian than Cree. Hanau helped me connect with my maternal lineage. My education took an unexpected turn. Together, we have worked to debunk indigeneity. Under Hanau's supervision, I have used my voice as a catalyst to educate the people about this false narrative. My philanthropic work got me recognized enough to speak at this event. My philosophy class has challenged me to become a humanitarian. I am going to reiterate a statement Hanau Bravebird once told me, 'People search for their indigenous roots when they take an ancestral test.

"'Genealogists claim it is a specific deoxyribonucleic acid haplogroup. That is a falsified statement. The reality is intrinsic. When the Far East Asians crossed the tundra, the tribes transported their deoxyribonucleic acid into the Americas. It does not change their race.'

"The American Indigenous can trace their roots back to a region in Far East Asia. Archaeologists have found footprints of the Indigenous crossing the tundra from Far East Asia to Alaska. That is where history begins. Individuals from Siberia were of Chinese origin. They moved to Lake Baikal. They made their ascent from Far East Siberia into the Americas.

"That happened during the prehistoric periods of history. Asia influenced the world. People began immigrating from Siberia to North Europe at least 3500 years ago. The earliest being 500 CE. Every American migration wave resulted in a new ethnic population influx. In Russia, there are provinces where they speak the Uralic language. That means they combined their indigenous language with Far East Asian languages. In Africa, Far East Asian influence is in surnames. Africans often have surnames related to these empires. Names such as Suleiman, Osman, and Sultana. The Far East Asian Empire influences are in locations and languages.

"In Africa, two rivers in Uganda and Kenya, Lake Turkwel and Lake Turkana, were named after this empire. The Far East Asians spoke a dialect of Turkic. Mongolians have been roaming the globe since the beginning of time. Far East Asians voyaged by boats to the Pacific Islands: Maori, Tuvalu, and Fiji. There are also three provinces in Far East Asia. In the Americas, they traveled by foot. In the Americas, they attempted to maintain their cultural lifestyles. Mongolians lived in Yurts.

"Indigenous lived in Teepees. You cannot differentiate between Mongolians and Americans. Thus, genealogists have grouped them within the same category.

"Ancestry companies have conjured up the Americas as an ethnicity. Being Far East Asian, I have felt insecure about stating my nationality. I am typically darker than the majority of the Indigenous ethnic group. Hanau reassured me that black Mongolians made their way to the Americas. They were not a monolithic group. Black Mongols conquered the Indian subcontinent.

"It made me feel accepted within my race. It connects Far East Asians and Indigenous. Before learning this, they could have had animosity toward each other. It will turn indigenous people into a fraction of the Asian community. The world needs more inclusion and understanding.

"It fosters a bond between Far East Asians and Indigenous ethnic groups. The religious component of the Indigenous is fascinating. I am also of Muslim descent. I found it interesting that there have been specific instances where indigenous women wore veils to cover their hair. The first documented case of a priestess wearing veiled attire dates back to 2500 BC. Women wore veils in Mesopotamia, Byzantium, Greece, and the Persian Empire. There are specific tribes in North America, such as Chakra, that originated in India. It dates back between 1500 and 500 BC. The Vedas are the oldest artifact that contains this document. In Peru, they celebrate the festival known as the Rama-Sitva.

"It is from ancient Indian and Egyptian cultures. Before departing for America, they kept certain traditions. They had been practicing in Asia. The practice seen in Peru is the Ramayana. The description showcased the Sanskrit language. It dates back to 200 B.C.E. American culture comes from the Mamluk era. The indigenous in Chile have documents dating as far back as the Araucanian tribe in 500 BCE. In the 1500s, Europeans arrived in the Americas. They saw humans as a deterrent. The Europeans viewed the Indians than the Aboriginals as people who halted their industrial projects. It resulted in their tribes experiencing a tragic systemic genocide by the European colonizers.

"The traumatic ordeal these tribes have faced has continuously haunted the community. It is a generational trauma. Canada needs to help the community heal from this cycle of systematic oppression. The Americas were subjected to residential schools, deportation, rape, and genocide to occur. My grandmother, Catori, went to a residential school. She received violent beatings. The trauma was passed on to my mother, Ayita. It hindered my upbringing. Regardless, they are wonderful people. Our community has endured forced displacement, enslavement, disease, and violence. It led to the decimation of entire communities.

"Indigenous peoples continue to face discrimination and marginalization. Their cultures and traditions were eroded. We must acknowledge the atrocities committed against indigenous peoples and work toward reconciliation. It includes respecting their cultures and traditions. Indigenous people looked to preserve their race. It puts them in an endless cycle of poverty and oppression. The indigenous community faces higher rates of domestic abuse, going missing, or getting murdered. They feel like they are a piece of history in a museum. As society advances, they get held back. It is part of their cultural erasure.

"An example of this is the Indigenous decreased job prospects in South America. Is maintaining their traditional practices a point of strength or holding them back? I do not want to sound like a defeatist. The community needs to find a middle ground. People should be proud to be from these ancient Far East Asian civilizations. Now I would like to speak about my paternal ancestry. I am half-Indian from Russia. I am proud of my heritage. Russian history needs to be more noticed. Russia is a country clumped together with a manifold of disenfranchised ethnic groups. Siberia has a shared history with the Indigenous in the Americas.

"The same empire occurred in Russia. People of the Mughal Empire often voyaged to the Caucasus to trade business deals. The Caucasus was the epicenter of world trade deals. Christian Europeans often travel there looking to make a capitalist investment."

Chapter 33: Shroud of Turin

"They stuck to their race and only engaged with business partners. There have been instances of Christian philanthropists in the Caucasus. They spent considerable time in Russia, doing missionary work. It includes Astrakhan. There was once a wave of Indians in the Mughal Empire who moved to Astrakhan. Astrakhan is in southern Russia, specifically in the North Caucasus.

"Interracial marriages between the indigenous of the Caucasus and those from the Indian subcontinent occurred. Most of the population in Astrakhan is ethnically mixed with Indians. The racial demographics are different in North Caucasus Russia than in Moscow. It has to do with migration patterns into the region. It is the reason that understanding the prehistoric migration patterns is critical. It provides insights. When an individual lacks prehistoric information, they are at a genealogical disadvantage. I am here using this platform to spread this message. There is no way to identify foreigners. Ethnic minority groups call foreign homelands their countries.

"Indians lived in Astrakhan as if it had been their own country, and their tombstones lay to rest there. It has been occurring for centuries. People are more alike than different. Religion alters their beliefs. The purpose of uncovering your deoxyribonucleic acid is to tell your story.

The largest subgroup in Russia is the Tatars. Tatars are individuals mixed with the Altai region. The admixture became advantageous. Russia Tatars display these Asian characteristics. The Tatars are a Turkic ethnic group with a long history in Russia. They first appeared in the region during the 13th century. They were part of the Mongol Empire. Over time, they became an integral part of Russian society and culture.

"The Tatars have made significant contributions to Russian history and culture. They played a role in the development of Moscow as a major city. Their influence is in Russian art and architecture. The Kazan Kremlin is the most famous example of Tatar architecture in Russia.

"Despite their contributions to Russian society, the Tatars have faced discrimination and persecution throughout history. During Soviet times, many were forcibly relocated or imprisoned for their perceived political views. They add to Russian cultural heritage. The Tatars have played a role in shaping Russian history and culture.

"Despite facing discrimination, they add to the rich cultural tapestry of Russia. The Seljuk Turks, founded in 1037, were Central Asians indigenous to the Altai. They made their way toward Russia and the Middle East. They were ethnic Kazakhs, Mongolians, or Russian Asians when they arrived. Interracial relationships would eviscerate the indigenous population. Cultural artistry is visible. Ancient artifacts have been on display. An iconic totem pole in Russia showcases its richness. The totem pole in Sverdlovsk survived the Stone Age. It is the oldest totem pole. It is called Shigir Idol. The Shigir Sculpture is a wooden-carved totem pole.

"The Idol was carved from larch. Stones were used for markings. In the Mesolithic period, individuals designed the Shigir Idol. Archaeologists discovered this artifact in the Middle Urals, Russia, near the village of Kirovograd. The geometric decorations are simple lines and zigzags. Researchers have detailed the artwork. The top had a face with facial features. The middle section was the body. The carver drew ribs. It also had hands. Other researchers suggested the artist make a navigational map. It got compared to *GöbekliTepe* in Turkey. *GöbekliTepe* got carved through three chisels using the incisor teeth of a beaver. The Shigir sculpture is consistent with early Mesolithic art in Eurasia.

"Archaeologists discovered many ancient totem poles in Asia. I hoped the attendees felt I made a compelling case for debunking indigeneity. It is my goal to help people. I spent my entire life thinking I was a bi-racial Cree. I am prepared to dismantle this false narrative.

"I have connected to my Indian and Russian roots. I desire to help the community overcome the difficult hurdles. This humanization is critical. It aligns with the vision for a beautiful future. I am focusing on shifting attention to the world's unique geography and racial dynamics. That is my time. Thank you."

The speech was fantastic. The crowd began clapping profusely, and half of the auditorium rose. The Master of Ceremonies appeared to be getting excited. He swung his arms and frantically moved his legs. Immediately, he rushed up the stairs.

The speech was fantastic. The crowd began clapping profusely, and half of the auditorium rose. The Master of Ceremonies appeared to be getting excited. He swung his arms and frantically moved his legs. Immediately, he rushed up the stairs.

The Master of Ceremonies, Lui Chan, reappeared. "That was a fantastic speech. Everyone, please welcome our next speaker, Marissa Mohamad."

When I noticed the large banner in the auditorium that read: We love Marissa Mohamad, I couldn't help but smile. The infectious energy of her friends' enthusiastic cheers when the Master of Ceremonies introduced her was palpable. Knowing how much she was loved and supported, I felt genuine happiness for her. However, a tinge of jealousy crept in as I realized I didn't have a support system as robust as hers

She walked up to the stage. "Hello, I am Marissa Mohamad. I am going to share a story about what led me here tonight. I was once a whitewashed Moroccan Canadian. I am 75% Moroccan. My father, Amer, is half-Brazilian. He claimed his indigeneity. Being a Muslim woman hindered my feminism. I became enraged. I felt victimized by the systemic oppression women in my culture face. I rejected my heritage. I chose feminism. One day, I went shopping with a Moroccan woman. Amal and I met in grade 12 history class. Amal shared similar ideologies as mine. It was a girls' day. I enjoyed my day until a racist ruined it.

"A European man started mocking my friend for her facial characteristics. We left the mall. Amal broke down in tears. It changed my perspective. I needed to be proactive. I found myself in a dilemma. I struggled to fit within my nationality. I felt mistreated for my ethnicity. I also felt a non-belonging in my religion due to sexism. I needed to assess what my beliefs were.

"I concluded that I needed to reshape my ideologies. I started thinking about my sister's two-year-old baby. What world did I want her to grow up in? I decided I would become a social activist. Since then, my life has become a whirlwind. I am a crusader fighting for social rights in Morocco."

Marissa took out her cellular phone from her pocket. "The world is interconnected with an endless amount of information. These sources come from all around the world. It is an excellent tool. It creates an inclusive environment. It can spread vitriol. What happens when these technological devices perpetuate hatred? One hate comment can spiral into millions of reposts. This dangerous rhetoric can target disenfranchised groups. The mental health crisis resulting from digitization is disastrous. We are at a crossroads. Wealthy oligarchs buy platforms to promote their conservative agendas. We are in the thick of battle. My boyfriend, Parker, is a conservative.

"I am a progressive liberal. I understand if the audience is afraid of confrontation. You can fight for your beliefs and foster healthy relationships. I am an advocate for safe spaces online. I have joined an organization to combat these issues. We have noticed that there is a spyware issue. Individuals get targeted with advertisements. Some of their methodologies are racist. Each website developer has their own political biases. Some websites have had political ideologies embedded in the website since their creation process. Websites will allow hate crimes to go unreported. The violation code of conduct varies. Our volunteer group has come up with a solution.

"A website should have to state its political affiliation through emoticons. It would foster a safer environment. Technical companies have created kids' adaptations of this. As grown adults, we have assumed that it is unnecessary. That is incorrect. We want to reinforce an inclusive atmosphere. I took it upon myself to assess the trends in the advertisements. The computer monitors your hobbies. The advertisements will show up on another platform. It is a money-making tactic. People also get bombarded with unrelated paid advertisements. The website transcends demographics. I have an example of a time when my online activity was monitored.

"I watched a video of an individual who reclaimed his Asian ancestry. Before his discovery, he believed he was indigenous to the Americas. I thought of my dad, Amer. Throughout my search history, I have received countless advertisements online to purchase a deoxyribonucleic acid kit.

"I knew that this was an infringement on my privacy. I pressed on with my genealogical research regardless. I wondered if Moroccan and American indigenous human rights issues overlapped. I noticed economic racism was a common occurrence throughout the world. Oppressive dictators have little interest in empowering their constituents. Dictators attempt to de-educate the public.

"History has become skewed. It favored the European race. A lot of social rights pertain to ancient civilizations. In America, the Europeans wanted to reprogram the children of the ethnic tribes. The Europeans wanted to create a disconnect between them to their culture. The residential school educators spewed misinformation. The Europeans destroyed most of their cultural books. They made a concerted effort to whitewash the culture. The religiosity component was successful. The majority of the tribal population once believed in Islam now. They converted to Christianity. There are a handful of people who rejected this.

"The medieval European tactics toward the ethnic tribes were questionable. The two ethnicities clashed. Liberal archaeologists scrutinize the actions of Englishmen and Spaniards. People of color were victims of violence, genocides, deportation, rape, and slavery. There are uncontacted tribes in South America. Preservation is critical to South American human rights. Individuals seek to know their ancestry. Some can track their heritage. Most cannot. It was the same issue I had when I was eleven years old."

Chapter 34: Minoan Bull Leaper

"I searched for my Moroccan history. I came up empty-handed. The injustice irritated me."

In grade four, "my mother, Nadia, distracted me with a trip to a water theme park. Her encouraging action enabled me to quit my genealogical research. When I became an adult, I learned about the importance of not being complacent. My interest was re-sparked. Being Moroccan meant that I went through colonization. To re-empower myself, I refer to myself as Amazigh. They are the indigenous ethnic group of Morocco. We were persecuted throughout the centuries. I do not hold any animosity toward the colonizers. It is progressive thinking. Thank you." Marissa left the stage. The Master of Ceremonies, Lui Chan, introduced Rina Gebara. We were distant cousins. I anticipated her speech.

"Hello. I am Rina Gebara. I am here to spread the word about colonization. I encourage the audience to research prehistoric colonization in their region. You may be surprised to learn about the history of your country. I suggest taking advantage of the academic journals posted online.

"It is an invaluable resource. My knowledge will empower people. A strengthened identity helps growth. I have connected to Arabs who used this knowledge to expand their ancestry. I hope that happens to someone here tonight. I hope people become well-equipped with academic knowledge and an understanding of their family history. The individual has a high probability of pinpointing ethnic origin.

"I have seen miracles. I watched adopted individuals find their heritage. The majority need to correct their understanding of their lineage. I felt inspired by those individuals who reclaimed their ancestry. I felt a restoration of justice. I stood there in admiration mixed with jealousy. I felt disenfranchised. I knew I was Syrian; my great-grandparents were born there. As a young girl, my naivety bought into this narrative. I realized that this was a miscalculation by both parties. I decided to resolve this. I knew my grandaunt accidentally joined the Kafala system in Lebanon. Kafala involves posting an advertisement online. The ads target people of African and Asian descent.

"Many people scurry to the Arab country seeking higher employment. In foreign lands, they realized the ads purposely misled them. They become fugitives, stuck in a country with no way out. Their treatment can involve physical, sexual, and verbal abuse. The level of torment varies." I stood there in shock. Rina was talking about my grandmother, Maya. I never knew Rina idolized my grandmother. *It is not shocking. My grandmother is a hero.* I hushed my internalized dialogue. I focused on Rina's speech. "I have a scenario for you. You are a foreigner in Syria, believing you're indigenous. Your features are stereotypically Asian. You have no logical explanation for this.

"Eventually, I realized they descended from past migrations. My grandparents are a mixture of Asians and Europeans. These traits differentiate you from indigenous aesthetics. Does it constitute being in the traditional Kafala system? Yes, unfortunately. My grandaunt received the same treatment as the foreigners. Together, we will work to overcome these barriers. I want to thank the audience for listening to my speech. It has been an honor to share my story with you. Have a great rest of your night." I had attentively listened to her speech. I went to get my bottled water and took a sip.

My behavior mirrored that of the other guest speakers, who shared the common desire to avoid a parched throat. Backstage, we all took turns replenishing our throats, a shared ritual that brought a sense of camaraderie. I felt at ease watching the presentations, but it was clear that each speaker, myself included, experienced a wave of anxiety at some point. This shared experience of public speaking anxiety is a challenge we can overcome, and we are determined to do so to deliver our best performances.

The Master of Ceremonies, Lui Chan, rushed to the stage. Lui Chan spoke. "Thank you for your eloquent speech, Rina. It is my pleasure to announce the next speaker, Amanda Karim."

The organization of this event appeared immaculate. Everyone was well prepared and accepted their dutiful roles. The Masters of Ceremonies fully controlled all the guest speakers, and the well-prepared participants added to the event's success. The event was a resounding success, thanks to the exceptional systematic structuring developed by the event planners. It is essential to acknowledge the hard work and dedication of the event planners, as they truly deserve credit for their efforts.

Amanda Karim walked up the stairs. She entered the stage. "Hello. I am Amanda Karim. I was born a Lebanese Muslim. I am here to talk about religious inequalities.

"It impacts Lebanese genealogy. I have European friends who became interested in their genealogy. I wanted to bond with them. I noticed the more I researched my ethnicity. Islam became a barrier. It is a recurring problem. French heritage is in Lebanon. French rule in Lebanon began in 1920, after the fall of the Ottoman Empire. After the First World War, the League of Nations stated that the French would oversee Syria.

"It affected Lebanon. Many French families voyaged to Lebanon. They settled in the region. Some were permanent. The others were temporary. The French mandate lasted until 1943, when Lebanon gained independence. During this period, France had an impact on Lebanese society and politics. The French introduced modern infrastructure and institutions to Lebanon, including roads, hospitals, and schools. They also encouraged economic growth by establishing industries such as textiles and banking. However, their policies were often divisive and favored certain religious groups over others. People date with the intention that they share the same personal values.

"Muslim men had a higher chance of mixing. Ancient history excluded Muslim women. Diversity in Lebanon has favored Christianity. My mom, Naila, told me that the

French came to the Middle East and were of the Catholic faith. They looked down on Muslims. Armenians are another example. The Armenians once worked in Lebanon within the Ottoman Empire. They maintained their Christian faith. Armenians started settling in Lebanon in the 1700s. They adopted the country as their own. In Lebanon, there is a neighborhood called Little Armenia.

"Living in Lebanon gives them the option to choose a Levant spouse. Armenia often chooses Christian spouses over Muslims.

"Their ideologies transcend when looking for a partner. The Armenians experienced genocide for their beliefs. Turkey was afraid that Armenia would side with the Russians. It resulted in genocide. It happened from 1915 to 1923. The Turks rounded up 600,000 Armenians and executed them. The genocide still goes unrecognized by Turkey. It fuels hatred between the two countries. Turkey apologizing for this tragedy is the solution. It has led to an inequality in diversity. Armenians fled to Lebanon to escape prosecution. Turkey decided that they posed a threat. Turkey was an Ottoman country. Armenians believed in Christianity. Armenians believe in Christianity.

"It causes sectarian conflict. There is no middle ground. Armenians are the target of hatred. Armenia is a vulnerable region. An exception is the Cretan Greeks. The Cretan Greeks resided in Lebanon. They are ethnically Greek and believe in Islam. It is Islamic history. It can assist Muslims in looking into their genealogical history. I think that it constitutes religious inequality. It is unfortunate. I am an Islamic human rights activist. I am a woman. I am demanding equal treatment, regardless of religion. It is a social rights movement. Allies encouraged. I hope you go home tonight and think about what I said. Thank you. for listening. Goodnight."

The Master of Ceremonies, Lui Chan, spoke, "Next up, Yura Jignyasu."

The moment I heard my legal name felt surreal. I had prepared for this moment by thoroughly rehearsing my speech. Despite how many times I rehearsed, it would not save me from stage fright. If I froze on stage, I might forget my speech and leave the stage humiliated.

My knees buckled. I walked toward the stage. I was staring at six hundred strangers. I tapped on the microphone. "H-H-Hello. My name is Yura Jignyasu. I have been making strides for social justice. It takes shape in the form of Arabic genealogy. I am an individual who has felt disenfranchised.

"My ancestors' hardships get reflected in my mental well-being. These deterrents cause emotional strife. I have a voice for the first time. I speak for those who are from an ethnic subgroup. Individuals are hesitant to change their race. In most cases, there needs to be documentation.

"No proof. I have created a method that changes this. I have assessed morphology and surnames. I have combined this with ancestral kits. It is possible to learn history. The forgotten story gets vaguely written in academic journals. I am proud to be Lebanese and not indigenous. My family has been in Lebanon for centuries. They were not there during the Syriac era. It occurred when Damascus seized Lebanon. It is the closest era Lebanon has to indigeneity.

Syriac gets learned and taught in academic institutions. You can learn about their ancient traditions. This knowledge is in high demand.

"The Seljuk Turks, an Islamic Empire, ruled from the tenth century until it morphed into the Mamluks until the final Islamic Empire, the Ottomans. The Ottoman Empire existed until the First World War. My family arrived at the end of the 17th century of the Ottoman Empire. It was a game-changer. A large percentage of Lebanon is indigenous. Learning about the previous empires in the region could help them heal. Colonization can be traumatizing. It will not heal individuals who came from elsewhere. They have an uphill battle. My ancestors had surnames from other countries. Russia was colonized by various regions. Then Russians moved to Lebanon.

"I want to challenge everyone in the audience. Think about the region of the country you come from. It is telling information. Chances are, the migrants stayed in that region. Assess their names. Names are an indicator. They do not give an accurate depiction. There are takeaways from learning your heritage. It shows war, slavery, and financial pursuits. There are drawbacks: it could cause an identity crisis. An individual must feel complete. People can adopt two cultures. A Middle Eastern subgroup should add to your life, not take away anything. A Lebanese individual may disregard what I say. I will say it anyway.

Chapter 35: Machu Picchu

"I was once you. I believed I was Indigenous. I am a part of the Ottoman subgroup. I am the master. I am a slave. I am a soldier. I am the renegade. I am Yura Jignyasu. I am an empowered woman. I am no different from millions of Middle Eastern people. Families are identical to mine without realizing it. It is possible to learn about your heritage. The Ottomans were once the most influential empire. The Empire got named after its founder, Osman. Osman had been born into the Mamluk Empire. He formed his own Islamic Empire with the existing Mamluk ideologies. Osman was of Far East Asian descent. He called his empire the House of Osman.

"That is how the Ottoman Empire came to fruition. Being an Ottoman comes with many riveting facets. I am a mixture of Far East Asian and European heritage. We descended from the Altai. These men were strong warriors. They received heavy resistance. They proved to be too great a force. Lebanon lost its indigeneity. Could I get a show of hands? Who is Middle Eastern?" Approximately less than a quarter of the audience. "Could I get a show of hands? Who is from an ethnic subgroup?" It was less than five percent. "Thank you. I count myself among you. A year ago, I would not have said the same. Ancestral kits helped me discover my heritage.

"An individual could be from a region and not know it. It needs to show the full historical context. My ethnic quantum remains unprovable. My grandma showcased Asian characteristics. Asians had not been in the region since the 1500s. It is an anomaly. The largest ethnic subgroup in Russia is the Tatars. Most Altai mixed with Iranians. There were two separate empires: the Mongol Empire and the Mughal Empire. The Mongol Empire was Middle Eastern. The Mughal Empire was Indian. It proved propitious in Pakistan and Afghanistan. This divided line was the region. It increased hatred and discrimination. It turned people against each other. It destabilized the region. That is my time. Thank you." I exited the stage.

I felt pride in facing the impossible challenge I had just conquered. The dream of becoming a public speaker has always burned within me, but the barrier of stage fright has always held me back. This milestone marked a potentially bright future as a public speaker and significant personal growth. I couldn't help but wear an electric smile, filled with palpable anticipation for the bright future ahead.

The Master of Ceremonies reappeared. Lui Chan made his final remarks. "That concludes the speeches. I hope you go home with inspiring takeaways. I want to thank the audience for purchasing their tickets. I hope everyone gets home safe." The rest of my college experience was good. The days flew by. There were occasional hiccups. Nothing was permitted. Everything had a solution. I had a positive support system to lean on. My friends, Lila and Elizabeth, were always by my side. I had also decided to start going to see a psychologist every month. My life was looking up.

Lila had decided to move back to the city after graduation. I was elated. I could not wait for college to be over. Lila made the decision based on employment prospects. It did not have to do with the fact that she missed me. Lila would have never done anything so sinister. Ugh! It wasn't delightful. I cared about being around her more than she cared about being around me. Lila planned to move back because Anthony got hired by a well-paid company. She was sure she could find employment. Regardless, I felt elated. I could not wait. No college friend had been able to replace her. My family dynamic was healthy. Elizabeth had improved her quality of life.

She had been experiencing a lot of personal wins. It included a Muslim man in her life. When Elizabeth came out as trans, the atmosphere felt eerie. I went to my parents' bedroom and put my ear against the door. I overheard them discussing their fears and concerns. My mother, Nadia, feared for her safety. My mother, Nadia, feared she would never have a love life. His sexuality and religion would ensure her fate. After her transition, Ahmed started noticing her. He only knew her in her later transitional stages. That was a blessing. Once Elizabeth was a fully transitioned woman, he felt attracted to her. Elizabeth entertained these thoughts. He upped his flirtation with her.

The mosque-goers realized what was going on. Transphobic outcries were stating Ahmed needed to be with a cis-gendered woman. They felt appalled by his attraction toward her. I believe they were jealous. Some of their daughters were single. There were several mean comments. One woman described Ahmed as a grisly part-time cashier. He only felt sorry for it. Ahmed could not get attracted to that. Bless his heart. I knew those comments were daggers in her heart. I wanted to remedy the damage. Her self-esteem took a hit. I attempted to restore her confidence.

I reassured her that she was a beautiful woman. I reinforced to her that being in love was amazing.

She deserved to be happy. Those women had unattractive husbands. Ahmed did not realize he was attractive. Humility is vital to a healthy relationship. Ahmed was an intellect. Chances were he would advance in his career. The two forged a path for young couples. It challenged the mosque for the better. Ahmed and Elizabeth are a modern liberal couple. Being pioneers meant they received backlash. People need to respond better to change. Ahmed did not seem fazed. Ahmed ignored the naysayers. He asked her to go out. Elizabeth accepted. Ahmed decided to take her to the movie theater. They went to an action movie, not a romantic choice.

Ahmed was a dichotomy of liberal and traditional. His uncle, Hassan, chaperoned his dates. The date quickly encroached. On the day, it took her all morning to get ready. She looked stunning. We eagerly anticipated his arrival. Elizabeth appeared flustered. I sensed it was butterflies. She had deep-rooted insecurities. Elizabeth thought she would be an old spinster. I felt stressed throughout her date. I wanted details. Elizabeth returned and informed me that it was successful. More dates were in her future. Love was in the air. Elizabeth fell in love for the first time. The relationship became serious. I suspected an engagement in her near future. I was correct.

One afternoon, his grandfather came to our house. He spoke to my Stepfather Omar.

I did not know what was going on. Later, the man came to the house to request Elizabeth's hand in marriage. My father, Omar, gave his consent. Elizabeth began to blush. Their union would change the upcoming generations. I had immense pride. I knew that my grandma would love this. Maya wanted the marginalized to experience love. My parents were beaming. I knew she would be a beautiful bride. This marriage is going to be a traditional union. Elizabeth was less religious than Ahmed. Her ideologies slowly shifted to his. They planned to get married at home. I was a bystander throughout the entire event. It was a fascinating experience. Elizabeth pleaded with my stepfather for religiosity. He told her no Imam would perform the ceremony. Despite not fully understanding Elizabeth's theology, I felt overjoyed at the thought of her having the wedding of her dreams. I knew she would reciprocate those emotions if I ever got married, and the anticipation of that future event was thrilling. It was my duty to fulfill my sisterly obligations, and I was ready to do so to the best of my abilities.

She came up with a way around this. "Misinform the Imam to exclude information on her transgender sexuality."

I felt conflicted. Happy yet hurt. I made a sly remark. "How does it feel to be a sellout? They stone the gay, Lesbian, bi-sexual, transgender, queer, 2Spirit community in the Gulf region." Elizabeth felt hurt. It did not go unnoticed

It caused my internal dialogue to stir; a part of me wished the stone would hit her, awakening her from her delusions. Elizabeth's longing for approval from the Muslim community seemed like a symptom of her past trauma as I muttered these words to myself; my intense desire for her awakening was a palpable presence in the room, the central theme of my narrative.

My stepfather, Omar, reassured her that he was a willing participant. "Listen, Yura, Elizabeth is going to heaven regardless. She wants to do the moral thing. I am going to help her achieve this." Omar planned to go to a mosque outside the city. He would invite the Imam to perform the ceremony. The Imam appeared to be a traditional man. My stepfather, Omar, gathered my family into the living room.

"The Imam may come to our house. When he comes, you need to do your best acting job. If the information got out, it would tarnish my name within the community." Everyone was silent. There was a unanimous decision that the Imam could not find out that Elizabeth is transgender.

It made sense; while asking for him to perform the ceremony, there was a risk he would find
out she was transgender and condemn her to hell. It would feel traumatic, considering her admiration for the religion. She needed to increase her chances of the Imam attending the marital union.

My stepfather pulled me aside. "Yura, could you be happy for your sister? It is the biggest moment of her life."

"I know, Dad. I told her that I would make a brief appearance. I want to be away while the Imam is here. I do not want to be around an Imam. Our views conflicted. I am modern. Why is it unacceptable that I am an atheist? The Imam has ideologies based on his religion that are not tolerant. Imams hate Elizabeth. This whole thing makes no sense. Remember our last encounter with an Imam? He ruined Elizabeth right in front of her eyes. He hurt her self-esteem. On the way home, she cried. Elizabeth does not see the Imam very often. Your defense of Islam is pointless. They hate her. She joined a religion based on hatred. The mosque humiliated her."

"Yura, this is not about you. It is not about any of us. It is about Elizabeth. I am a father. I am not religious. Tomorrow is Elizabeth's wedding day. I expect you to be on your best behavior."

I looked at the pure innocence and excitement on Elizabeth's face. I knew she had waited for this special day for her entire life. Bound by a deep and unbreakable bond, Elizabeth and I used to stay up talking about her wedding day. Our parents had their expectations to marry and for Elizabeth to stay single, not vice versa. Despite our theological differences, I loved my little Elizabeth wholeheartedly.

I reluctantly said, "Okay."

Chapter 36: The Winged Victory of Samothrace

I walked into the wedding hall. I noticed that Carter was there. I did not think that he would have been there. It was my sister who invited him without telling me. I ducked into the ladies' room. I was hyperventilating. I had been throbbing in pain ever since we broke up. I did not know why he would have agreed to come. It was Elizabeth's wedding. She is my sister. I felt jarred.

I thought about this rationally. What if I was overthinking this? I went back into the main hall. Carter was staring at me. His cheeks seemed rosy. I got shy. I did not want to speak to him. I sat in the back. Carter approached me. "Yura. You cannot avoid me forever. I am sorry for the way things ended. I miss you. I got scared. Our relationship moved too quickly. You were the best love I ever had."

We both had relationships in the past but recognized this was the most profound love we had ever had. Many eligible bachelors on campus were tied down and on track to get married. I realized the probability of finding another love like ours decreased as I got older. Our love story was a rare, once-in-a-lifetime experience. We formed a beautiful relationship that was rooted in friendship.

"Carter. I cannot. You broke my heart. It took me forever to put it back together. You were the love of my life." He attempted to kiss me. I pushed him off. He found it off-putting.

He could not understand the devastation his rejection brought upon me. It was a pain that reverberated through my entire being. That night, the shock was immediate. I was sure my arm became forcefully wrenched from its socket. I was left paralyzed in a whirlwind of anguish. The days that followed were a deluge of uncontrollable sobs. I was unable to function. But I summoned every ounce of strength the following week to piece myself back together.

"When I want someone, I become relentless." Carter left. I was blushing. I did not know how Elizabeth kept this from me. I watched her plan her entire wedding.

That was a big thing to keep under wraps. I phoned Lila. "Guess who is here?"

As I let out an excruciating gasp under my breat, I hoped it was inaudible, but I couldn't be sure. I tried to ignore my unwanted sound and histrionics, just as I had seen Lila do in her conflicts with Anthony. I hope for the same understanding and lack of judgment I always gave her.

"I do not know, Yura. Who?" I responded anxiously. would have assumed that Lila would have been able to correctly guess the individual based on my voice, which had a hint of excitement, terror, and sexual tension. I realized I had overjudged her ability to interpret my communicative skills. I decided to ignore the tinge of disappointment that I felt.

"Carter, he says he wants to take me back. I do not know what to do."

The words felt surreal. I never imagined his day would come. I felt a burst of energy combust through my entire body. The wide range of emotions was challenging to describe. I have felt this way in the past. The only way to rectify it was for me to settle down and determine what I was feeling. It would be impossible to describe my emotions accurately while I felt frazzled.

"I do not know what to tell you, Yura. What does your heart want to do?"

My impulsive heart was reckless when dealing with emotions. I needed to make a practical and analytical decision. It would ensure that I did not fumble my future. As with many young women, I struggle to find a balance between love and practicality. I thought about this momentarily before I broke my well-thought-out silence on the matter.

"That is the problem. I want to run to him. Carter broke my heart so badly. I feel guarded."

I knew Lila could relate. When Anthony and she temporarily broke up in high school, she contemplated refusing to take him back and finding a new romantic relationship. She ultimately knew she wanted to salvage their relationship. Since then, Anthony and Lila have improved their communication skills and formed a stronger bond.

"Yura, if you do not take the risk, you will regret it. You got over the first heartbreak. You can do it again. It might turn out differently. Take the risk. I hope it pays off."

Her response replicates her past decision. Her forgiveness blessed her with happiness and a flourishing love story. Lila is love-oriented. I would have received a different reaction if I had asked someone who felt jaded about love. Anthony was not Carter, and neither was the situation able. I need to reach my conclusion on the matter.

"Thanks for nothing, Lila." I hung up. I stared at Carter for a few minutes before going to my seat.

I saw other girls attempt to flirt with him throughout the evening. I got a tad jealous. I managed to keep my composure. Carter could not keep his eyes off me. I found that enticing. He asked me to dance. I shrugged him off multiple times. Eventually, I agreed. "Carter, even though we cannot get back together, I want you to know I have forgiven you," Carter seductively responded.

My jaw hit the floor, and I stood tongue-tied. I could not believe I had lost the man of my dreams and wished for him to return to me. I never suspected this day would come, but I am delighted it finally has.

He used every arsenal in his toolbox to persuade me to realize that he is essential to my life. MAs he looked at me, my heart began racing. He could withstand my flirtatious attempts; however, I could not display the same level of restraint. I felt like the weaker sex; however, I wanted to be with him, and I could not deny it. I felt my willpower crashing down all around me.

"You cannot? Yura, I think you can. I am worthy of forgiveness." Carter kissed my collarbone. I pretended like I did not feel the sensation. I continued speaking. I needed to be serious.

He could not use physical touch to convince me to forgive him easily. I felt it was emotional manipulation. Getting touched by a man who thinks you are sexy is the best sensation in the entire world. He caused me insurmountable psychological trauma. I was not opposed to falling in love. I needed to respect myself.

"It was a painful heartbreak. It felt more tasking than going to school. I went through emotional turmoil. I felt depressed for a month. Every night, I called out your name. Throughout our breakup, I texted you, and you ignored them. It tormented me. Lila gave me a new perspective on the situation. I knew that you made that decision to have a prosperous career. I was the collateral damage. All I wanted to be was by your side. I knew you did not deserve the hatred I was harboring for you. I knew that it was important for both of us."

I attempted to make direct eye contact with him, but it became too much to bear. His piercing eyes seemed to see right through me, exposing my vulnerabilities, and my face began to feel hot with embarrassment. I looked down, feeling a sudden wave of self-consciousness. Carter sensed my distress about the situation. I noticed him fumbling around, trying to alleviate that awkward tension.

Carter spoke. "Yura, that takes strength. The pain I caused you was monumental. It takes courage for you to tell me."

Recalling the memory was painful. The initial pain I felt during the breakup resurfaced in my mind. Carter was a man who could raise me and tear me down at the drop of a dime. His power over me was terrifying. It exposed me to the potential of being abused but still attracted to my abuser. I needed to develop a healthy relationship where I had control over my moments yet still had a whirlwind romance.

I gave a thoughtful response. "Forgiving you doesn't mean I will not always have those scars. I want to release myself from my resentment toward you. It enabled me to move forward. My friendships had been shaken. I spent time with my family. Eventually, I began hanging out with my friends. After you broke up with me, I forgot how to laugh. Re-learning to laugh again was a huge accomplishment. My overall happiness diminished without you. I felt joy only through my humanitarian work."

I saw the breakup from a different perspective. It assisted me in pursuing endeavors I would have become too preoccupied with to put my total effort into, and I felt grateful for that. It also helped me grow and learn tactics and mechanisms to overcome adversity. In those regards, the breakup was beneficial.

I saw the breakup from a different perspective. It assisted me in pursuing endeavors I would have become too preoccupied with to put my total effort into, and I felt grateful for that. It also helped me grow and learn tactics and mechanisms to overcome adversity. In those regards, the breakup was beneficial.

"Yura, I am sorry. It was painful for me too. I went to the gym to keep you off my mind. My exercise regimen did not help me. I focused on Kegel exercises." Carter winked. He made a sexual innuendo. Carter told a joke, and I received it awkwardly.

It is a trait Lila customarily exhibits due to her Asperger's

Syndrome. I do not struggle with this. I wondered if the excessive stress had hindered my cognitive capabilities. I felt embarrassed and realized this was how Lila felt daily. I wanted to use this moment to help me resonate with Lila in the future.

He resumed. "Can we try again? I know that it will take effort. I am willing to put in the time. I will take my time in other ways too." I knew he was overcompensating. His humor is immensely sexual.

This time, I laughed. Carter spoke. "I hope to have a future with you in it." I fell silent. I smiled. Carter attempted to kiss me a second time. I let him. Carter made a pathetic joke. "I have not had any form of sexual contact for months. It was hard on me. I fantasized about having sexual intercourse at a mosque." I let it slide. Carter continued speaking. "I got a job as a medical consultant and purchased a home." Carter has the career he strived for. I knew that he was miserable.

It was visible on his face. I liked that he could not be happy without me. I always believed that he was capable of accomplishing great things. The music stopped. I went back to my seat. I watched my sister. The bride and groom looked enamored with each other. Carter tapped on my shoulder. "Yura, can you please come with me? I have something I would like to show you." I left the mosque early. Outside, there was a limousine. My jaw hit the floor. It was straight out of a romantic comedy. Carter opened the door for me. I got in. The limousine took us back to our first-ever date. It was at an arcade. Arcades may seem like a thing of the past, but they made for our perfect first date.

I knew a manifold of my classmates took their dates here. It was a popular destination for dates seeking a fun and playful atmosphere. It made our date memorable. As we walked into the arcade, the first thing that struck me was the atmosphere. The arcade was empty. I immediately heard the rumblings of the machines. The arcade had neon lights and flashing screens illuminating the space. Music filled the air, creating a lively and energetic vibe. Simultaneously, the room was echoing. There were rows of games and attractions, ranging from classic arcade games to modern adaptations.

We played countless games. I observed Carter's behavior the entire time. Carter looked pure. Almost as if he was a little boy. He seemed happy.

Chapter 37: Olmec Colossal Heads

I was smitten. I wanted this moment to last forever. Carter spoke. "Yura, I messed up. I do not know how to live without you. Having a prosperous career is not enough to suffice my appetite. You are!" Carter bit his lip. He resumed speaking. "You are the best addition to my life. I am sorry for breaking up with you. It was the biggest mistake of my life. It will not happen again."

I began to blush. "Yura, I promise to give all of myself to you. I will put effort into our relationship. The relationship may crumble. That is the risk you take when you fall in love. It was not because he did not give himself to the relationship. It would be the same as dating any other man. I have never felt this chemistry with another girl." I attentively listened through his spiel. I saw his sincerity as he spoke to me. Carter has built a positive relationship with me. He was an honest man. I felt enamored by his face. Carter is a sexy man. I saw his sincerity as he spoke to me. It was an unfair fight. I believed him when he said he would give our relationship everything. I was captivated by him. I still felt worried that he would get cold feet again. My hand was quivering. I did not want him to leave me again.

I was on the brink of tears. I have felt sick since we split. Now Carter was here, saying all the words I wanted him to say. I had not moved on. I could not believe he was willing to give our relationship everything. Carter is a persuasive individual. I began caving at the mosque. I did not expect to be weak. Carter makes me feel sexier than most men could. I knew that he was irreplaceable. I played with the claw machine. I picked up a wedding ring. Immediate tears rolled down my cheeks. I was unaware that it was occurring. The wedding ring got stuck. Carter opened up the machine with a key. He got the wedding ring from the claw.

Carter returned and got down on one knee. He proposed.

I said yes. I sent a group message to my entire family. "I just got engaged. I am going to be Mrs. Yura Gosling." There was a flooded congratulatory response. It reaffirmed that I made the right decision. Carter guided me to the ball pit. He playfully started throwing balls in my direction. I countered by throwing balls at him. We made out. I told Carter I had figured out who I was. I no longer experienced an identity crisis.

"I knew you could do it, Yura. I never doubted you. I cannot wait to see all your accomplishments as my bride." I spoke.

My accomplishments felt void without Carter assisting me in this endeavor. I missed sharing moments of ancestral wonder with him, and I knew I would not reap the full benefits I would have had he been by my side.

Thanks, babe. The next stage would be uncovering your heritage. You said that you were Norwegian." I am fascinated with Norwegian culture. Our relationship has expanded my horizons about other cultures. Carter has taught me a few words and how to cook essential dishes. I cannot wait to explore his culture and ancient emigration patterns further.

"Thanks, babe. The next stage would be uncovering your heritage. You said that you were Norwegian."

Carter nodded. "You told me you do not have a family tree. Norway is full of wonder." Carter silenced me with a kiss

The kiss took my breath away. The taste lingered in my mouth, reminding me how much I missed myself. It is the most effective method of halting a conversation without getting into a tiff.

He spoke. "Yura, you should create an archeological-themed wedding? You will have your hands full planning a wedding. You will have no time to dissect my genealogy."

Genealogy has provided me with solace as I made my ascension into womanhood. I want to share it with the love of my life. We need to discuss this further.

I started blushing. "Carter, when do you want to get married?"

He stared into my eyes. The palpable attraction from the direct contact caused me to blush. He kissed my lower lip, adding to the jubilation of the moment. He still has not responded, so I

prompted him to do so.]

"As soon as possible, Yura. We cannot spend too much money. We need to save for the future. Not to mention paying off my loans from purchasing our house." I immersed myself in the balls. I resurfaced.

"Okay. I want to get married here."

I looked around the room, filled with anticipation, as I mentally prepared for the wedding reception. The cafeteria hall would witness our union, and the arcade would be the stage for our celebration. Each guest would receive an allocated number of tickets for the fun and games.

"Yura, be serious." He continued to tease me until I couldn't contain my laughter. I was on cloud nine, knowing I was about to marry the man of my dreams. This moment, which I had been dreaming of since I was a little girl, was finally here. I didn't want it to end. I wish I could freeze time and live in this joy forever.

"I am being serious. It has a deep meaning for both of us."

Carter thought about it. "Okay. Yura, we will get married here. Yura, this is a new chapter for the both of us."

Notes

I wrote my book intending to advocate for the truth. Growing up, I heard the saying that the truth can set you free. It prompts honesty. Later on, it took on a double meaning. I started using it for social activism. I found my passion for learning about ancient civilizations. I educated individuals about the prehistoric events that led up to their existence. One day, I went to the shared kitchen of my college dormitory to get a snack. That is when I met my new roommate, a white Peruvian woman. Paulina! It changed my perspective on the world. Together, we assessed what defined someone as Peruvian. The concept of indigeneity was present throughout our discussions.

We debated Peruvian social rights. Our conversations transcended into immersing myself in the ancient American empires. It changed my perspective on America's whitewashed history. It had been falsified. Paulina and I had both gotten deceived by the concept of indigeneity. Archaeologists debunk this theory. The Indigenous originally came from Far East Asia. The scientists' work tends to get minimized. Scientists also tend to be conservative with their work. The acceptance of their work by the government is off-putting. Governments have reverted to traditional courses of action. It leaves the public in the dark for a stark period. Social activism gets hindered.

People must be involved in the political process. My discovery was life-changing and monumental. Word of what I was doing made it to the crown of the Canadian government. It made headway in the crown of Aboriginal Affairs. That was the most liberating moment of my life. I had a voice that could enact change in the government of Canada. That would change the construct of Canada's history. In turn, politicians have used the information I acquired to call for policy reform. It made headway in the crown of Aboriginal Affairs. I never thought that changed. My research led me down a new path. My life began intertwining with the Canadian government restructuring process. I felt empowered. I was vocally speaking on a large scale. That is the basis of my book.

Glossary

A

Adulation: To praise someone.

Aesthetics: Designs that are visually pleasing.

Affiliation: A connection one has to something.

Aggrandize: To enhance a reputation of a being.

Ambiguous: Doubtful or uncertain.

Ammunition: It enables people to shoot from a weapon.

Animosities: To hold high amounts of hostilities.

Annihilation: To cause mass destruction.

Araucanian: A tribal ethnic group found in Chile and Argentina.

Atrocious: Very dreadful.

Attest: To verify that something is valid.

Avail: To assist and take advantage of something.

Avars:. Renegades that travelled and moved to the Caucasus, Russia. They were once indigenous to Mongolia

Aymara: South American tribal ethnic groups in South America.

B

Bamiyan: The city of Bamyan once had carved Buddhas into cliffs.

Bipartisanship: When prejudice favors a cause.

Boisterous: An energetic behavior.

Bolshevik: Russian Social Democratic Party, 1917.

C

Cahoots: To form a partnership with someone to achieve something.

Calligraphy: Writing as visual art.

Callous: Cold-hearted.

Catastrophic: A disastrous event.

Cathartic: A form of psychological cleansing.

Chechen: The people from Chechnya, Russia.

Chippewa: People part of the Algonquin tribe.

Collateral: To give the lender something of value as payment.

Complacent: Expressing pride in one's achievement.

Conveyance: To transport from one location to another.

Culminated: To reach the desired outcome.

D

Dargins: An ethnic group in Dagestan. Indigenous to the region.

Decimation: The destruction of giant proportions of a group of beings.

Deformities: A part being disproportionate or malformation.

Deoxyribonucleic: The molecule that is responsible for organisms to function and develop.

Deity: A god.

Deterrent: To   discourage   someone   from accomplishing something.

Digitization: A computer system with an internet connection.

Discrepancies: It is the compatibility of two or more objects.

Disintegrated: An element breaking up into pieces.

Disjointed: The disconnection of something.

Dismantling: To take pieces apart.

Dzungaria: It is a region in Northwest China.

E

Elicit: To bring out a response.

Encapsulated: To encompass the essentials of something.

Epicenter: A focal point area.

Encroached: To intrude on someone's territory beyond acceptable limits.

Enticing: The temptation of something alluring.

Entity: It is an independent existence.

Eroded: For something to crumble.

Erupted: An object exploded.

Exuberant: A lively energy and excitement.

F

Falsified: Something that is disproven.

Fret: To worry about something.

Fruition: When a plan comes into actuality.

Fugitive: A person in danger that flees or escapes a region.

G

GöbekliTepe: This is a monument in Turkey. It is a human-built structure on top of a mountain.

Grandiose: Appearing to be magnificent.

Gravitated: A moving force that pulls someone to the center.

H

Heterozygosity: To having different one or two versions of DNA sequence for character traits.
Homogenization: A process of making things similar.

Hyperventilating: To breathe at a rapid pace.

I

Illuminating: Getting clarity on something.

Incan: A ethnic tribal group in South America. Most common in Bolivia and Peru.

Incentivized: Give someone a reason for doing something.

Indigeneity: Genetics trace back to one region across the globe.

Indistinguishable: To not be able to differentiate between two things.

Infringed: To breach the terms of agreement.

Infiltrated: To gain access into a place.

Insinuated: Hinting at something indirectly that would maneuver their views favorably.

J

Jalairs: An ancient Mongolian that created the Khalkha.

Janissaries: The Ottoman's (ancient Turkish empire) army made up of slaves.

Jargon: Vocabulary and language.

Jarred: A disturbing occurrence.

K

Kafala: The Middle Eastern modern-day slavery system.

Kaffiyeh: A male Arab headdress associated with Islam.

Kalmyks: Stems from the Altaic language Kalmuck. There are also Mongolians living in Kalmykia, Russia.

Kirovograd: A city in Ukraine.

Kumyks: These people are of Turkic descent. They are prevalent in Dagestan, Chechnya and North Ossetia.

L

Larch: It is a part of a tree.

Lethargic: When someone feels sluggish or lifeless.

Lezgins: These people are an indigenous ethnic group to Dagestan and Azerbaijan.

Litmus: Test that gets used to see if something is acceptable.

M

Manchu: An ancient Far East Asian tribe.

Marginalization: A group of people with shared commonalities. They tend to be peripheral.

Marital: Marriage.

Mesolithic: The middle part of the Stone Age. It was between the Paleolithic and Neolithic.

Monetary: It is money or finances.

Mongol: A person that descended from Mongolia.

Monotheistic: Believing that there is only one god.

Monotonous: To be dull and repetitious.

Monumental: To have enormous importance.

Mughal: An ancient Islamic empire in the Indian region.

N

Nikah: An Islamic marriage contract.

Normalcy: Something considered normal.

O

Oirat: An ancient Far East Asian tribe. Indigenous to the province of Oirat in Mongolia.

Oligarchs: They are wealthy businessmen.

Orchestrated: An arrangement to produce a desired outcome.

P

Palpitations: A rapid heartbeat.

Pachamama: A South American fertility goddess.

Pascha: A Jewish holiday. Passover.

Perished: To die.

Perpetuate: To preserve and keep going.

Philanthropists: A person that donates time and money to a cause.

Polytheistic: Believing in more than one god.

Prosperous: Being successful.

Q

Quantum: This is a percentage.

R

Raggedy: Shabby.

Rama-Sitva: Is a Peru holiday to represent the winter solstice.

Ramayana: This is a scripture in the Hindu Sanskrit.

Rambling: A long wordy speech.

Ravaged: A shabby object.

Reconciliation: To reunite in a friendly manner.

Rectify: To correct a situation.

Refute: To debunk a statement.

Reminisced: To remember past events.

Renegades: A person who acts unconventionally.

Repertoire: The collection of skills that a person uses.

Replica: A duplicate copy of something.

Rhetoric: Effective writing. One example would be figures of speech.

Riveting: To become captivated by something.

Rotation: A revolving series of actions.

Rummaged: To search in an untidy manner for something.

S

Sanskrit: Ancient Hindu scripts.

Saulteaux: Are a branch within the Ojibwe tribe.

Semblance: It is the external appearance of something.

Sentiments: An attitude someone has in regards to a situation.

ShedrubLing: Is a Tibetan monastery in Nepal.

Shia: Is a minority sub-sect of Islam.

Shigir: It is the oldest totem pole in the world.

Sovereignty: It is the region's ability to govern itself.

Sufi: A form of Islam that originated in Pakistan.

Sultanate: It is a geographical area ruled by a sultan.

Sunni: It is the largest sect of Islam.

Sverdlovsk: It is an oblast located in the Uralic part of Russia.

T

Trajectory: To be on a route course.

Trope: A figure of speech.

Tsar: A Russian emperor. It describes a policy adviser.

Tuva: A republic within Russia that once belonged to Mongolia.

U

Undomesticated: Untamed or unaccustomed.

Unification: To become a unit, a merger or form a coalition.

V

Vengeance: To get revenge for past wrongdoings.

Verbatim: An exact translation.

Viracocha: A Peruvian creator/god.

Virashaivism: Those devoted to Lord Shiva.

<u>Vitriol:</u> Harsh/malicious vocabulary spoken.

W

<u>Wean:</u> Trying to remove something an individual has become dependent on.

X

<u>Xinjiang:</u> This is a province in China.

Z

<u>Zygomatic:</u> The cheekbone.

Appendix

Lidz, F. (2021, March 22). *How the World's Oldest Wooden Sculpture Is Reshaping Prehistory*. The New York Times. https://www.nytimes.com/2021/03/22/science/archaeolog y-shigir-idol-.html

Boehnke, K., Galyapina, V., & Lepshokova, Z. (2021, June 10). *Sage journals*. Values of Ethnic Russians and the Indigenous Population in North Caucasus Republics of the Russian Federation:
An Exploratory Three-Generation Comparison. https://journals.sagepub.com/doi/epub/10.1177/00220221 211020444

Elias, S. A. (2014, March 4). *First Americans Lived on Bering Land Bridge for Thousands of Years*. Scientific American.
https://www.scientificamerican.com/article/first-americans-lived-on-bering-land-bridge-for-thousan ds-of-years/

Sood, S. (2020, November 15). *Here's How Ancient Indian Civilization Survived for over 5000 Years*. The Collector. https://www.thecollector.com/ancient-indian-civilization/

Jiang, F. (2022, January 19). *History of China: Timeline Summary, Dynasties of China, Maps*. History of China: Dynasties of China, Timeline Summary, Maps. https://www.chinahighlights.com/travelguide/culture/china-history.htm

Waterson, J. (2018, September 5). *Who Were the Mamluks?* History Today. https://www.historytoday.com/miscellanies/who-were-mamluks

HISTORY.COM EDITORS. (2020, February 28). *Ottoman Empire – WWI, Decline & Definition*. History.com. https://www.history.com/topics/middle-east/ottoman-empire

Bonesh, F. (2022, January 25). *Religious and Ethnic Groups in Lebanon*. Al Bawaba. https://www.albawaba.com/opinion/religious-and-ethnic-groups-lebanon-1463785

Hashemi, N., & Qureshi, E. (2022, May 26). *Islam and Human Rights: A 50 Year Retrospective*. De Gruyter. https://www.degruyter.com/document/doi/10.1515/mwjhr-2022-0007/html?lang=en

Reedsy editor Salima Ali Khan has verified Brianna's book, Hidden Ancestry in the Middle East. Our ethnic backgrounds connected us to make a socially inclusive book. Brianna McMahon is a 2nd generation emigrant from Lebanon. Salima Ali Khan's father descended from India.

We both have an academic background. Brianna attended the University of Ontario Institute of Technology. She obtained her Bachelors of Arts in Early Childhood Education. Brianna understands promoting social acceptance in the formative years will transcend to healthier race dynamics later in life.

She is an innovative artist. She uses her writing to brush up on a wide array of topics. Upon graduating, she intended to work to improve the lives of young families. She spent time engaging with the Incan community in the Greater Ottawa area. It was the first time she started comprehending the issues of the South American indigenous community.

She understood that the community feels deeply shaken by past events. People have not hea'ed from these past events. It is due to the need for more education this community receives on their issues. It has left them vulnerable. It has held them back as a community. My goal is to uplift the community. I met an indigenous man who feels attached to his roots.

He struggles with generational trauma. He cares about his community. Our lives are intertwined. We formed an unexpected friendship. He focused on educating me on the problems his community faces. Together, we will continue to fight for the truth. Being a third-party journalist meant I worked to help the Incan community heal from past traumas.

Brianna's research is groundbreaking. She is a resilient individual who persevered. She only knew why when she reached twenty-seven. Her philanthropic work became recognized in a big way. She has spent the majority of her twenties doing undeniable work. She worked to change her own life for the betterment of society. It was through her love for others. She has made a name for herself.

Her research was going to lead her to other endeavors. She is a racial equalizer throughout the world. Her goal is to be the change that she wants to see in the world. She hopes you can sense her passion for success. It inspires someone to overcome the hurdles that they face. She hopes you get solid takeaways from her book. Thanks for investing in her book.